FOR WHEN I'M GONE

Rebecca Ley

ORION

First published in Great Britain in 2020 by Orion Books,
an imprint of The Orion Publishing Group Ltd
Carmelite House, 50 Victoria Embankment
London EC4Y 0DZ

An Hachette UK Company

1 3 5 7 9 10 8 6 4 2

Extract from 'Spoken For', from *The Undressing* by Li-Young Lee,
published by W. W. Norton & Company, Inc, and reprinted
with their permission.

A CIP catalogue record for this book is
available from the British Library.

ISBN (Hardback) 978 1 4091 9537 5
ISBN (Export Trade Paperback) 978 1 4091 9538 2
ISBN (eBook) 978 1 4091 9540 5

Typeset by Deltatype Ltd, Birkenhead, Merseyside

Printed in Great Britain by Clays Ltd, Elcograf S.p.A.

www.orionbooks.co.uk

For my mother, in gratitude.

'And my death is not my death,
but a pillow beneath my head, a rock.'

from 'Spoken For', by Li-Young Lee

I

Sylvia's Manual

It's definitive now, you heard him. 'Nothing more we can do,' he said, before using words like 'comfortable', 'time' and 'family.' Soothing sentences, carefully chosen.

He didn't find it easy, I'll admit that. Dr Z: young, earnest frown, getting it right. But it was a job to him. And I resented that. Never mind his sweet professionalism, his unblemished skin. It turns out dying hasn't made me a saint after all, you see. I so wish it had.

Anyway, now we know for sure, I'm doing this. Since it turns out that all the treatment and trials, the cannulae and caffeine were for nothing, it seems right.

I'm not going to tell you that I'm writing this. Not yet, anyway. I don't think you've accepted things, even after what Dr Z said. You seem to be operating on your own flight path, denial holding you in mid-air. I know that's what is making it possible to get out of bed, get the children to school, hold my hand. But I miss feeling like we're heading to the same destination.

You don't want to talk about it. What we've lost. And all I

want to do is chat. About what happened to us, the good and bad. Our everyday tale of love and mutilation. That ordinary, precious happiness we stumbled upon. The times you surprised me out of surliness with a dropped kiss on the back of my neck as I made packed lunches. The unsolicited cups of tea, sofa suppers, hugs where soaking up the other's radiant warmth felt like sunbathing.

And when I try to turn to what happens next, you shush me like a child. Make me feel morbid. That focus on the present, always your way. An accidental Buddhism. I've always envied you for it, but now it leaves me dissatisfied.

So, I'm writing this. A manual for when I'm gone. The how-to guide nobody ever wants to write. It's all the rage nowadays, don't you know? There seem to be so many of us going through the same thing. Clustering on chatrooms, like masses glowing on MRI scans. Swapping tips about the best hiking socks to keep our feet warm and which disgusting tea really has the most antioxidants.

And lots of us are writing guides for our families. In order that they remember when to de-flea the dog and where the window keys are and, in turn, to remember us. It's a vain attempt to weave ourselves into your future, just like we did the present.

Yet, I've debated endlessly about whether to write one. Knowing the exact brand of plastic cheese that Jude favours isn't going to change my absence. But that's not all. There's the other stuff too, the things I should have told you before it was too late. Like a furball lodged at the back of my throat.

Now, ironically, I've got time on my hands. So many hours to fill. I'm bored of box sets. At last. Tired of novels. And I can't do social media any longer. Those sunsets, salads and smiling children have lost their allure. Frankly, it's a bit of a relief. I'm starting to draw in.

I did wonder briefly if I should do this in the form of a vlog instead, so you and the children have me talking to you, properly. A hologram from the other side. But I'm so reduced now. I side-eye mirrors and shun fierce daylight. I don't want this to be how you remember me, as fragile. You helped me find a strength and purpose I didn't realise I was capable of. That's the woman I'd like you to fix in your mind, forever.

There's a pathetic corollary to that, one it embarrasses me to admit. I assumed that after all of this I wouldn't care about how I look, but vanity still lingers. I miss my hair. My breasts. You do too, don't deny it. That look on your face, when I unveiled the reconstruction, like a child biting into a chocolate bar with an unexpected filling.

So, look at old pictures to remember my face. Those thousands of snapshots stored in a digital cloud, like unshed raindrops. Photographs pre-diagnosis, pre-treatment – maybe even pre-kids, when I was soft-faced and still thought life was easy and circum-scribable. And then read this, to remember the rest of me. Who I am now.

I'm just so sorry to leave you in this position. I wouldn't want to be you, trying to be me, facing those tantrums and parents' evenings on your own. The food on the floor. The detritus on the stairs. The flotsam of family life that washes in every night, like a tide.

But I'm angry, too. I can't bear the unfairness. I'm not done. After what happened to Rosa, I thought our bad luck was done. It is unjust that you can't euthanise me like your animals. All those

3

cancerous cats, submitting to your gentle touch and murmured words, oblivious to their sheer good luck.

I know I'm supposed to say that I hope you move on. I have said that. And I do mean it. Or at least part of me does. My best side. But there's another bit of me too and, in the spirit of full disclosure, I'm going to lay it down here. I struggle to bear the thought of you with someone else. If she's nice, it will be even worse. The children will forget more quickly, I'll be bottom-drawered.

Sometimes, in the small hours, I imagine this faceless woman holding them, when I can't. Sitting in our kitchen, where we shared so many happy times. I'm worried she might be a better mother than I was, perhaps the one they deserved all along. Calmer and more organised, adept at reward charts and batch cooking. But I know she won't love them as much as I do. For all my short-comings, my many faults, of this one thing I am sure.

And, I expect – encourage – you to find her anyway. I'm just offering up my honesty as a final love token, like a lock of the red hair that I should have harvested for you before it was gone forever. All I have now are grey chemo curls. The new me. So, my candour is my gift. Please take it as such.

2

Then

The pug had been chomped into like an apple, leaving a livid wound in the black plush of his flank.

'Did you see who did this?' said Paul, glancing up at the dog's owner, then back to her pet's squashed, pleading face.

'It was a Staffie,' the woman replied, gesturing towards the door, her breath frayed. 'At the park round the corner. Some boys. I thought they would call it off but ...' Her shoulders rose as she ingested a sob.

Paul nodded, gently probing the animals abdomen, fingertips grazing tiny, useless nipples. It was the third such injury he had seen in practice that week. High summer was coaxing the city towards crescendo, a scream of satisfaction or anger – or something between the two. But he usually treated the fighting dogs themselves, brought in by slender, quietly furious youths, rather than those caught in the crossfire.

'Can you fix him?' she said. 'Will he be ok?' Paul noticed her then, his focus momentarily diverted from the animal. A wide mouth and patrician nose, Lucozade hair, a constellation of freckles on thin arms. Twin stains of high colour on her cheeks. He felt freshly aware of the smell of urine in the small room. The hairs from his last patient littering the table between them.

'I'll do my best,' he said, wanting to reassure her, but far from certain of the outcome. It was clear the dog had lost a lot of blood. It was a deep injury, the aggressor casually intending to kill.

'He's called Ted,' said the girl. 'I'm Sylvia. It was my little joke. Our passion knows no bounds.' She stroked the dog tenderly on its nose, in the centre of its smashed face.

Paul normally despised owners with breeds like these. Style over substance. Bulldogs with sclerotic arteries, cats with dreadlocks, obese house rabbits with pressure sores. But her love for her pet was obvious, this animal no mere fashion accessory.

'Leave him with me,' said Paul. 'Ring the surgery in a couple of hours.'

'Please save him. I couldn't bear it if something happened ...' She trailed off, looked at him, a frown fissuring her forehead. 'He's my best friend.'

Paul didn't answer but watched her go as he squirted antiseptic spray onto the examination table. The room freshly bleak in her absence.

*   *   *

'So, he's going to be all right?' Sylvia banged through the swing door, heading for the bed where Ted sat recovering, still dazed. 'My darling.' As she kneeled down, bangles crashed together, tiny cymbals.

'He should be,' said Paul, cautious. The surgery had gone surprisingly well and Ted had woken from the anaesthetic and eaten. Good signs. When Sylvia had rung the previous evening, he had told her that she could collect him the next morning. 'He'll need a course of antibiotics, of course. And lots of rest.'

'Thank you … so much,' said Sylvia. She stood, jangling again, the corners of her too-large mouth turned downwards, like a child trying to be brave.

'I'm just relieved it looks like he'll …' Paul paused. 'Survive. Those dogs are lethal. Why the police don't do more is beyond me.'

'I don't know what I would have done,' said Sylvia. 'If …' She made no attempt to brush away the plump tear tracking down each cheek.

'Let me sort out that prescription for you,' said Paul, turning to his computer, abashed. 'The next few days are still critical. Here.' He signed the slip and handed it to her. 'Three times a day. With food.'

'Thank you,' said Sylvia, extending a hand for it, her face mottled. Then, before he had quite realised what was happening, she drew him into an embrace, pressing her damp face against his shoulder surprisingly forcefully, imprinting her features through his shirt.

'It's all right,' said Paul, awkwardly. He hesitated, before bringing his hands loosely around her back, into what he hoped was a reassuring, platonic pat. He could feel her rib cage, fragile as kindling.

'I know,' said Sylvia, drawing her damp face back from him, unembarrassed. 'Can I buy you a coffee or a drink or something? To say thank you properly.' She stood back from him, assessing. There was something plausible, familiar even, about this man.

'Um,' said Paul, thinking of Alice, the girlfriend he had only just broken up with. She would be neatly tapping away at her computer, hair pulled off her face. It had been her plan – theirs, really – to return to Melbourne in a year, via Thailand, then try for a baby. But he had woken one morning with the inconvenient conviction that he wanted something else.

'Sorry, is it inappropriate to ask?' said Sylvia. Occasionally she overstepped, she was told. Danced over invisible boundaries. But she was going to be thirty on her next birthday. Thirty! Then, what? This man, safe and sensible, but not unattractive, looked like someone a thirty-year-old would have a relationship with.

'I'd love to,' he finally said, reluctantly smiling. The girl with the paintbox-hair presenting him, irresistibly, with another version of himself to try on.

* * *

The truth is, nobody thought for a second it would last. Sylvia had many boyfriends. And as a couple they were too dissimilar. Sylvia's friends, a feckless and charismatic bunch, etiolated from lack of sunlight, were perplexed by Paul's solidity.

'Does he give you money?' her friend Ariadne, with the heavy fringe, wondered aloud, as the girls sat on their decaying sofa in their flatshare, smoking.

'No,' Sylvia replied, sweeping her face down to kiss the top of Ted's head, where he sat in her lap, his scar still knitting together. 'I just ... like him. He's nice to me and he's ... he's good. You can just tell.' She flushed, internally wincing.

'He just seems a bit boring,' said Ariadne. 'Sorry.' She shrugged.

'Don't be,' said Sylvia, recovering. 'Just don't worry about it.' She inhaled the smoke from her cigarette and considered Paul. She still couldn't articulate what she liked about him precisely, aside from his goodness, the fact he had saved Ted. Then she thought of his astonished smile when she had asked him out. The warm, clean comfort of his shoulder. Even Barbara, her mother, who valued exoticism, thought Paul was dull, not that she said as much. Rather: 'He's not exactly what I pictured, darling. He seems ... quite *ordinary*.' Then, pushed: 'He is what I would have hoped for you in some regards, but not in all.'

Ted made his disdain for Paul evident at every possibility, although that was straightforward jealousy.

In turn, Paul's friends, many of them Antipodean exiles in London, thought of Sylvia as an exotic fruit, like a custard apple or a lychee. Attractive, certainly, but at the end of the day you'd rather just eat a banana in the morning, surely?

And Alice. Poor Alice! When she found she had been re-placed so quickly and by such a shimmer of a thing, she rang his parents in Melbourne and told them he was throwing his life away.

'Alice is a good girl,' said Paul's mother, Miriam, that night, her voice needling on the phone. 'You have a great history together. I thought she was the one.'

Only Paul's father, who he spoke to afterwards, proffered any support. 'You like this girl?' he said.

'I really do,' said Paul.

'Then it's the right decision,' said Mick, who was to die of his pancreatic cancer, hidden deep in his core, a mere six months later.

The thing was, it wasn't a matter of choice, for either of them. Sometimes it isn't. The universe conspires, the planets align, those things we read about are true. That's how it was for Sylvia and Paul. Stitched together from the start, different as they were.

* * *

The street was a gelato counter of pastel colours, hushed with wealth.

'Where is it? It's definitely on this road somewhere. Oh yes, that's the one.' Sylvia was triumphant. 'My dream home.' A pistachio townhouse, wreathed in a creeper, with a port-hole window on the third floor. 'It's so pretty. Completely ridiculous. Just imagine living in such a place. You couldn't worry about anything in a house like that.'

'It is sort of ... sweet,' said Paul, slowly, reaching for the correct response. He wasn't sure why he so badly wanted to impress her. She was clearly what his mother Miriam would describe, in scathing italics, as *emotional*. He avoided people like that, usually, as he'd been taught. His parents' relationship had always been contentedly undemonstrative. He remembered as a child once seeing a couple arguing in the street on a Saturday afternoon. He had been riveted by their abandon. Visible veins in the man's throat, the woman shrieking like a car alarm. Angry, but thrillingly free. As Miriam had tugged him away, he had looked back over his shoulder to see the man kneeling on the pavement, imploring the woman. To hit him or kiss him, perhaps, by that point Paul was too far away to tell. He often thought of what he had seen, but in the face of his own family's placidity, it took on the air of a cautionary tale.

Yet here he was, at Sylvia's suggestion, lingering in a postcode smarter than either of them could afford, courting excitement as if he didn't know better.

'I love it,' said Sylvia. 'Maybe one day.' She moved her arms out in an inclusive gesture, as if she was trying to hug the air. Ted's lead was pulled taut and he looked up, long-suffering but adoring, at his mistress. 'Of course, my sister – Tess – thinks all property is theft. She's a total hippy, lives in a shed in Cornwall. But you know she would come and stay like a shot all the same.' Sylvia rolled her eyes. 'She's always tried to save the world. When we were kids she used to spend hours roping me into making posters about the ozone layer, or organising litter-picks on the beach. She's so different from me, but … she knows me better than anyone.'

Paul smiled, indulgent. He had scant interest in the house. Or the off-grid sister. His main point of focus, at that moment, were the bands of flesh Sylvia had exposed for their sojourn. Her arms, calves and, unexpectedly but delightfully, her stomach, flat and white as a sheet of A4.

'You don't like it?' said Sylvia. 'Sorry, is this a stupid idea?' She glanced at the ground. 'We don't have to hang around.'

'Not at all,' said Paul. 'It's great. And it's good to see you again.' He had been unsuccessful in his attempts not to think about her.

'Thanks,' said Sylvia, nodding and holding his gaze.

'So, how's the patient?' said Paul, suddenly awkward, leaning over Ted, looking for where the neat stitches he had made extended around the dog's trunk. Ted glowered at him, ungrateful as a beloved child.

'He's fine,' said Sylvia. 'Thanks to you. I still can't believe what you did. So clever.'

'What do you do then?' said Paul, straightening up, trying to avoid looking too obviously at Sylvia's mouth, her hair, that stomach. Focusing directly on her eyes, where he couldn't go wrong.

'I make babies,' she said. 'Kind of. Well, I work in a lab. A fertility clinic on Harley Street. I'm an embryologist.'

Paul was silent. It wasn't what he was expecting from this girl. He imagined her as an artist, an actress, a waitress. As flaky as filo. He re-calibrated his view of her, twisting the kaleidoscope to see her in a different pattern.

'That's not what I was expecting,' he admitted.

'It doesn't pay to have too many expectations,' said Sylvia, smiling, evidently pleased to surprise him.

'Sorry,' he said. 'I didn't mean ...'

'Don't worry. You aren't the first to be shocked that I'm a woman of science,' she said. 'I'm a mass of contradictions. Shall we walk up the hill? There's an amazing view.'

A short climb and the city was spread in front of them. The faux-pastoral of their immediate locale contrasting with the greedy glitter of spires on the horizon.

'Gorgeous, isn't it?' said Sylvia, sighing slightly. Paul didn't respond but watched her contemplate the skyline for a moment, before reaching for her hand.

3

Now

He had found the document in the boot of the car. Next to his spare kit, the wellies, a tartan blanket and a huge golfing umbrella, with a spiked finial, like a weapon. A place he was certain to come to, eventually.

Laminated, bound, neatly formatted. Sylvia had clearly meant business. How she had found the time, or the strength, he couldn't imagine. He thought of her towards the end. How she had slept for hours, propped up in that high bed. Sleeping Beauty felled by an enchanted spindle. Intermittently he had stood to kiss her forehead, half hoping it would wake her, but she didn't stir, seeming already to be somewhere else.

'She's not in pain,' the nurse had said. The nice one with the big cow-eyes and the tattoo of a star on her inner wrist. 'I promise.'

Megan had nodded solemnly, then looked at the ceiling, as if trying to tip back tears.

Jude was impassive, for once, sitting in a chair next to Sylvia's bed, silent. Outside the city night, sirens keening, lives changing.

'Shall we play some of those stories again?' Paul had suggested, keen to regain the calm that had mostly presided in the last few weeks. Instead of music, Sylvia had asked for audiobooks as she grew weaker. Classics from her childhood, mostly. *Peter Pan. Anne of Green Gables. Little House on the Prairie.* Stories she had both read to herself and been read to, in the house by the sea a lifetime ago, when everything was still to play for.

But Megan had shaken her head. And Jude was starting to circle the room, like a shark. So, he had taken the children home, put them to bed. Or rather, they put themselves. Even Jude.

And that's when it had happened. The hospice rang him at 10 p.m.

'She slipped away ... just now,' said the hospice manager, Khadija, a kind woman whose eyes, beneath her headscarf, sparkled constantly, as if with unshed tears.

'But we were just with you,' Paul had said, stupidly. 'I just came home to drop off the kids and take a shower.'

'It's often the way,' said Khadija, apologetic. 'They wait until the family aren't there to ... let go. I'm so sorry for your loss.'

'I ... I understand,' said Paul. But he didn't. The idea of any volition was laughable. And the thought of Sylvia leaving quietly, by the back door, was incomprehensible. She was someone you heard coming, usually from halfway down the street – heels, her percussive jewellery, that brittle laugh. She had presence, the kind you couldn't ignore. An emotional weather system that could alter a room's atmosphere in seconds. Animated, even sitting down, constantly jiggling her knees, stretching her arms above her head with every yawn, tucking tendrils of escaping hair behind her ears.

Afterwards, he had sat on the stairs, where he had taken the call. His mind oddly blank, pain deferred. His eyes ached but remained dry.

'What's the matter, Daddy?' Megan appeared, then curled around him like a cat. He looked at her and a sound, not a word, came out of his mouth.

Knowledge formed in Megan's eyes. She climbed onto his lap and sat there, curled up tight, head tucked into his chest. He had held her then. Comforting her, comforting himself. He was not sure for how long.

* * *

The hours since had blurred. Full of people. Sylvia's mother, Barbara. Friends, acquaintances, neighbours. The house busier than it had been for months. The children alternating between sullen, hidden behind their screens, and animated, talking to the visitors as though nothing had happened.

Sitting in the front of his car, outside the funeral home, Paul looked at the pages. From just reading the first sentences, her voice struck him with force. It made him realise how long it had been since he had heard her speak like that, so frankly and like herself. For almost a year, it was as if she had been behind a pane of glass, visible but unreachable. The easy intimacy they had once shared creepingly incomprehensible. The times they had fallen asleep holding hands, exhausted but content after another day in the parenting trenches, or stood together, Sylvia's head resting on his chest, watching the children play in the garden. For after that conversation six months ago, when Dr Z had gently said there wasn't any more they could do, she had started to retreat, inexorable as a tide. It had almost been the most painful thing. Losing her before she actually died.

There had been different Sylvias through the course of their marriage. The glamorous, unlikely wraith he first met. The surprised newlywed. The accidental mother-to-be. The devoted mother. The depressed housewife. The invalid. It had been hard to keep up. Throughout, he felt he had remained the same.

He hated admitting to himself that the Sylvia he liked best was the one that came first. The caustic girl who drank flaming sambuca and carried a book of poetry in her handbag. It wasn't her body he missed – or not only – but the sense of optimism, before it was knocked out of her.

But here she was, another Sylvia, in his hands. A legacy he wasn't expecting to find, tucked under his spare syringes. So unmistakably her. Loving, but tart, like those sour sweets that make you wince and then reach for another.

She saw things that he hadn't even admitted to himself. Both of them looking for the other but unable to find them when it mattered most.

Maybe she would tell him how to cope. He honestly had no idea. Their family had pivoted around her for so long.

17

4

Sylvia's Manual

Just a reminder. This manual is for you alone. Not for Barbara. Or Nush. And definitely not for the children. Don't leave it lying around.

To help you navigate our family life, I necessarily have to be honest. And I know you can cope with such frankness, that you'll take it as it's intended: an act of love. But I fear that anyone else would find it too brutal. I don't want Jude and Megan to think that this can adequately convey my feelings for them. It couldn't begin to. The glorious, dizzying, humbling wonder of being their mother is as unfathomable as outer space.

Does it make sense for me to provide advice for each child separately? I think so. After all, they have always been so distinct. Two different species, from their respective first nights in hospital.

I'll start where we began. Megan. Always so calm and self-contained. She slept for hours after the birth, as I lay looking at her. I couldn't believe she was mine. As the years went by, that slight sense of disbelief at my luck, in getting such a girl, never faded. I'd watch her drawing, a perfect pincer grip, the tip of tongue slightly protruding as she concentrated, and feel an overwhelming rush of love. She was so easy is so many ways, but always just slightly unreachable somehow. Her father's daughter.

First of all, don't assume that she is as grown up as she seems to think. She's always been what they call an old soul, but that doesn't mean she can't make present-day mistakes. I know she's only eight and we haven't had to deal with teenage stuff yet. But it's coming, it's just around the corner. I can see it now, in the way she moves, the arch of her eyebrows. As I've got plainer, first in the everyday way we're supposed to accept and then drastically, almost overnight, she has started to unfurl, a premonition of womanhood, like a warning.

I can admit that, even before this, I've been nervous about the future. How I'd take her growing up in the face of my decrepitude. It's that vanity again, running through me like the name of a seedy seaside town in a stick of rock. I wasn't relishing the prospect, but now the idea that I won't see it happen at all is agonising.

Her effortless social dominance at school has surprised us both, but don't assume everything is always fine. Watch out for Eliza Jenkins. That girl is trouble. I knew it at Megan's fourth birthday party. If parenthood has taught me anything, it's that people don't change. They can't. And Eliza is not who we want Megan to drink her first alcohol with. Eliza won't hold back her hair.

I know I've bored you with this kind of thing enough already at bedtime, in the 'pre' days, when I still bothered to smear my face with oil each night, while you flicked through your phone. I would conjure countless future scenarios, gently catastrophising as I sat at my dressing table. Really, I was waiting for what you always did next, when you would finally stand up, cross the room and laughingly kiss my hair, telling me that everything (imagine it, everything!) was going to be ok. That rush of relief I reliably felt. For, deep down, behind my show of anxiety, I trusted you were right. You were supposed to be my happy ending, you see. My lucky full stop.

Make sure she eats enough vegetables. Try not to let her get away with picking at tuna pasta. I know it's not a body-issue thing at the moment, just an innate distrust of food that was there from the first sweet potato I pureed, but try not to let it become one. I don't think she ever realised what my own unbothered attitude to food concealed.

Encourage her to try different things. Sashimi, watercress, blood oranges. Take her to the seafront in St Malo and encourage her towards a seafood platter, with prawns, oysters and razor clams sitting on a bed of ice. Try to promote a healthy appetite, such an essential thing for a teenage girl.

Foster her reading. I love to imagine her devouring the same classics that I did, following my breadcrumb path through yellowing pages. She's made a good start, but there are so many I haven't had a chance to introduce her to yet. Lots are in the bookcase in the spare room. *What Katy Did. The Hobbit. Jane Eyre.* My collection of Diana Wynne Jones. Then Flaubert, please. When she hits fourteen. There's a lot a young woman can learn from Emma Bovary. I know she still sees herself chiefly in Hermione Granger, but that needs to change. She's a perfect role model for a little girl, but Megan is going to need fleshier, more fallible literary mentors.

Give her my jewellery when she's old enough to look after it. I left it all in the left-hand drawer of my dressing table. Tell her the stories behind my rings. The amethyst engagement ring, of course. That beautiful diamond from your gung-ho Melbourne grand-mother. But also the one with the nugget of Mexican turquoise, which you gave me in the early days, when we were tentatively dipping our big toes into the hot water of commitment.

There's another one in there too. A black opal. I don't know if you've seen it – I never wore it – but it's worth quite a bit and you should sell it. Stunning as they may be, opals are for tears. I can't say that ring ever brought me any happiness.

Teach her to treat my mother with a healthy degree of caution. You're all going to need her, but don't let Megan rely on her too much. She will only end up getting hurt. If this wasn't happening, I would have taught her to build a shell around herself with regards to Barbara. To keep the tenderest, most vulnerable part of herself safe. To manage expectations.

But Barbara will be good for career and cosmetics advice, cer-tainly. She can teach her how to paint her nails, to apply lipstick so it doesn't bleed, to dust powder onto grease. To ask for pay rises with aplomb and stab colleagues in the back so stealthily they soundlessly crumple to the floor.

I couldn't have coped with my mother without Tess. Our close-ness was like a shield, it saw me through so much when we were growing up. We quarrelled, yes, but I took her presence for granted. So reliable and sweet. Tess seems enigmatic if you've only just met her, but I could always read her expressions and gestures as well as any book. Her trying-to-be-brave face and bored eyebrow raise. The glottal giggle that preceded a cheeky plan. The contraband thumbsuck that meant she was especially tired. Maybe it's naïve to think, but I hope that taking me out of the equation might make it easier for Megan to form a close relationship with her aunt. An unexpected silver lining. Summers in a yurt in the valley, perhaps? I can see it already. Maybe wait to send her until she's sixteen, just to be on the safe side. At that point, my sister's perspective on the world might be just the thing for Megan, our little corporate lawyer in training.

Try to make sure she doesn't shut off from Jude. I can see it happening already, as she spreads outwards, upwards. Her intellect sucking her towards her future. Sometimes she treats him with something almost like contempt. I can't bear that, don't let it happen. I know how different they are, but they are going to have to rely on each other.

Show her that picture of them in the garden, when they're arm in arm laughing. You know the one. They were playing some mad game of spies, but it was the closest I ever saw them. One of those afternoons when motherhood feels like a benediction.

No phone please, until she's at least eleven. I know Eliza Jenkins will get one sooner. I also know that Megan will probably be sensible enough to handle it. But I can't bear it. That radiation beeping into her little brain. That portal into the entire universe, in the palm of her hand. Fend it off for as long as you can.

You need to speak to the genetic counsellor at the hospital. I know you were there when they said my illness had implications for Megan, but just in case it didn't stick. I never know what you are taking in these days, how much you've heard. That smile you do, that easy tilt of your head, while your thoughts are light years away.

Megan will need to decide for herself about being tested when she's older. She needs to be aware of her options. And by that point, they'll know more. After all, I don't have the most common genetic markers for breast cancer, but by then maybe they will have deciphered the genes that doomed me, that combination of DNA that sealed my fate. Maybe not. Tess should be tested too, but she won't, I'll bet money on it. She's been with Danny so long that his distrust of modern medicine has become entrenched. Barbara won't either, but then she's invincible. Good luck to the cancer that tries to take up residence in her chest.

Take her to my dad's bench as often as you can. He would have loved her. They share so much. Her innate dignity isn't just from you, you know. Even cleaning away fish guts with his knife, my father had it in spades. Why do you think I liked you in the first place? Daddy's girl. I'd been looking for him in all the wrong places until I found you.

So yes, take her there. Wait until September, when most of the crowds have gone, so you don't have to share it with lovers, picnickers and twitchers. Clear off any bird shit, please. Persuade Tess to come too, if you can, to talk about our father. And me, of course.

5

Then

The thing between them grew, despite the whispering nay-sayers and their own reservations.

Paul found that all he truly missed of Alice was the roast chicken she cooked and their shared commitment to picking things off the floor, while Sylvia tentatively identified the soft feeling in her chest as contentment.

They started to meet all the time, staying over in each other's rooms, spending Saturdays playing at adulthood. Brewing cafetières of coffee and reading the newspapers, getting drunk in the evenings with one of their respective groups of friends, never commingling the two.

Sylvia was delighted to find that she desired Paul, despite the fact he was nice to her. She traced the scar that extended across his back with her fingers, ghostly filigree branded by a jellyfish. While he was simply dazzled, as if he was trying to sneak a look at the sun, eyes half-shut.

By the autumn, a relief to Paul who still enjoyed the

novelty of changing seasons, they never spent an evening apart. Ariadne rolled her eyes at Paul in the kitchen in his boxer shorts. Sylvia gawped at the monastic tidiness of his studio flat.

But after six months, Sylvia's sister Tess and her boyfriend Danny came up from Cornwall for the weekend.

'You'd better sleep at yours or it could get a bit crowded,' Sylvia said.

'Sure,' said Paul, compliant but disappointed nonetheless. Separation, even for a single night, hard to bear.

He arrived on the Saturday morning armed with a greasy paper bag of cornershop croissants and a newspaper across his chest, like a shield. From outside Sylvia's flatshare he could hear raised voices. Two of them. Startlingly similar, as if Sylvia was having an argument with herself. As he stood there, bag in hand, wondering whether to knock or to ring Sylvia's phone, a man opened the door from the inside. He looked like so many boys back home – triangular torso tapering to skinny legs, sun-bleached hair stiff with salt, a pendant on a leather loop.

'All right mate,' he said, extending his hand. 'You Sylvia's new bloke?'

'Yes,' said Paul. 'You must be ...?'

'Danny,' said the blond man. 'Tess's ... well, I've known them both for a long time. Since we were all kids.' He pulled his rubbery face into something between a grimace and a grin. 'They're saying hello to each other by having a huge argument.'

'You always expect me to do that!' shouted Sylvia, from

25

upstairs, and Danny stepped out into the street nimbly, like a cat, shutting the door behind him.

'They usually do this,' he said. 'We may as well go and get a coffee. It'll be a while.'

Paul considered. He was thrumming with anticipation about seeing Sylvia, after the eternity of a night away, but she probably wouldn't want him to meet Tess in the middle of a fight.

'Ok,' he said, reluctantly turning away. 'Are they really always like this?'

'Well … not always,' said Danny. 'But often enough.' He squinted at the busy road in front of them. 'Can't handle the city, don't know how you stand it, mate. What do you do on a sunny day? At least where we come from, we've always got the beach.'

'You get used to it,' said Paul, thinking of the life he had once lived, which revolved around the sea. He had known plenty of boys like Danny, back then. Had been one of them, even, in the days when he and his brother Ed used to surf every day after school. But he didn't miss the ocean, or the high, blue skies that trapped you like a spider under a glass. There was something soothing about London's muggy grit.

'Where's good for coffee?' said Danny.

*   *   *

By the time the men returned, the flat was quiet. Upstairs, Sylvia's face was flushed and Tess was nowhere to be seen.

'She's gone out for a walk,' said Sylvia. 'To Highbury

Fields, I think.' She looked at Danny and he nodded, as if she had communicated an order: heading back out to look for Tess.

'Did you hear us arguing?' said Sylvia. She was painting her toenails, angry but precise, Ted curled up alongside her. The pug opened an eye to glare viciously at Paul before resuming his pretence of sleep. Relations between them were still frosty, but Paul worked hard to conceal his antipathy towards the dog. He had met few animals in his life he didn't warm to, let alone actively disliked. It was a sadness that the first should be Sylvia's pet. He hesitated but then nodded. There was little point in hiding it.

'Do you think I'm awful?' said Sylvia. 'She does. She thinks I'm a selfish nightmare.'

'No,' said Paul. And he didn't. Sibling relationships could be difficult for some people, he knew that. He was grateful he and Ed had seldom argued, although the flip side was a certain detachment. And as the weeks passed, he had started to sense the insecurity that lay behind Sylvia's confidence. Sometimes it troubled him; she was like a quagmire of neediness. But it was also true that he ached for her, would say anything to soothe her.

'We always argue,' said Sylvia. 'It clears the air and then it's fine. We'll be ok later.'

'What was it about?' said Paul. He longed to touch her. But she was agitated, shaking the bottle of black-red polish angrily.

'She thinks I need to go and see Dad more often,' said Sylvia. 'She says he's getting vague, keeps locking himself out

27

of the house. I don't know.' She shrugged. 'It's such a long way. It's all right for her, she doesn't really have a proper job, she's much more flexible. I don't think it's right that she tells me what to do. And I don't find it easy down there. It's beautiful, of course, lovely fresh air. But half an hour off the train and I start to get The Fear.'

Paul smiled. He was discovering that all sorts of things gave Sylvia The Fear. Utility bills, leafy vegetables, flat shoes, early mornings. Now the place she had been raised was added to the mental list he had started to compile.

'We can go together if you want?' he said. 'I'd love to see where you're from and meet your dad. It sounds like you should see him.' Sylvia was such an urban creature in his mind, he couldn't imagine her growing up in the countryside, by the sea no less. Like he had. But a different, colder sea. He had seen a photograph of the childhood home where her father still lived. A granite farmhouse on a cliff, orange lichen spreading across the slate tiles like a skin condition.

She frowned, surveyed her toenails and lit a cigarette. 'Maybe,' she said. 'I'm not sure you're ready for it. I'm not sure I'm ready to take you.'

'You could try me,' said Paul. 'Do you want a hug?'

Sylvia shook her head. 'Not right now. I need to calm down. Sorry. I'm sorry. I didn't mean it to be like this.'

'It's ok, Sylv,' said Paul. 'I actually went for a coffee with Danny.'

'Oh yes?' she said, bristling. 'Well, he's a dick. I wish they had stayed at home.'

* * *

It was later, in a bar under a railway bridge with a curved ceiling, that Paul met Tess for the first time. She was unmistakable as Sylvia's sister. They shared the same colouring and oval faces. Modern Modiglianis. But instead of make-up and high heels, she was bare-faced, wearing grubby plimsolls with holes fraying the sides. Her hair, unbrushed, was threaded with extensions, purple acrylic skeins. She was also noticeably prettier than Sylvia, he observed, guiltily. Her nose slightly less piratical, her mouth neater.

'Tess!' Sylvia was already on her way to drunk. 'Can we just forget about earlier? I'm sorry.'

'Ok,' said Tess, nodding, a brief smile. She sat down as Danny went to the bar for their drinks.

'Nice to meet you at last,' she said to Paul. 'I've heard so much about you.' She looked at him, gravely, and he noticed the irises of her eyes, one brown and one blue.

'Likewise,' he said, offering his hand to be shaken and then feeling stupid. But she responded and her palm was dry and cool, her grip loose. She had none of Sylvia's puppyish enthusiasm, the desire to be liked that she wore on her chest, like a brooch.

Danny came back with two pints of lager and a packet of crisps, the shiny skin of which he split like a mackerel's, to fillet the contents.

'Cheese and onion, help yourselves,' he said. 'Looking forward to tonight. A night on the town in the big smoke! I'm taking my T-shirts to a couple of places tomorrow so I can't go too crazy.'

'You're making T-shirts?' said Sylvia. Her eyes glittered

and Paul sensed, confusedly, the question's underbelly of scorn.

'Yeah, I've made up some with my logo on. They're selling pretty well off the website, but I just need to get them in a few shops ... Got some meetings set up,' said Danny.

'What an entrepreneur!' said Sylvia, laughing.

'They're pretty good,' said Tess, and Danny looked at her gratefully.

'I might not be winning many surf competitions any more,' he said, 'but I've still got my fans out there. It's all about diversification these days.'

'And you're a gardener?' said Paul to Tess.

'That's right,' said Tess. She didn't elaborate and Paul glanced at her hands. Her fingers were longer than Sylvia's, oval nails unpainted.

'Tess gives amazing massages, too,' said Sylvia. 'With all these different aromatherapy oils. How is the business going?'

'It's more energy healing, really,' said Tess. 'Reiki. I'm working at the salon in town on Tuesdays.' An image of Tess pummelling flesh sprouted in Paul's head. He couldn't fathom it. She seemed far too dignified and remote.

* * *

'After she had a few drinks last night, Tess told me she had a miscarriage,' whispered Sylvia, in bed the next morning, glancing towards the door. Even when they were alone, her statements often had a stagey note, as if performed for an audience.

'God, poor her,' said Paul. 'That's rough.' He propped himself up against the wall. 'How far along was she?'

'Ten weeks,' said Sylvia, then shrugged. 'Rough. But I was just so surprised that they would even consider it, I didn't know what to say. I mean, Danny, a dad. That's madness.'

'Why?' said Paul, equably. 'He seems like a decent enough bloke. Haven't they been together since they were teenagers? Maybe it's what they want?'

Sylvia frowned and climbed out of bed, moving to look out of the window.

'Tess has never been with anyone else,' she said, her back to him. 'Neither of them works full-time. They don't even have an indoor toilet.' She turned to look at Paul, almost pleadingly. 'Surely you can see it's a *ridiculous* idea?'

Paul didn't answer. He never knew how to disagree with Sylvia. Instead, he stood up himself and walked across to where she stood, standing behind her and squeezing her waist with his hands, like a ketchup bottle.

'Stop! That tickles,' said Sylvia, laughing and forgetting.

6

Now

'I'll give you a moment,' said the woman. She was kindly, practised.

Paul nodded. She shut the door behind her. The room was small, windowless and spotless, a vase of lush chrysanthemums on the mantlepiece too perfect to be real. He looked towards the table where Sylvia lay. Another impossible task. Like the manual he had left in the car, expecting to be read.

She looked more like herself than she had towards the end in the hospice. Her hair still in grey curls, no hint of its previous colour, but her face softer somehow. She wasn't in pain, he realised. That was it. Yet her cheeks were starting to hollow inwards, to collapse in on themselves. She appeared ancient, timeless, the scaffold of gender stripped away.

He couldn't really see her body, it was covered with a sheet. A *shroud*. But the terrain under the fabric was familiar. The hillocks and mounds of his wife's shape achingly familiar. Although it had been reconfigured lately, her new breasts perter than the old ones that had slid under her armpits. But she was right, he hadn't liked the renovation, would probably have preferred a simple scar, acknowledgement of what had happened.

Like this, without make-up, he could see every freckle on her lovely face. Her polka-dot skin, eyebrows translucent, eyelids shut, lips sealed. So unlike her. She was such a chatterbox. Even after she was ill, she filled most silences with words. Observations, asides, disquisitions.

There was no breath, no soft inhalation, no shuddering release. He had seen it a thousand times before, in his surgery, with animals, of course. And although you never quite get over the fact of death, he thought he knew about mortality. But just like birth, like those ecstatic moments when Megan and Jude emerged, it turned out witnessing death in your own species was different.

Looking at her was categorical. She was gone. The first human corpse he had ever seen. Mick was already six feet under in Australian dirt by the time he made it back to Perth. His death had been so sudden; Sylvia had been pregnant. But it was no excuse, he should have got there in time.

But still, this wasn't like what other people have said to him. He didn't find himself expecting Sylvia to sit up. To shuck off the shroud and start chattering away about her day, Jude's reading record, the latest drama in Megan's social circle.

By contrast, she was so obviously absent that what he felt most keenly was a crushing loneliness. How could you do this to me? he thought. I did everything I could for you, gave you all I could and then you just go and die on me. She had given

33

him the slip, again. Slightly out of reach, like always. He had tried so hard to tether her to him. For a while it had seemed to work. There was that sweet spot in their history, when she lost her restiveness, but retained her joy. He thought she had finally grown up, that she was his to keep.

Those had been the days he would never forget. The sweet normality of raising their children together. Blithely speculating about Megan's graduation, Jude's prospective BMX career, grandchildren – as if the future was their right.

But then, after Rosa, she floated away into a yawning abyss. They never regained that confidence, that sense that they were building something. And then she was diagnosed. And now this. Always slightly in front of him, looking back over her shoulder.

He bent down and pressed his head to her chest. The spot he loved so much, just beneath her clavicle. The place that used to feel like home. Her body, once so precious, endlessly enthralling, but just an object now. Still, the last time he could ever do it, could ever feel her flesh.

'How are you getting on?' The woman was back, standing in the doorway. Paul straightened, awkwardly embarrassed.

'I was just …'

'Don't worry,' says the woman. 'Do what you need to do.'

* * *

'You know, sometimes I like to imagine that Mummy has just gone on holiday,' said Megan at bedtime, Paul sitting on the edge of her bed. 'That she'll be coming home soon.'

'I know what you mean,' said Paul, cautiously. Perhaps he should have taken the children with him to see Sylvia's body, he thought. To know that it was definitive. That she was never coming back. Barbara had counselled it, first in the hospice and then the funeral parlour, but he had put his foot down. Sylvia herself hadn't wanted it, she had been very clear.

'I know it's what the books say you should do,' she said to him, when it had just been the two of them, him spooning her tentatively, terrified of hurting her. 'But I don't want them to see me like that. I can't bear it. Please.' And he had capitulated, as he so often did when it came to his wife.

'It feels like if I wish for it really, really hard, then maybe it will come true,' said Megan. She had half-buried her face under the duvet, embarrassed. Paul swallowed. This was unbearable.

'It's hard to believe that she has truly gone,' he said, carefully. 'But sometimes even if we really want something to happen, it still doesn't.' He swallowed. He knew exactly what his daughter meant. Even if it didn't make any sense, he too had one ear half-cocked for Sylvia clattering towards the front door. Megan was silent then and he bent over to kiss her forehead.

'Night-night,' he said.

'Call me chicken,' said Megan. 'That's what Mummy used to call me. Or little rabbit.'

'Ok … my little rabbit,' said Paul, leaning over Megan. Even to himself, he sounded wooden. He never could access the warmth Sylvia found so natural. It wasn't his way, wasn't how he was brought up. Certainly, Miriam and Mick never called him pet names. His family weren't big on showing emotion; they kept their cards close to their chest. The love was there, in the way his mother pasted his skinny boyhood shoulders with sun cream, checked his limbs for ticks after another long day tearing around in the sunshine, but it wasn't articulated freely, spread around. Sometimes he worried that Sylvia belittled love, by tossing it about. But most of the time he was glad that his children were left in no doubt.

'You didn't say it right,' complained Megan. 'It sounds stupid.' She sighed deeply, making Paul's parental insufficiencies clear.

'I'm sorry,' said Paul.

Megan had turned from him by then, was settling for sleep. And Paul stood. He had brought the manual in from the car in his work bag. It called to him and yet he felt reluctance too. Once he had read everything Sylvia had left for him, she really would be gone forever. Outside his daughter's room he bent over, as if winded, his hands on his knees. Trying to fight back the urge to weep, the terror that threatened to wash over him.

Eventually he gathered himself and went downstairs, past the pile growing on the stairs. The things that needed sorting around the house. The work that his wife did constantly, without appearing to do anything. He hadn't realised. He sloshed rum into a glass and sat down on the living-room sofa, Sylvia's laptop on his crotch. He seldom checked his own social media accounts. Despite living so far from home, he found them tiresome. The dinners and marathons of old school friends merely induced a kind of listlessness. Such a naked pageant of ego and insecurity. Besides, his work was of the old-fashioned kind you didn't need to promote and, despite the time difference, his mother only ever used the phone.

But Sylvia had been addicted. She was the perfect storm of vanity and insecurity. She checked it constantly and posted pictures of Jude and Megan, waiting for the validation of the likes. They were beautiful children, he knew she enjoyed presenting a controlled image of motherhood, one that legitimised the sticky, chaotic reality.

When she tired of it he finally knew, incontrovertibly, that she was dying, drawing her horns in. Shortly afterwards, she had passed him a slip of paper. 'My log-in details. For all my accounts,' she had said. 'You should have them. So you can tell people.'

'Tell people?' he said, then realised what she meant. She wanted him to announce her death to her online network, like a flyer on a village noticeboard, or a death notice in a local newspaper.

'You might want to check it too, sometimes,' said Sylvia. 'People will write things. These things are like memorials now, online. If you don't delete my page, it will stay there forever, so you may as well check it.'

'Oh god, Sylv, you know ...' he groaned, 'I'm not sure I can.'

'Please, Paul,' she had said. 'Do it for me. And the children can look at it when they're older too.'

So, he had taken the slip of paper and now he logged in

to Instagram – her favourite – curated images, the bits of her life she wanted the world to see. Flat whites, peaches, stippled skies, Jude's bare feet, Ted's silly, roadkill face. The sepia-filtered selfies where she pouted, unintentionally, trying to look casual.

He had chosen a picture of her. Far more natural than those self-conscious photographs she took of herself. It was from a trip to the park, when she was pregnant with Rosa. Their lives steady but still full of possibility. A smile in the evening light, her hair like a beautiful shawl spread over her shoulders. It was hard to remember her ever looking that young, yet it was only three years ago.

He started to type the caption. '*I'm just writing to let you know that my beautiful wife Sylvia Katherine Clarke died on Sunday, after fighting cancer for almost a year ...*' He paused. Sylvia wouldn't like the use of 'fighting'. She hated any battle metaphors when it came to her disease.

'So, if I don't get better, it will basically mean that I didn't fight hard enough?' she would say, angrily.

He deleted 'fighting' and wrote 'suffering with cancer' before continuing. '*We are heartbroken. Sylvia had a unique ability to light up a room and was a brilliant mother. We cannot imagine our lives without her. Paul, Megan and Jude xxxx.*'

There. He had done it. He felt nauseous and flattened. As he took another swig of his drink, the heart button started flashing, as Sylvia's digital community, so much more malleable than her real-life one, started to respond.

The comments started. 'A bright light taken too soon.'

'Thinking of your precious family.' 'Only the good die young.' 'Love and light.'

Sylvia would have hated the virtue-signalling sentimentality of it, he knew, while also revelling in being the centre of attention. But he was conflicted. He knew how lonely she had been, even before Rosa. Aside from Nush, the mother of Jude's best friend, Ryan, she had struggled to form meaningful relationships at the school gate. She was torn, finding deep personal fulfillment in motherhood but struggling with the humdrum social requirements of raffle tickets and bake sales. It went back to that problem she had had in younger life, of not easily discerning convention. He didn't recognise many of the names commenting; Sylvia herself had probably never met them in the flesh.

Another one. 'She brought happiness wherever she went.'

Paul frowned at the name. What did this person – Emmy35 – know about the pointy happiness that Sylvia could bring, he wondered? He thought of how Sylvia used to make him laugh until his belly ached, with a skit she used to do just for him, where she flawlessly impersonated an Australian accent, an unreconstructed bloke desperate for a beer. He was never quite certain if it was him she was sending up, but they both found it hilarious, giggling until tears leaked from their eyes.

He thought of how she waited for the children at the front door if they had been out, squawking with delight when she saw them, even if they had only gone to the swings. 'My babies!' she would say. 'I missed you so much.'

He remembered a summer evening on the sofa, a square of golden light on the wall opposite, when she lifted her top, unselfconsciously, so secure in her allure. She took his hands and placed them on her skin, looking him straight in the eyes all the while. Challenging him.

Yes, she could bring happiness all right. But he was certain this person, whoever they were, had no idea about the specifics of it. And she could also impart upset, anxiety, anger. She had a unique ability to say the one thing you didn't want to hear, as if placing her manicured fingernail on a bruise.

Certainly, he didn't recognise this one-dimensional portrait of his wife as a saint. But who was? Sylvia had often been selfish, vain and preoccupied with some of the wrong things. But those character insufficiencies made her good points shine, like gold in dirt. Her honesty, her sense of humour, her courage.

He wanted to post something to reflect this, the complicated reality, but couldn't find the words.

He wandered to the kitchen, looking for more alcohol and something to assuage the gnawing in his stomach. He was living off sandwiches, crisps in a tube, instant noodles. After Sylvia's death it was a shock to him to find that he was still hungry. Dinner rolled around and his disloyal body screamed for something to eat.

He fished a piece of ham out of the fridge, chased it with an olive, and refilled his glass. It was a muggy evening and he pushed open the door to the garden, that concertina of glass that Sylvia had demanded, before stepping out into the night.

It wasn't a big plot, but they had used it hard. Another room, really, rather than anything like the disparate wildernesses that both he and Sylvia came from. Quietly, never really articulating it, both of them thrilled to its sense of containment. They came from opposite sides of the earth but had seen nature close up and knew how vicious and unrelenting it could be.

In their garden they were in control. It was a place for spontaneous barbecues and drinking rosé. A square of plastic grass ('Tess will disown me when she finds out,' Sylvia had laughed when it had been installed) and the ubiquitous trampoline, a futile bid to contain Jude's energy. The only notable plants were a large lavender that scented the night, and an unlikely cherry tree that yielded hard, slightly frightening fruit that fell to the ground and festered.

On an evening like this, Sylvia would sometimes perch on the step by the lavender and slowly eke out a single cigarette for as long as she could. Less in the years since becoming a mother, but she had never quite fully jettisoned the habit, even if she gave up while pregnant. A tiny act of rebellion after a day of wiping noses, stacking plates, lying on the carpet playing with Jude, praising Megan's latest story. Precise smoke circles sent skyward like a distress signal.

Paul moved to his wife's preferred spot and sat down himself, as if by mimicking her movements, he could feel closer to her. He stared at the flower bed, not sure what he was doing. But, sure enough, a discarded cigarette butt was tucked in the edge of the flower bed. He put down his glass and picked it up, pincered between thumb and forefinger. Smoked right to the filter, a smear of coral lipstick against deathly white.

He tucked the relic in his pocket and stood. It was time. He couldn't put it off any longer. His wife had left him something to read.

7

Sylvia's Manual

Parenting Jude has been a bit like trying to tame a leopard. The constant motion, the unpredictability, the ferocity that winds me afresh each day.

He's feral, our son. But you know that. Spirited is what they say, these days, I think. A timid euphemism.

It's been hard to keep up, even before I got sick. Being his mother is exhausting.

But I've loved it too. Life is never dull with Jude around. I used to worry that motherhood meant mundanity, but Jude's finely tuned sense of the surreal precludes it. Still, I can't deny that a perk of my current situation is that I'm finally getting to sit, very still, in sunlight from an open window, for the first time in five years. Even in the depths of my pain at what we've lost, I can appreciate that.

Just like the croissant you brought me this morning, the sight of birds soaring in the patch of blue sky visible from my chair. Unexpectedly beautiful moments strung across my day.

I was so reluctant to come in here, to St Luke's, but now I see it was the right decision. I can focus on these instants more clearly, they become sharply defined. I miss our bed, the fake-monsoon of our shower, our battle-scarred kitchen table, but it's easier to rest here.

Even as a newborn, Jude demanded constant motion. That jerky, sleep-deprived dance I used to do to stop him roaring. Then chasing him around as a toddler, the way he would immediately scale the perimeter of wherever we went, heading for the hills. More recently always scooting ahead, just out of sight, as I ran behind shouting, 'Jude! Jude!' He always did make me look like a bad mother.

Sometimes – often – I used to worry what I'd done. To create such a hyperactive child.

But, in fact, it was Megan that I wasn't prepared for. I drank wine, ate soft cheese, smoked for weeks before I knew I was pregnant with her. Then, with Jude, I was so careful from the beginning.

But there's nothing like motherhood to make you realise how little in life you really control. Aside from breast cancer, perhaps.

Despite how he is, his contrariness, I've always found Jude so loveable it's like a skewer through my heart. I can relate to him, we're made of the same stuff. It's been harder for you, I know that. You would never admit it, you're far too nice for that. But you pictured a son as calm as you, as measured. I know you don't shout – I'm the shouter. But sometimes I can see you disengaging from him, disinterested, like when you've been seated next to someone at a dinner party whose political opinions mean you could never respect them.

Your template of masculinity was Mick, after all. Jude's emotional blowsiness unsettles you – more than it should. I can see it so clearly, although you try to conceal it. I know you're wondering if perhaps your son is a bad seed. Like his mother.

But Jude has a kind of crazy charisma. I still can't picture who he is going to become. Drug-addicted drop-out or prime minister, the jury is out. I so wish that I was going to get to find out.

I read somewhere, in the 'pre' days, that our children are sent to teach us something. Rubbish, I used to think. More soppy bullshit, like all those other Instagram truisms. 'Everything happens for a reason', or 'What doesn't kill us makes us stronger'. Please. But I think there is something in the idea of our children educating us, for you and Jude. Listen to what he is trying to say to you, really listen.

I've started to see the love I have for my two children in different colours. Maternal synesthesia. Megan's is the gorgeous indigo of a Cornish night sky, Jude's a bright, orangey-red. Another secret of motherhood you won't find in the books – you may well love your children equally, but the love itself will be different, with feathers or claws.

Behind his restlessness is a savage intelligence. I've glimpsed it. Less academic than Megan's, certainly, more unconventional. But it's there in his stubborn refusal to do what he doesn't want to do, his quick parsing of every situation to see what he can get out of it.

I'm starting to suspect he might be dyslexic. Like Tess. When I can get him to sit down and practise his reading, the letters seem to bunch and wriggle on the page for him. He gets so frustrated. I do too. So lately I've given up. There doesn't seem to be much point. I'm not going to be the one to teach him to read now, there isn't enough time. I don't want to spend my last days with him asking him to do things. Trying to get Jude to jump through hoops, to conform, is not my job any more. It's yours, I'm afraid.

I just get to soak him up. Watch his fire burn. And it does. When he comes in here to visit me, the energy of the place changes immediately, shifts and crackles. Our boy is alive. He arrives in a blaze of energy, chatting about his day, about rhinos, the moon, what he had for lunch.

My friends here, the dying, look forward to the times you bring him. For Jude is quite the tonic in this place. Constantly propelled forwards, with no time to savour mundane moments, he reminds us all of another way of being. And while I'm enjoying my newfound love of the small stuff, grateful for it, I miss what he embodies. That carelessness towards life. I used to be like that.

I don't even mind when he kicks his football out into the corridor for the tenth time. I've stopped aggressively whispering, 'Stop! Jude!' I'm just letting him be. I wish I'd thought to do it sooner. If only I hadn't minded so much about what other people thought.

And when he stops moving, for those precious moments, to climb onto my lap and put his hot arms around my neck, I feel like a queen. He could always make me feel like that. I remember wrapping him in a towel after his bath and carrying him to his bedroom. He would lock his eyes on mine and whisper, 'You're the best mummy in the world.' It got me, every single time.

Yesterday, I sat there, trying to fix the sensation in my mind. He still hasn't lost that caramel smell on the top of his head. A relic of his babyhood, like the barely visible crease in his thighs. Six months tops and they'll be gone. Just like me.

Leaving him – and Megan – is the thing that I just can't square in all of this. I let go of my own future quite quickly, such as it was. I've even – reluctantly, of course – let go of you, the love of my life. But I just can't see how I'm going to let go of them. They were my future, my shot at immortality.

And I'm guilty too. So guilty. I should have been a better mother when there was still time. I tried so hard, but I made so many mistakes. Not just the commonplace failures. The times I lost my temper or burrowed into my phone instead of looking them in the eyes. Skipped downstairs at bedtime for a glass of wine, just as Megan was opening up. There was other stuff too. Things I can't forgive myself for, that you had no idea about. When I got my diagnosis, it felt like karma. But I never told you that. I couldn't.

I wasn't cut out for motherhood. I did try to warn you. I wasn't good enough, pure enough, strong enough. I tried so hard to be, I loved them so much, but I unravelled.

And I never had a role model in domestic drudgery. Barbara was very clear about that. I didn't grow up watching a thwarted woman peeling potatoes and dabbing stain remover onto collars. Instead, I watched my father, struggling.

The cliff house was always filthy. Did you know that? Actual dirt. Strips of black on the skirting board and yellowing sheets. Camus on the bookshelves, crap spatters on the toilet bowl. Genteel, middle-class poverty. Of course, we should have thought to do something about it. Tess and me. Should have snapped on the Marigolds and helped William stay on top of things. But we were children. We didn't know anything else. It was our home.

You made me feel so safe, I thought maybe it would be all right. Maybe I could learn normality by osmosis from you, so good. Forged in Australian sunshine, with open skies and saltwater running through your veins, you shone a light in my dusty corners. Made me feel normal. For a while, at least.

47

8

Then

An empty packet of Jaffa Cakes. Crisp packets. The hind of a plastic loaf. A pile of slimy chocolate muffin cases that looked as though they had been sucked. Crumbs, foil balled into angry little cannons.

Paul surveyed Sylvia's kitchen in dismay. He had let himself into her and Ariadne's flat with the newly cut spare key she had presented him with the week before. 'Here you go – the key to my heart!' she had said, laughing throatily and changing the subject, but Paul had been touched at the intimacy.

Sylvia never ate food like this. It must have been Ariadne, stoned. There was a sound of a toilet flushing. Sylvia emerged into the kitchen. She was wearing a towelling robe that looked as if it had seen better days and had mascara stains under her eyes.

'You didn't say you were coming over.' Her voice was

exhausted. She didn't leap towards him and encircle his neck with her arms – her usual greeting.

'Are you all right?' said Paul.

Sylvia nodded, not meeting his eyes, fractionally. 'Yes.'

'Somebody's had the munchies!' said Paul, eyes sliding to the rubbish. Sylvia didn't respond but moved towards the wrappers and started bundling them all into the bin. Shiny, sticky plastic and cardboard. A junk-modeller's dream.

'Was this all Ariadne? You shouldn't have to tidy up after her.' Paul forced a laugh. Sylvia said nothing, but tears started tracking down her cheeks. She rummaged under the sink for cleaning products and then produced a spray, which she started dousing the kitchen countertops with. It smelled of synthetic lemon. Fake cleanliness.

'Steady on,' Paul said. 'Where's my hello? What's going on?'

'It's nothing.' Sylvia shook her head.

Paul stepped towards her, put his arms around her waist.

'It doesn't seem like nothing,' he said, quietly. He could smell distress on her, rank and adrenal, like the scared animals brought in to see him.

'Don't, get off,' she said, jerking him away. She smelled of toothpaste and, faintly but indisputably, sick.

'Please,' wheedled Paul. 'I've missed you.'

'I'm disgusting,' said Sylvia.

'You're not,' said Paul. Her eyes met his.

'I am. You don't realise how disgusting. You've only seen the best of me.'

Paul thought of the months they had been together. It

49

was true that he still couldn't believe his luck. It was as if a unicorn had wandered into his life. Everything seemed more exciting than it had before. Trips to the cinema, walks in the park, Friday evenings in the pub were all strangely enchanting. Nobody had ever made him laugh – or come – as hard. Was this the thing he had been waiting for, with slight unease? The catch.

'I've got to get ready to go out,' said Sylvia. 'You should go. You shouldn't have come over without telling me. I know you've got a key but I don't want you just bursting in on me. It makes me feel claustrophobic.'

She was retreating now, towards the kitchen door. She just wanted him gone. Couldn't bear to look at his expectant, in-nocent face for another second. Paul lived in a world without dark corners; hers was full of spidery recesses.

'We can talk about this,' said Paul. 'It's not a big deal. You were hungry and you ate some rubbish. Who cares?' He thought of the meals they had eaten in different cafés. Sylvia's careful portions. He assumed she had a bird-like appetite. Many girls did, didn't they? That was how she maintained her pin-up waist and pipe-cleaner arms.

'I don't want to talk about it,' said Sylvia. 'You haven't got a clue.'

'What do you mean?' said Paul.

'You are so straightforward, Paul, everything in your life has been easy. You don't know what this' – she gestured towards the bin – 'has been – *is* – like.'

Sylvia thought then of Paul wolfing down a burger, unself-consciously. He ate it and then it was gone. It didn't weigh on his mind for days afterwards. He didn't write it down in a notebook that he carried everywhere with him. In that moment, she churned with fury for how little he understood. How hard she had to work to appear carefree, to ignore the hunger that rose inside her like a dragon.

'Try me,' said Paul. 'It's not a big deal. And not everything in my life has been easy.'

'It is a big deal, Paul, and that's exactly why I don't want to talk about it.'

Sylvia was cornered. She had always been so careful. Perhaps Paul thought her breath naturally smelled of mints, just as her eyes were constantly perfectly ringed in kohl. Like most men, he had no idea of what went on behind the scenes. The shaving, bleaching, plucking. Smearing foundation onto alabaster skin. Vomiting until the blood vessels in her face popped.

'Ok, I'll leave,' said Paul. 'I don't want to pressure you. But this doesn't have to mean anything for us.' He sounded sad. 'I just wanted to hang out. Call me if you want to talk. You don't need to be ... ashamed.' The word hung in the air.

Leaving, he couldn't stop himself from taking the stairs two at a time, loping back out into the bright afternoon and normality. To Sylvia, the swift clattering sounded as if he were running away. But even as he sighed with relief at being out in the street, Paul felt something slotting into place in his mind. So this was it. He had known there was something. There was that expression of weary horror she had when she encountered mirrors, before she remembered to paste on a smile. Her dislike of talking about her past.

Sylvia stood in the kitchen with Ted at her feet. His paws were deliberately positioned to graze her bare feet, so she knew he was there. She had got careless. Paul had said he might call over at some point on Sunday. She had given him the key. It was almost like she wanted him to find out.

But nobody could love her if they knew what she did.

She had thought that perhaps being with someone like Paul – a good person who was nice to her – might stop the habit. It had, for a bit, but the voice in her head had slowly started whispering to her again. This internal critic belonged to a bitchy female that Sylvia, in an effort at disassociation on the advice of a counsellor, nicknamed Magda.

She couldn't visualise her exactly, but she was thin, certainly. Thinner than Sylvia would ever be. All elbows. And while Magda wasn't always vocal, in the times she was silent Sylvia knew she was still watching. Totting up how repellent she was.

Sure enough, Magda hissed to her now, reminded her of how undeserving she was of someone as whole as Paul. Sylvia started to cry again. Hopelessly, almost silently. Ariadne wouldn't be back for hours. She thought of the half-eaten cake in the bin.

Maybe she should finish it off. That was just the kind of thing someone as disgusting as her would do.

Sylvia stood by the sink for five minutes, engaged in an internal battle, before turning to the bin and rootling inside, among soggy tea bags and cigarette ash, for the cheap corner-shop Battenberg. Squares of fondant pink and vanilla-yellow. She crammed it into her mouth, not really tasting it, staring out of the window at the blue sky. Magda was silenced, archly satisfied, but Sylvia was desperate for this to be the last time. Now she had found Paul, it had to stop. Ted watched her, not judging. He had seen it all before.

9

Now

The pills were tiny and bitter. Animal sedatives intended to be crushed into pet food, concealed in chunks of cheap meat and jelly. Paul took three at a time. Enough to knock out a Labrador or afford him a few sweet hours of oblivion.

He should have gone to his GP for his own prescription, he knew that, but he couldn't bear to. He'd had enough of doctors in the last year to last a lifetime. They hadn't been able to help when it counted. And he was sick of their blithe arrogance. They thought themselves superior to him, invulnerable.

Insomnia was new to him. Unlike Sylvia, he had always been a deep sleeper. But things had changed. His worldview had admitted the unimaginable in so many ways, why not this, too? Each night, since she had left for St Luke's, he remained perched on a ravine, unable to drop into the abyss of unconsciousness. And each night, he gave in and swallowed the tablets.

They usually worked until the small hours. Then he would roll onto Sylvia's side of the bed, where there was still a depression, moulded in memory foam, to the shape of her body. He would turn his face to her bedside table, left exactly how she'd had it with a pile of dusty paperbacks, a spatter of hairgrips and a glass for water, ringed with limescale. Impossible to believe she wouldn't be coming back.

Lying there he was briefly comforted. He could steel himself for Jude's inevitable arrival at 6 a.m. Every morning he would barrel in shouting, 'Mummy!' as if he had forgotten and still expected to find Sylvia in bed, blearily extending her arms. Every single time, Paul felt the pain afresh in his chest.

But the night after reading the manual, the sedatives failed. There was some constriction, deep inside, that overrode the chemicals and his brain buzzed with static, as if he were trying to tune into a distant radio station.

He kept turning over, as if a new position would yield a different result. Eventually he switched on the bedside light and sat upright in his bed. He hadn't bothered to put the blinds down – he woke so early anyway – so he stared out at the muddy orange phosphorescence of street lights. A place where you could never see the stars.

He had told Jude, in a fit of fancy when it first became clear that Sylvia wasn't going to recover, that Mummy was going to become a star in the sky. He realised his mistake the night after the one in which she died, when Jude strained his eyes at the window at bedtime.

'But I can't see her, Daddy, I can't see any stars!' Jude had shouted.

'It's the city,' Paul had responded, desperately. 'We'll have to go to Cornwall to see her star properly. Sorry, Jude, I promise we'll be able to.'

Eventually, Paul turned off the light. He was almost inebriated with exhaustion and he felt himself finally starting to drift, warm water closing over his face. But then an image of Sylvia towards the end appeared in his head and he was hooked back, wide awake.

He moaned softly. Not this. He had always viewed Sylvia's emotional vacillations with incomprehension, even, he was ashamed to admit, some condescension. He had tried telling her once that he believed mental control was anybody's for the taking. You just had to train your thoughts. Focus on the positive. She had looked at him and smiled sadly, before saying, 'Oh Paul. You don't have a clue.'

But now, just when he needed it most, his own mastery was slipping. His previously compliant mind wouldn't afford him the respite of oblivion. He turned over, towards the door, and lay very still, curled in a foetal position, in the dark. He struggled to catch breath, his sore heart throbbing like a rotten tooth. It must be the pills, he thought, groggily, the grief. Never mind the manual, which, when he had finally sat down to read, he had whipped through hungrily, unable to restrain himself. It was all sending him over the edge. He was losing it.

As he lay there, he noticed that the room still smelled of Sylvia's perfume. That cloying scent that would never have been his choice – he preferred cleaner, ozonic smells – but was apposite and so he grew to love it. Pavlov's dog, trained to respond. It was around him, up his nostrils, at the back of his throat. He pushed himself up slightly in the bed.

'Sylvia?' he said. But there was no one there, of course, and he lay back. Yet it was inescapable, the fragrance blooming in the darkness. It couldn't be on the bed linen, which he had clumsily changed since Sylvia had gone into the hospice. Megan must have been playing around earlier in the day, spritzing the remaining bottle that sat on Sylvia's dressing table. Trying to summon a sense of her mother. He shut his eyes and inhaled. So strong he could almost taste it, but comforting, as if Sylvia were tucked up next to him, passed out without bothering to take off her make-up, half-cut after a night of negronis, cadged fags and idle gossip. He felt something inside unclench.

* * *

The next morning, at breakfast, Jude staged a show for Paul and Megan. As if nothing had happened. He stood on a chair, thrashing an air guitar, singing a song he had clearly just made up. He was wearing an old pair of Sylvia's sunglasses he had found somewhere, white-rimmed bug shades.

'Stop it, Jude,' said Paul. 'I've got a headache.' Megan barely glanced at her brother.

'One last number,' said Jude, in a flawless American accent, his voice husky, like the craggy rocker he was impersonating. 'Just one.' He scanned the room as if playing to a large audience, waved at Ted, who watched him narrowly from his basket.

'Ok,' said Paul, reluctantly, buttering the toast he didn't want. Jude turned around, wiggled his bum, started singing again, looking over his shoulder to catch Paul's eye. Despite everything, Paul found himself smiling. His son so completely ridiculous. Jude grinned back, satisfied, then dropped into his chair, finally deigning to eat.

Later, at the surgery, exhaustion slowed Paul down. Behind everything he did – stuffing depositories up the bottom of an ageing greyhound, conducting a routine neuter on a young tom cat, eating a disappointing egg cress salad sandwich – lurked a sense of oddness. Sylvia's sentences spiralling around his head.

His receptionist Carla noticed it and asked if he was all right. 'You shouldn't be back at work yet, Paul,' she had said gently. 'It's insanity.' Her eyes were wide, concerned. Carla would do anything for him, he intuited that. Always had. Plump, with acrylic nails that changed colour weekly. Currently a grey-brown of a mouse's fur.

She had never liked Sylvia, he knew. She disliked the panicked mid-morning phone calls after his wife had locked herself out, the way she sometimes deposited Jude and Megan with him before he had even gone home, so she could go straight out, the casual dismissal of Carla's own significance to Paul's business.

But he had shaken his head, demurred. The only way he could continue was by hanging his days on the skeleton of what had gone on before. The crematorium hadn't been able to offer them a spot until the end of the week, Barbara had the children, there was work to be done.

Later, his mother rang him, to ask, in hushed tones, how he was coping, whether Jude and Megan were all right, if there was anything she could do to help with the funeral preparations.

'I should have got an earlier flight. I should be there right now helping you hold the fort.'

'Ma, it's all right,' said Paul. Part of him wanted to cry out for her, in a way that he hadn't since she had taught him that wasn't what big boys did. Yet he couldn't. Miriam would think he was losing it and, above all, his mother had taught him the importance of keeping going. Of putting one foot in front of the other.

Once he got home, Barbara wanted to discuss the order of service. The readings, music, catering. With time to prepare, Sylvia had formulated a clear idea of how the day should go. She had decreed that everyone wear bright clothes in different colours of the rainbow. She wanted upbeat music. Sushi.

She essentially wanted it to be a party, as if she were going to be attending herself. But although it had given her some small consolation to plan it, from her sick bed, Paul had always thought her ideas wrongheaded. Somehow, even in death, Sylvia prevailed. A funeral should be sober and sad, giving people a chance to say goodbye, he thought. Not a proxy rave. Sometimes conventions were useful. He sensed that Barbara thought this too. She was trying to insert her own readings. To add quiche to the sushi platters.

She was in full flow when Paul produced the envelope that Sylvia had left for her mother, paperclipped with several others to the back of the manual's floppy pages.

'Sylvia wanted you to have this,' said Paul, handing over the letter. Barbara stopped talking.

'She left me something?' was all she said, but she went home quickly after that, to read the missive from her daughter alone. Sylvia had also written to the children, letters for their eighteenth birthdays. And there was something for Tess too, an envelope marked in his wife's distinctive sloping scrawl. But after reading the manual, Paul dreaded passing it on. He would have to, of course, at some point. But as yet hadn't felt able to entertain the prospect.

Tess had come up from Cornwall to stay with Barbara shortly before Sylvia's death, warned that the end was imminent. She managed to make it to her sister's bedside, although after Sylvia had already slipped into unconsciousness. For reasons Paul had never fathomed, the sisters had grown distant as the years passed. They hadn't even bothered to argue with each other as they once had; a new formality precluded it. And although lip service was paid, Megan and Jude scarcely knew Danny and Tess's daughter, Flora.

Paul could trace the schism, even if he hadn't understood why it had occurred. It had happened shortly after Jude was born. Tess and Danny had come to London, to meet the baby, pink and simian, swaddled in muslin. But catastrophe happened while Paul was at work. He came home to find Jude screaming and Sylvia pacing up and down, both their cheeks slick with tears.

'Where are they?' he had asked, expecting to find Danny and Tess installed on the sofa, or smoking roll-ups on the balcony. They were such a pair, his sister-in-law and her boyfriend, with their tangled hair and knitted jumpers smelling of woodsmoke.

'They've gone,' said Sylvia. 'We had an argument.' But instead of the fury she usually demonstrated after a fight with Tess, she was wearily subdued.

'I'm sure you'll sort it out,' Paul had said, annunciating the words over the roaring of his son. Sylvia had shaken her head.

'I don't think so. Not this time,' she said. Then, looking down at Jude, 'He just won't stop. He's overtired. You need to take him out for a drive or something. I just need some sleep, a couple of hours.' Her tone wheedling, subject closed.

Paul had expected a reconciliation, as usual, but none came in the days that followed. Then, scarcely a month later, they heard via Barbara that Tess was expecting a baby herself. At last.

'God. She must have been pregnant when they came up, when we had that huge row,' said Sylvia, head in her hands. 'I had no idea. The timing ...'

'You should ring to wish her congratulations,' said Paul. 'Put it behind you.'

'I don't think she'll want to hear from me,' was all Sylvia would say, trying to plug a dummy into Jude's roaring mouth. 'God, this baby.'

But she did call. Paul heard her do it – a bright, brittle 'Congratulations!', so different from the unforced tone Sylvia usually dropped into during her and Tess's frequent phone conversations, which Paul had always thought sounded like her truest, unvarnished self. It was followed by a muffled, 'I'm sorry, Tessy.' After that, the relationship was defined by new parameters. They no longer shared the inconsequential details of their lives, some spark of sisterhood extinguished. And it remained so, even as significant life events stacked up. The birth of Tess and Danny's daughter, Flora. William's decline. Rosa. Even the breast cancer diagnosis. They were cordial, outwardly supportive, but the intense familiarity had gone.

Paul raised the change with Sylvia, several times, but to no avail.

'I thought you wanted me to be more like you,' she would say, not meeting his eyes. 'Less emotional … Maybe I've finally got an adult relationship with my sister. You should be happy about that. I really can't win, can I?'

He could hardly counter that, so he left it. Their lives were so frantic and then fractured, he didn't have time to go digging for answers. A small part of him enjoyed the fact he had Sylvia all to himself.

For so long, he hadn't been able to comprehend it. It was only now his wife was gone that she had finally filled him in.

10

Then

Megan's conception had been an accident. It wasn't as if they were meticulous, but they had a system. But a few particularly hardy spermatozoa lingered in the plush cavern of Sylvia's womb long enough for one of them to fertilise the egg when it appeared.

Sylvia didn't realise until she was almost nine weeks gone. Megan the foetus, the size of a pistachio by that point. Still a cluster of cells, but one with a spine and, though she couldn't know it then, a Megan-ness already running through it. An embryo with aspirations.

Afterwards, they tried to work out which occasion it had happened on, settling on the time they had both been laughing, lazily lost in the moment, forgetting themselves.

Eventually, after two weeks of all-day nausea, Sylvia deigned to take a test at Paul's insistence.

'I can't be pregnant,' she said, dead certain. She had an innate distrust of the body that she had abused for so long.

Surely it couldn't do something as naturally wondrous as conceive. Tess's miscarriage only made it seem even more unlikely.

Paul, in contrast, had faith in nature, normality and the cycle of life. He was used to probing the bellies of pregnant cats and had delivered a foal during his training that was still held in the amniotic sac.

'You don't know that,' he said. 'There was that time.'

Sylvia scrunched up her face. 'It's just not possible.' She didn't mention that she hardly had periods. Hadn't for years. That part of her had been relieved when they stopped.

But pregnant she was. After the initial home test, a trip to the doctors and an early scan confirmed that she was just shy of nine weeks. Megan, miniscule but incontrovertible, exerting her dominance over her mother's body.

'Was this a planned pregnancy?' said the ultrasound technician, pressing hard on her stomach through cold jelly. She was Spanish, her accent husky, her movements precise.

Sylvia didn't answer. She didn't see why that was anyone's business, really. She was hardly a teenager. At that point, she wasn't yet used to her body being public property. Then there was that sound. A cantering, whooshing music like a space horse striding across the galaxy.

'That's baby's heartbeat,' said the technician, smiling at Sylvia's look of amazement, at the tears that sprung into her eyes.

'We can still get a termination,' said Paul, afterwards, his arm linked through hers as they left the hospital. 'It's not the end of the world. These things happen all the time.'

But Sylvia knew, as soon as she had heard that otherworldly noise, that she wouldn't be doing that.

'Nope,' she said, certain of something, for almost the first time in her life. Such a relaxing feeling, to know that she had no option, understanding for the first time Tess's desire to have a life grow inside her.

'Are we really going to do this then?' said Paul. There was a note of excitement in his voice and Sylvia realised that he was secretly thrilled. It wasn't as if they were that young after all, although she, at least, had been living as though they were.

'Yes,' said Sylvia. 'We're going to do this.' Never mind that they still didn't live together, yet. Never mind that Barbara would tell her that she was throwing her life away, that she should do another couple of years at the lab first. That William would frown, perplexed. That Ariadne would giggle and mutter, 'Shit. Really?' That she'd once told Tess that she wasn't planning on children for ages, perhaps never.

Never mind that Paul's mother lived on the other side of the world.

'Are you going to be all right?' said Paul. 'With everything, I mean?'

They hadn't talked much about Sylvia's guilty habit. After that first time, when he rushed out back into the afternoon, there had only really been one conversation.

'Are you sure you don't want to break up with me?' Sylvia had said. She was penitent, muted. She had arrived at his studio later that afternoon, fully made-up, determined, despite Magda's needling, that she wasn't going to let Paul escape.

'Break up with you?' he had said, as if the idea hadn't oc-curred to him. 'Why would I ever want to do that? I want to know every little detail about you. Even the bad stuff.'

'Really?' Sylvia had been doubtful.

'Really. Let's just get all our secrets out there.'

'I don't know if that's a good idea,' she'd said, quietly, moving to sit down. 'I'm not sure you'd feel the same way about me.'

'Try me,' Paul had said, sitting next to her. But she had shaken her head, looked towards the door. 'Ok, I'll start,' he had said. 'I used to steal Tim Tams from the corner shop when I was eleven. Little crim that I was.'

'That's nothing.' Sylvia had shaken her head.

'Ok. Well, this is worse: I shagged my best mate Jim's girlfriend, Colette, the summer before I went to university. I mean, he was only seeing her, but ...'

'Really?' Sylvia had replied. 'Your best friend's girlfriend. That is *quite* bad, I suppose. I mean ...' Her face had opened up, relief and curiosity commingled.

'So, you see, I'm no angel.' Paul had been satisfied.

'Did he find out? Your friend, I mean?'

'Oh yes, eventually, and then he went after this girl I liked – Stephanie Pickering. So, he got his revenge. We ended up laughing about it.'

Problem sorted, Sylvia had thought, marvelling at male simplicity. The sense of solace ebbed away.

'So, now it's your turn.' Paul's face had been eager. 'Tell me anything.'

'Well, I've had this *thing* with food.' She'd had to give him something. 'For a while.' She hadn't been able to use the words. Eating disorder. Bulimia. Too hard to retract.

'Uh-huh,' Paul had said, his face receptive. 'What kind of thing?'

'Sometimes I ... binge.' The last word whispered.

'Come here.' Paul had pulled her towards him. 'That's ok. I mean, we all do that – I used to shove down all the Tim Tams I nicked. Hiding the evidence. One time I even made myself puke.' Sylvia had jolted a little in his arms, discerning where he was leading her, but unwilling to say any more. 'Don't worry, is what I mean,' Paul had said, watching her closely. 'You are perfect to me, just as you are.'

Since then, he had ignored empty wrappers in the bin, the sound of Sylvia flushing the toilet and running the tap late at night. The marks on her bottom teeth – enamel distressed by stomach acid. He had initially resolved to fix her, but then found out how much help she had already sought, over the years, so concluded his best mode of support was just loving her as hard as he could.

And his knowledge of it had taken away some of the power. But Sylvia still did it, regularly, dancing to the tune that played in her head, submitting to Magda's jibes.

'Yes,' said Sylvia, enthralled again by her new sense of certainty. And, remarkably, something about the pregnancy finally stopped her binge-and-purge treadmill, when even Paul's acceptance hadn't. It wasn't just her any more; she couldn't do that to the baby. She had permission to care for herself, to silence the sniping of her interior critic.

She started cooking herself proper meals and eating

vegetables. Drinking water and getting early nights. And just like that, like a pilot light going out, her ambition seemed to flicker off. Whereas once she agonised over the clinic's success rates, staying abreast of new IVF technology to impress her boss, the driven Dr Vittorio, now she had a new interior focus. Her own baby was taking over from all those other babies she had made for other people.

Her body softened and her stomach swelled. And just as he had loved thin Sylvia, Paul found he adored this new iteration. It was just Sylvia he loved, he realised, however she came.

'Any day now?' offered waggish passers-by when she was barely five months, starting to waddle.

*   *   *

Girls' lunch in a restaurant in town. Tess up from the West Country, Barbara's hair like a legionnaire's helmet, cast in bronze.

'How are you feeling, darling?' said Barbara, as Sylvia sat down heavily on a chair.

'Not too bad,' said Sylvia. 'The sickness has mostly passed, although sometimes if I don't eat a biscuit quickly enough first thing I can still end up puking. Paul brings me one up.' She thought of how tenderly Paul was looking after her, how exhilarated he was.

'You look terrific,' said Tess. 'Radiant. Doesn't she, Mum?' Sylvia was struck by her sister's reliable generosity but she detected the note of longing that Tess had tried to bury. The flip side of sisterhood's closeness being the fact there was nowhere to hide.

'Gorgeous,' agreed Barbara. But she was full of trepidation. She thought she had conveyed carefully to her girls the pitfalls of motherhood and yet here was Sylvia, her brightest hope, casually straying into domestic quicksand. And it was obvious from Tess's face that she was keen to follow suit. It wasn't that she didn't want her girls never to have children, but just not yet. She couldn't face grandmotherhood and what it might demand of her. It had come around so quickly.

'What will you two have?' she said, surveying the menu. 'My treat. I can't be long as I've got afternoon conference in a bit.' Barbara's column would wait for nobody.

'I'll have the lentil soup,' said Tess, vegan long before it was fashionable.

'I'll go for the shepherd's pie,' said Sylvia.

'You know that eating for two is a myth, don't you?' said Barbara, grinning. 'I fell for it and I was like a beached whale by the time you were born.'

'Thanks, mother,' said Sylvia.

'How is your and Paul's new flat?' said Tess. 'Are you enjoying living together?'

'It's great,' said Sylvia. Hard to explain the safety she felt in her new home. The joy at creating their own space. Everything from changing the bedding to taking out the bins was infused with novelty. And there was that sense of peace after so long on her own, trapped in her flesh. Now, suddenly, her body wasn't a prison any longer. 'What about you and Danny? Everything all right with the chalet?'

'We have got a bell tent too now,' said Tess. 'You should come and stay before you have the baby.'

'Yes,' said Sylvia. 'That would be great.' She pictured sleeping on a pallet in a tent in Brean Valley, crystalline air cut through with wafts of marijuana, and inwardly shuddered.

'And Dad is getting worse,' said Tess, quietly. 'You need to come and see him.'

'William?' said Barbara, sipping the glass of wine she had ordered. A little drink never affected her copy. 'Is he completely losing his marbles or something?'

'Barbara.' Tess's expression was stern. 'You shouldn't take the piss. I'm pretty sure it's ... dementia, or something. I am trying to get him to go to the doctor, but you know what he's like ...'

'I'll come,' said Sylvia. 'Me and Paul. We can help.'

'I would help,' said Barbara. 'But I'm not sure if he would actually want me involved? I don't know if he would *want* me seeing him like that? He was always such a strong man, so controlled.'

'I don't think he cares how anyone sees him any more,' said Tess. 'That's the point. The house is a mess. He isn't eating properly. He hardly goes to the Logan Rock any more. He's not well. Just because you left him all those years ago doesn't mean you can't help him now. He was your husband, once upon a time. He's our father.'

She shook her head and Sylvia noticed how thin and drawn her sister was, her jawline crisp. Her bright extensions had been replaced with dreads snaking down her back.

'I feel like you've both just left me down there to get on with it,' said Tess.

'Darling,' said Barbara. 'I simply had no idea that things were that bad.'

'He's on his own,' said Tess. 'In that stupid house.'

'It's more than twenty years since I left,' said Barbara. 'We haven't really spoken since. I know it's hard but he isn't my responsibility.'

'He's the father of your children,' said Sylvia. She felt guilty herself, for failing William, but it was easier to direct her discomfort at her mother. 'He was the one that brought us up. We all owe him a lot.'

Barbara was quiet then; the fleshy pit of her neck quivered. 'No. You're right,' she said. 'I should come down.'

Later, drunker, she expanded on motherhood while waiting for the bill.

'I don't have much advice. As you know, I wasn't always the best mother,' said Barbara. 'I loved you both so much, I loved William, but I realised that if I stayed I was going to completely lose myself ... That wouldn't have helped anybody. Sometimes it's kindest to look after yourself so nobody else has to pick up the pieces.'

Sylvia and Tess exchanged a glance. They never talked about Barbara's flit from the family home when they were nine and seven. It was one of the immutable laws of their family, the only way they could survive.

'We were so passionately in love,' said Barbara. 'You know I met him writing about the Cornish fishing industry and he was just so ... so real ... I had never met anyone like him

71

before. I gave it all up to be with him. But sitting around waiting for a man to come back from sea was never my style, you know that. I had to work. I missed the city.'

It wasn't an apology, but it was the closest she had ever come. Sylvia wanted more. She wanted to know how it felt to leave two little girls without explanation. To board the train to Paddington 'for work' and never return.

She thought of photographs of her parents from when they first met, black-and-white snaps for the feature that Barbara wrote for a Sunday supplement. Thin and sexy, William rugged beneath his cap, Barbara in a twinset, hair cropped, silk scarf knotted at her throat.

'It was a long time ago,' she managed, eventually.

'You can't change the past,' said Tess. 'But you can come and see him now. Danny is the only one who is helping me look after him. Without him, I wouldn't be able to cope.'

'And you're still set on a child yourselves?' said Barbara.

Tess nodded, sadly.

'But it doesn't seem to be working,' she said.

'I could get you a consultation at the clinic?' said Sylvia. 'I mean, if you wanted. To see if there's any reason why?' She realised that her hand was curled around her stomach. She had always looked askance at pregnant women who cradled their bumps, as if it were performative, never understanding how instinctive it was.

'It's all right.' Tess shook her head. 'You know, Danny doesn't ... There's a brilliant herbalist in Zennor I've got an appointment with.'

Sylvia bit her tongue. She knew Danny was distrustful of specific technology. He would never use a microwave and fretted about Wi-Fi.

'Motherhood isn't easy,' said Barbara. 'I don't know if anyone else will tell you girls that, but it's better if you're prepared. It's hard.'

Sylvia looked at Barbara with something that felt like pity. She wasn't going to let her own baby down. She would never leave her.

II

Sylvia's Manual

Three is the magic number. That's what you used to say, in the dark, when the others were asleep. Fingertips doodling circles on flesh.

It wasn't planned. We were hardly surviving as it was. But from the minute I felt the hormones roll in, sensed that I had Rosa on board, I felt as if it was going to be all right.

It was the easiest pregnancy of all. Do you remember?

I glowed, like you are supposed to. I didn't spend eight months constantly nauseous like with Megan, or balloon with fluid as I did with Jude. She measured right for dates. Passed all her scans with full marks. Turned somersaults in my stomach like a happy little fish.

I had been so unsure, but she made me certain, carried me through, with the strength of her nature. I sensed what she would be like from the first weeks. Hair like mine and chocolate button eyes. Jude's charm and Megan's intelligence, but her own person, from the beginning. I'd lost all notion, by then, that babies came out like lumps of clay, waiting to be fashioned into somebody. I knew she would be herself, from day one. But that seemed even more miraculous, somehow. I couldn't wait to meet her.

And you seemed so happy too. I know you had felt me starting to sink in domestic drudgery before. The novelty of pregnancy and breastfeeding had worn off and the endorphins leached out of my blood.

This gave me new purpose in the domestic sphere. I could see the relief on your face. A third baby! Back to sleepless nights, milky spit-up, swollen nappies. You'll have your hands full, they said. Those other mothers with their questioning eyes. But that's what I wanted. Full hands, clean conscience, calm mind.

I was determined to do it right, third time around. I took folic acid daily and ate whole heads of broccoli. Breathed my way through pregnancy yoga, listened to the hypnobirthing CD so many times I knew it by heart.

The drama of having two children receded a little. I felt closer to Megan, less wrung out by Jude. I was freshly tethered to motherhood. Since Tess and I grew apart, after that awful row we had, there had been a sadness at my core. I know you sensed it. But the pregnancy dulled it, drew me into the everyday.

Sometimes anxiety would needle its way in. I knew by then that childbirth was a roll of the dice, never mind the nature of the person you made. But I was so confident, you see, that's why I did it. She made me sure of myself, our girl. Our surprise.

I wish I thought I was going to get to meet her properly, see her face, where I'm going. But I'm not sure that's the case.

Visit her holly tree once a week, won't you? The one we chose because it reminded me of Christmases in Cornwall, when William would go up the valley and come back with huge cuttings from the holly bush to fashion our Christmas tree. That's what all the fishermen did. Make Megan and Jude go too, please. None of you have been for so long. It's getting so big now, just like she would have been.

She would be three next week. Of course, you know that. We haven't mentioned it, although I still get the email alerts from one of those pregnancy accounts. The ones that used to say, 'This week your baby is the size of a plum / peach / watermelon.' Except now they say things like, 'By now your little one will probably be starting to make friends at nursery and learning more about their place in the world.' 'Practise counting to ten and learning colours with your child.' 'Get ready to meet your three-nager – why tantrums aren't just for the terrible twos.'

I haven't had the heart to unsubscribe. It seemed disloyal somehow. Keeping her alive in my head was the only thing I could do, since I wasn't able to keep her alive in reality.

You need to do the same thing, for me. Not the emails but the remembering. I know it's easier not to think about painful things. You're so adept at easygoing denial. But for her, you have to change the habit of a lifetime. I'm not going to be around to do it. It has to be you.

Promise me. Even after my replacement comes along – and more children too, if you've got the stomach for them. I expect you will have. Men usually do. It's women who get bogged down in the blood and guts of parenthood.

You're going to be a widower, quite the catch. Still hot, despite the silver hairs and the deepening wrinkles. Slightly helpless. Women are going to love it. Before I came in here, I saw them circling already, those traybake bitches with their oven dishes full of mince and their faux-solicitude. Emma Davey from number 11, with her stale marriage, compliant children and sideline in fish pie. Moony, fat Carla fetching you endless coffee at work.

Abigail Blackwood with her demanding role as a fund manager, still finding the time to drop around homemade banana bread and ogle our sitting room.

Even Natalia P, not as odious as the others, admittedly, more consistent with her generosity despite having the least to give, but still, I'd warrant, more fascinated by me than genuinely concerned. I could see it in her eyes, as she handed over all those hearty meals I felt too sick to eat. To her I was some kind of fantastical beast. A maenad wandering the streets of Hackney.

They played a good game. They pretended I was one of their own. But I caught them sneaking glances at my ankle tattoo, my poison-smoothed forehead. Deep down they hated the fact that I hadn't let myself slide into their version of motherhood.

Only Nush, dear, sweet Nush, accepted me for who I was and truly liked me. And she never bothered to bring us nourishing food in our crisis, always opting for a bottle of wine instead – what I truly wanted. She liked my sense of humour, didn't judge my mothering. Just like Ryan has never judged Jude.

But aside from Nush, I know those other mothers felt scintillas of schadenfreude after I lost my hair. Refusing a wig, a headscarf, for so long. Let them look, I told myself. But I know what they thought. How did lovely Paul, such a nice man, end up with some-one like that? And now she's dying and leaving him to raise the children on his own. Poor Paul.

There was some sympathy for me too, after Rosa. For a while.

But I didn't play it quite right and so I lost their pity. Fair enough. I hated them for it anyway.

When you have cancer there are rules that you are supposed to follow. Number one, wear a scarf to cover your shiny pate. Two, look for positivity in the pain. Very important, that one. Three, stop drinking. I mean, nobody said as much to my face, but there were eye-rolls when I sank half a bottle of wine at the parents' quiz. It barely touched the sides. Four, keep your focus on the children, make much of how they're your everything.

That's one, at least, I managed. In fact, the cancer brought me back to them when I had drifted, after Rosa. In that sense only, it was a gift. I remembered what was important.

12

Now

The celebrant was a beatific woman in her middle years, plump body sheathed in baggy, wrinkled linen. She was good at her job, respectful yet somehow uplifting, but Paul was minded to hate her.

The summation of Sylvia felt all wrong. Like the syrupy tributes still pouring onto social media. As soon as he started thinking of his wife in such terms, she would be lost. Better to hold the complicated reality in his mind. The manual helped with that. Since reading it, grief for his wife had been undercut with a layer of incomprehension. How could she not have told him?

Like some kind of deviant anthropologist, he was also seeking out any physical remnants he could. There was the cigarette butt. A ticket stub for an afternoon cinema showing that he had found in the pocket of her denim jacket, still hanging in the hall. Then real treasure – a single, long hair he had noticed glinting on their bedroom armchair that very morning. The colour of Orangina. Undoubtedly one of Sylvia's from the days before she got ill. He had wrapped it around his forefinger, tightly until it cut into his flesh, leaving a tiny mark he could just about still see.

He stared at the coffin on the platform. It was impossible.

'And now we will hear "The Folly of Being Comforted" by WB Yeats,' said the celebrant, 'read by Sylvia's close friend, Nariya Patel.'

Nush, Sylvia's only true friend, apart from him. They had so many acquaintances through the children, a network of people they greeted, arranged play dates with. They were always busy. But the thought of revealing their true selves to most of these people they spent their time with was laughable. Most of Paul's friends from the early days in London had moved back to Australia. While Sylvia had her digital friends, of course. The ones who swallowed her sumptuous depiction of motherhood, avatars in their living room, egging her on. With their dip-dyed hair, avocados and similarly impossibly angelic children.

But Nush was an exception. A friend in real life, or IRL, as the digital acronym would have it. Another woman who sat slightly on the periphery of the school gate scene for her single-motherhood, her cropped grey hair, her shift work as a paramedic. Ostracised twice over – once by her conservative family for leaving her arranged marriage and then, again, by the mothers who didn't know what to make of her and didn't really want her at their coffee mornings and barbecues. Despite the cultural diversity of its inner-city location, or perhaps because of it, the school was a pastiche of idealised

Englishness, with jumble sales, chess tournaments and nativities playing out under the chug of police helicopters.

Nush's son Ryan was far calmer than Jude, much more manageable. But from the start the two boys had a connection and so their mothers formed one too, tentatively at first, but then joyously, with a sense of relief. Despite Nush's plain appearance, she had a succession of boyfriends and Paul knew that Sylvia found the trials and tribulations of her love life compelling. He understood that part of his wife missed the drama of romantic entanglement, of starting afresh, of being desired by new eyes.

In the days when Sylvia started to get short of breath, shortly before she moved to the hospice, Nush had come over every day, expertly adjusting the cushions on her bed, taking Sylvia's pulse, smoothing her hair, getting her fresh water. She padded through the house, like a cat, letting herself out silently. Paul was always surprised to find that he missed her quiet presence after she had gone.

She read the poem quietly, without much expression, gazing at the people in the room. The acquaintances that filled their lives.

> *When all the wild summer was in her gaze.*
> *O heart! O heart! If she'd but turn her head,*
> *You'd know the folly of being comforted.*

Paul glanced at his mother. She was standing next to Megan, familiar hands clasped in front. They were dusted with sun spots he had never seen before. The flight had clearly been exhausting, but when he had woken that morning she was already up, presenting him with coffee and a hushed injunction to eat.

He felt Jude start to wriggle in the seat next to him. All day he had discerned how hard his son was trying to behave, but Jude couldn't sit still for long, his very being was kinetic and explosive.

'All right?' he whispered.

Jude nodded, solemn, and stopped squirming. Paul smiled.

'Good boy. You're doing such a great job. Mummy would have been so proud of what a big boy you're being.' It was true and he wished that Sylvia could see her son, in the little pastel-blue suit that Barbara had bought, his hair neat, for once, his face scrubbed like an apple. The thought accompanied by a punch of pain.

He wouldn't have to worry about Megan making any kind of scene. She was utterly still, her eyes filling with tears. Although that very containment was troubling in itself. Since Sylvia had first become ill, Megan, always a responsible child, had started to insist on doing everything she could for herself. As if she could stave off chaos through good behaviour. While it was undeniably useful in some ways, Paul worried about the sight of her bedroom, the soft toys lined up like mournful sentries, the desk clear of clutter. She had done her own plaits, clumsy pigtails that framed her face.

He glanced around the room. Tess was standing next to Barbara, holding Flora's hand and with Danny at her side. She wore a bedraggled purple dress, her usual stacks of silver jewellery. A teenager's ying-yang rings and bangles. She hadn't felt strong enough to do a reading. 'I just can't,' she had said, shaking her head, subject closed. 'It's too raw.'

Paul struggled to look away. The manual had given him a fresh perspective. Both Tess and Danny looked older, less gilded than he recalled. No longer flower children but drained parents, like him and Sylvia. He finally pulled his eyes away. He wasn't going to let unwanted thoughts ruin this day. He had to keep things clear-cut.

It was Barbara's turn next. She was good at this, this was her thing. She was armed for battle, with heavy make-up, hair thick with hairspray. And she began well.

'Of all the people I have ever known – and I have known a few ...' she said, 'my daughter Sylvia had the greatest gift for making things exciting. It was a talent that was there since she was a baby.' A pause. 'She was a very talented girl. We were all certain she would end up doing something worthwhile, from the beginning ...' said Barbara. 'And, indeed, she developed a terrific scientific career. But she wasn't just a white coat, she had incredible style. And everybody who knew her, loved her sense of humour. In short, she could have done anything. But, in the end, she focused on another course and found a true vocation in ... motherhood.'

You can't even appear pleased in the eulogy, thought Paul, rancorously. Barbara had made no more mention of her letter from Sylvia; he knew he would never know its contents.

'She found true happiness in her family,' said Barbara. 'And her approach to family life was inspiring – especially for an old reprobate like myself. She made me very proud. Her father William died last year. He had a long struggle with dementia, but I know that he too was very proud of the woman Sylvia became ...'

* * *

'Such a beautiful service,' said Miriam. She was clutching a glass of prosecco in one hand and a paper plate in the other. Barbara had organised smoked salmon blinis from her smart caterer in the end. 'It really did her justice.'

'Oh god, Ma, I hope so.' Paul shook his head. His most valiant attempt couldn't stop the tears gathering in his eyes.

'Paul.' Miriam was aghast. 'Oh Paul.' She reached out to touch his arm, her own eyes brimming. Paul shook his head, pulled himself together. This close he noticed a faint blue line around his mother's irises that he had never seen before. She was getting old.

'I'm all right,' he said. 'We'll be ok.' He couldn't bear his mother's grief. Not for Sylvia, whom she had never truly known, but for himself. 'Thanks so much for coming. All that way.'

'Ed wanted to be here as well, but things are so tricky with the garage at the moment. It was just impossible for him to get away.'

'It's fine,' said Paul. 'I've spoken to him. He's going to come over in a couple of months, once things have settled down.'

Paul understood his brother's absence as an act of kindness. Ed shirked displays of overt emotion, as they had both been taught. He would postpone his visit until the point that they could once again watch sport and drink beer together without it seeming inappropriate. And Paul knew how soothing that would be.

'You're a good boy,' she said, nodding and blinking at her canape. She wasn't used to food like that, Paul knew. He looked away, guiltily, not wanting to see her attempt a bite.

'I sent the kids upstairs with the iPad,' he said. 'I figured they needed a break from everyone.'

'I'll check on them,' said Miriam. Grateful for something to do, she moved quickly, setting down her drink and the blini with evident relief. 'You've got all your friends here. I'm in the way.'

Paul looked around the room. There was Danny, Abigail Blackwood, Carla. Were they friends, exactly? He wasn't sure. Certainly, he didn't want to talk to any of them. But then he noticed Nush. She, at least, wouldn't make him feel worse.

'You did a good job, thanks so much,' he said. 'Sylvia would have been so grateful.'

'Do you think so?' said Nush. 'I think she would have been well bored, honestly. Desperate to move on to this stage. The fun bit.'

'Yes,' said Paul. 'If you can call it that.'

'She would have made her own enjoyment,' said Nush. 'Remember that time at the school disco? When she decided to learn how to do the floss from a group of seven-year-olds?' She smiled broadly at the memory. 'Maniac.'

'Oh god,' Paul said, smiling too, despite himself, at the thought of his wife trying to master the dance move, limbs flailing, while the children looked on in delight.

*   *   *

'You surviving?' Danny had slipped outside. 'Do you mind if I ...?' He gestured to the hand-rolled cigarette he held.

'S'pose not, mate,' he said, slipping into the laddish tone that he had always used for Danny, even after all these years. Paul stood up, dropped the lavender head he had been crumbling to dust in his fingers, waited an awkward beat. After chatting to Nush for a while, he had retreated to the garden. To the spot where Sylvia used to sit. 'How is Tess bearing up?' said Paul, finally. There were so many other things he wanted to say, instead, but the words presented themselves.

'Not good,' said Danny, who glanced at Paul, bright blue eyes appraising, before fixing his gaze on the trampoline at the back of the garden and sucking hard as he smoked. 'She's devastated. Can't sleep, won't eat. It's like William all over again.'

'It must be hard for her,' said Paul. 'Especially since they grew apart.' I know, he thought to himself. I finally know why.

'Hmmm?' said Danny, tapping ash delicately into mid-air.

'Of course, after she got really ill, Tess finally came to visit her,' said Paul. 'That meant everything to Sylvia.' He remembered the look on Sylvia's face when Tess turned up unannounced at the house. It had been a bad day, one of those where getting Sylvia out of bed and downstairs onto the sofa was like mounting a polar expedition. But after Tess arrived, the atmosphere had shifted. Paul had left them to it for a while, busied himself in the kitchen making tea. He heard them talking, then laughing, before walking into the room to find them both in tears, holding hands on the sofa. Sylvia had been admitted to St Luke's two days afterwards.

'They always loved each other, those two – even when life got in the way.'

'Life?' said Paul.

'They had that bust-up, but there was also William. The end was hard and I think maybe Tess felt Sylvia didn't always do as much as she could have, at times. Tess felt like we were left to get on with it. Down in Cornwall.' Danny's face reddened and he cleared his throat. 'Sorry – I'm not trying to cause trouble. I had too many glasses of prosecco.' He held up his hands in apology.

'She tried,' said Paul. 'She did her best. But after Rosa ... well, things kind of fell apart.' He thought of William's funeral. So different from Sylvia's own. Soberly Cornish, everyone in standard-issue black, pasties and Doom Bar in the pub afterwards. Sylvia had been drunk, trying to pretend she wasn't, and started sobbing in the middle of her eulogy, hacking tears that had made Paul wince. Eventually, Tess had gone up to the lectern and ushered her sister down.

'I understand that,' said Danny, nodding slowly. 'Of course.'

Paul squinted towards the back of the garden, towards the cherry tree, as if he might spot Sylvia sitting in the branches, long white legs dangling.

'You surviving, though?' repeated Danny.

'Yup,' said Paul. 'Don't have much choice, really.'

'I just can't believe it,' said Danny, softly. 'She was such a force of nature, that one. A hellraiser, in her day.'

Paul grimaced and nodded.

'Mate,' Danny said slowly, cautiously. 'You've been under a lot of pressure. More than any person should have to cope with. And she was so young. It shouldn't have happened.' He took a final, regretful drag on his cigarette and stubbed it out on the wall, the neat roach all that remained. Then he reached a square, tanned hand out to grip Paul on the arm momentarily. A sharp squeeze that almost hurt. 'We are all going to miss her.'

From inside came the sound of someone laughing. The timbre of the conversation lightening as more alcohol was consumed. Paul smiled, as if he had been joking. The easy finality of Danny's statement made him furious.

'I know that, of course,' said Paul. 'I'm just exhausted.' He was alarmed to feel self-pity rising like vomit in his throat and his eyes stung as he blinked.

'Here,' said Danny, clapping his arms around Paul and holding him tight. Paul was surprised to find himself, despite everything, submitting to the embrace. It was so long since another man had held him. The last time must have been Ed. Aeons ago. When they were still boys.

'Ssssh,' said Danny. 'Everything's going to be ok.'

Paul thought of all the times he had said that to Sylvia. Despite her apparently Teflon-coated cynicism, she had always believed him. And look where they were now.

'You two all right?' Tess had slipped outside, a questioning note in her voice. She had a grease-spocked paper plate in one hand with a mushroom vol-au-vent on it that Barbara had assured her was vegan.

'Yes.' Paul and Danny spoke in unison, pulling apart. Danny moved over to Tess.

'Are *you*?' Danny asked, placing a palm on her shoulder.

'Um. Not really.' Tess's voice wobbled and she kneeled down to put the plate on the ground. 'Not that hungry.'

Paul felt a clutch of sympathy for his wife's sister as she straightened up. She looked so spindly and wan. She must feel as broken as he did himself. But pity was swiftly replaced with something else, spiky and bitter. After reading Sylvia's manual, Tess and Danny evoked strong feelings. But today wasn't the day for expressing them.

'It was a beautiful service,' said Tess. 'Really special. I think Sylvia would have ...' Here, her voice snapped and she started to sob. Danny enfolded her in his arms and rested the bridge of his nose on the crown of her head.

'I better get back inside,' said Paul. He told himself that to stay would mean intruding on a private moment, but the truth was that he didn't trust himself to spend another minute with the pair of them.

13

Sylvia's Manual

I've made a start on how to look after Megan and Jude, but to look after them properly, you are going to have to look after the house too. Our family home. My palace and my prison.

You have got no idea what it takes. The constant bending and sorting. Bleach in the toilet bowl. Limescale remover doused on glass. Mulch cleared from the dishwasher filter. Even before my diagnosis I had become a kind of ghost, haunting the stairs, toting dirty mugs, discarded apple cores, hair clips.

I didn't recognise myself. Where was the girl who stood on the banquette of that bar and danced while everyone watched? I was both relieved she had gone and sorry for her passing. But the truth is that I never expected to be in a supporting role.

By the time Megan came along, I had acquired quite the taste for melodrama's sugary thrill. My metamorphosis into housewife was a surprise for both of us. My ego transferring from my looks, my success rate in the lab, to my domestic prowess. Yet you loved the clean sheets, the meals, the mopped floors, while taking a stunning disinterest in their production.

Barbara and Tess mocked me for it. Barbara never really cleaned, you see. But then she never really had to. Other people did it for her. She was at the newspaper so many hours every day and then often went straight out. Home alone, she would boil an egg, under extremis.

And Tess always lived how we grew up. Her and Danny's chalet in the valley charmingly bohemian, but filthy with its smeared surfaces, overflowing ashtrays, damp walls. Even after Flora came along.

So, for me, cleaning became an act of rebellion. A way of distancing myself from the past and defining my choices against those of my family. Then later, after Rosa's birth, it became a way of atoning. Of keeping order.

Even with alcohol in my bloodstream I could fold laundry and prove sourdough. Even on the comet trail of a comedown, I could scour the pan clean of your scrambled eggs. Playing the happy mother.

Until this, this thing I'm writing for you – I still don't know what it is exactly – our house was my most faithful autobiography. I'm there in the details. The coasters strategically positioned for coffee mugs. The tasteful seagrass baskets bought to store toys. The bentwood chairs hunted down on eBay. The pencil marks on the kitchen wall recording Megan and Jude's heights.

Maintaining my story was hard work. And that's what I worry about now, stupidly. Who is going to care enough to clean the grout with an old toothbrush? Or wash the front steps? Or any of those tiny, mind-numbing tasks that no cleaner you hire will do for you, ever? I know that gradually those cracks will fill with dirt and I can hardly bear it. It will be as if I never existed in the first place.

You were oblivious to the woman hours that went into it. Near impossible to have a full-time job and run a family home, as I discovered.

So, it's going to be a shock for you, running the house. You're going to need help. You'll need Svetlana. She's a hard worker, that one. Her number is in my phone. She will iron too, if you ask her. Make your shirts nice for surgery. But remember not to be too friendly or she'll get confused. Don't be too nice or things will fall apart.

You need the windows cleaned every few months. That's Luke. His number is in my phone too. He's disarmingly handsome, the window cleaner, as I'm sure you noticed. But don't worry, I was never tempted. Nor by the postman, luckily enough. Or any of the stream of young couriers who beat a path to our door every day, bearing tiny objects in disproportionately huge cardboard boxes.

That's not to say nobody ever caught my eye. But after you, I can honestly say I was never really bothered by anyone else. My head wasn't turned.

My password for my phone is 141117. Our children's dates of birth.

Sheets are in the cupboard in the spare room. A Jenga of fresh bed linen. I labelled the different sizes. Lego on the floor is Satan's gift. Watch out for that. I'd normally cleared it away by the time you got back from work.

You won't find the bottles. Once I slipped up, once the anxiety came crowding back, so too did the alcohol. Wine, mostly. Not the civilised pinot noir we'd slowly share on a Friday evening, but cheap, white plonk, bought in the online shop and squirrelled away. It didn't need to be chilled. What mattered was the warmth it gave me after it slipped down my throat, radiating out into my chest. The comfort and the sense of possibility. A glass of wine is a beginning of something, however you look at it.

There is a monthly veg box subscription. And I've got one of those supermarket loyalty cards that will get you money off. It's in my wallet, in the drawer in the bedroom.

When it comes to my things, my clothes, ask Nush if she wants any. She probably won't. Our styles couldn't be more different. I know that she regards my floaty dresses with absolute disdain. 'Boho crap', I think the expression was. So take them to the charity shop. Don't leave them lingering in the cupboard please. Except, perhaps, save that green dress for Megan when she's older? The silk one. It was stupidly expensive. Wait until she's eighteen though. As her father, you won't want her wearing that dress until you can handle it.

As for the underwear, just throw it away. All those lacy bras, a satin rainbow. I should have thrown them away myself; they've been taunting me since my diagnosis. My breasts no longer for fun, but grenades, even after the reconstruction. Now shrouded in a sensible heavy support bra. The first bit of me to die.

All the cosmetics, the moisturisers and lotions. Those should be tossed. All that bottled hope that in the end is so meaningless. One of the few things I shared with my mother, a taste for all that stuff. Tess couldn't be less bothered and the irony is that her skin has aged the best.

There's a box of old photographs and letters in my wardrobe. On the top shelf above the hanging space. From the analogue days, heady as they were. You are welcome to look in there, but please wait until you've finished reading this, if that's ok? There are some letters from my past that might take a bit of swallowing. You knew so much about me, more than anyone ever did, but it still isn't everything.

My guitar is in the spare room. Keep that. Give it to Megan when she gets a bit better at playing.

For Jude, I bequeath my copy of *On the Road*, complete with self-conscious, sixth-form annotations. Barbara was always so sniffy about Kerouac, but that book spoke to me once upon a time and I think it will be just the ticket for our wild son.

For you, I am leaving this. Not that exciting, I know, but perhaps a more enduring autobiography than my housewifely efforts. And it means that even if you do find someone else – probably a good idea with all that cleaning to do – you'll still have me in the back of your mind, or literally in the bottom of a drawer.

14

Then

They married in the autumn. Sylvia was eight months gone, her swollen stomach fit to pop in a strawberry-red bandage dress. Paul, shyly suited, still unable to believe his luck. Barely able to look at her. All his ships had come in.

It was quite a wedding. Paul's friends could drink, sinking pints steadily at the bar, and Sylvia's friends loved obliteration in whatever form it took. So, they met in the middle, bonding for the first time through free alcohol. Ariadne ended up kissing Dane, a shy Kiwi wearing sunglasses on the top of his head. She was an angry kisser, all teeth and tongue, but Dane didn't mind. Kissing wasn't the important bit, as far as he was concerned.

The dance floor a tapestry of drama beneath soft fairy lights. During the course of the evening, there were tears, a scuffle. Three babies were conceived, two relationships ended.

'It must be any day now,' said the guests. 'Have you seen

her stomach?' 'Aren't they sweet.' 'The salmon was all right.' 'I give them two years.'

A sense of slight outrage lingering, still, at the union, the pregnancy, the hasty nuptials.

Barbara stood and spoke at the reception, champagne glass in hand, mouth thickly lipsticked.

'I didn't see this one coming, Sylvia,' she said, nodding at the married couple. 'I have to say. You never struck me as this ... conventional. But,' and here she raised a finger to quell the ripple of surprise that had spread through the room, 'I honestly think you've made a good choice. A sensible choice.' More surprised laughter. A pause here, as Barbara looked around at the crowd. 'As many of you here know, Sylvia's father William and I divorced when Sylvia was quite young. So, I wasn't around that much. I hope that I've made it up to you ...'

As if, thought Sylvia, smiling tenderly at her mother, cradling her stomach. She felt a sudden, fleeting urge to sink her face into the wedding cake, to suffocate in buttercream icing.

William seemed oblivious. He looked vague and uncomfortable in his suit, too far from the sea. Probable vascular dementia, the consultant had said. That was why he kept losing his house keys and forgetting to wash. But with Tess's help he had made it to the city for the wedding. Part of Sylvia was pleased he was there, but it also crushed her. The man dressed in a navy suit looked like her father. When you hugged him, he smelled right. But the minute you looked into his eyes, or heard his speech, a maze of meandering non-sequiturs, you realised that her real father was long gone. She missed that man so much. She knew he would have approved of Paul, would have sensed a kindred spirit. It was such a shame there hadn't been the opportunity for him to take Paul out in his boat, looking for mackerel under the yawning Cornish sky. She should have made more effort.

'And throwing this party for you,' Barbara gestured around the room of the smart hotel she had chosen, 'I hope to show you just how much you mean to me.'

Of course, you had to get the money in, thought Sylvia. She hadn't even particularly wanted to get married, but Paul was insistent. 'My mother will die of embarrassment if we don't,' he had said. But Miriam had no savings and William nothing, save the cliff house, so it had fallen to Paul and Barbara together to pay for the event.

And there she was. Miriam. Sun-worn and thin, staring around her as if she had landed on the moon. Her son, so recently just about to move home, marrying a strange, red-headed woman who he hardly knew. Her first grandchild set to grow up in this crowded, damp country, far away from the wide skies of home.

'To the happy couple! May domesticity treat you well,' said Barbara, raising her glass in a toast.

'To domesticity!' roared Danny, sunglasses pushing back his saltwater-crispy hair. He had caught a few waves just before getting the train and his arm was slung loosely around Tess's shoulders.

* * *

Later, on the dancefloor, Sylvia leaned in to Paul. Her bump – Megan – sat between them. They slow danced self-consciously, while Barbara looked on with amused interest, and Miriam dabbed her eyes.

'Beautiful couple,' Miriam finally said to Barbara. 'It's going to be a beautiful baby.'

Barbara nodded, looking at her daughter. 'I hope motherhood treats her well,' she said. 'It's such a lottery.'

'It's the most precious thing in the world,' said Miriam. 'Since my boys left and Mick died, I haven't known what to do with myself. I miss them being young.'

Barbara nodded again. She didn't understand. She had always known exactly what to do with herself. It was motherhood, babies and small children, with their incessant, infernal demands, that she hadn't been able to get to grips with. The crushing responsibility, as noisome and all-pervasive as the smell of a dirty nappy.

Others started to join the dance floor, including Tess and Danny. Tess, an exotic bird in a bright-pink, batik dress, Danny dancing confidently, flamboyantly for a man.

'Another gorgeous pair,' said Miriam, gesturing at them. 'That's Sylvia's sister? It must be. They are so similar. That wonderful hair and those freckles.'

'Yes,' said Barbara. 'To look at. But they're such different characters. It's as if I gave birth to strangers. Tess is much more content to go with the flow. Sylvia likes to … set the tone. I hope your son won't mind that in the years to come. It has plus points. She's terrific fun. Still angry with me for leaving her all those years ago, mind, whereas Tess found it easier to forgive.'

'The leaving must have been difficult,' said Miriam, taking a sip of her drink.

'Funnily enough, it wasn't,' said Barbara. 'Not really. The leaving was the easiest thing to do. I wasn't built for country life ... or family life. It's the years afterwards that have been difficult. But I'm not complaining. I made my bed. I just hope that this baby might help Sylvia to realise how hard it was and how much I always ...' Here Barbara turned away. If you didn't know her, you might have thought there were tears in her eyes.

Miriam just smiled. 'We all do our best.'

On the dance floor, Sylvia whispered into Paul's ear. 'I love you. I love our baby. I love our life together. You make me happier than I ever thought possible.' Thoughts of the wedding cake, of filling her mouth with sugar and fat until she almost choked, were almost entirely absent.

15

Now

'I thought they would never leave.' It was Ariadne, in his kitchen. So many years since Paul had seen her. After Megan's birth, she and Sylvia had drifted apart. Motherhood had driven a stake into their friendship and eventually the sporadic meet-ups had withered away to nothing.

But here she was, still with the heavy fringe and knowing eyes, but wider than he remembered, marionette lines carved nose-to-lip. Dressed in crumpled canary silk. She was wiping the countertops and picking up plates as if she belonged.

'Catering was good,' she said. 'That sushi was fantastic and the blinis – yum.'

'Yeah,' said Paul, too tired to smile politely. Why was Ariadne still here, of all people? Even Barbara had eventually gone, heels tottering into the night.

'It was a lovely tribute,' said the woman, who he was remembering he had always disliked. 'She was a special person. We used to have such a laugh.'

Paul shivered at the use of the past tense. He could never think of Sylvia in the past tense.

'Life sucks,' said Ariadne. She stood and moved over to the kitchen counter, glancing at the half-empty bottle on it.

'Would it be terrible?' she said, gesturing towards it. 'If I have another? I just don't quite feel like being on my own. Not yet.'

Paul gulped. 'I'm pretty tuckered – I should head up.'

'Go on, just one.' Ariadne handed him a glass of wine and went to sit on the sofa in the kitchen, which looked out into the garden. Paul capitulated, following her to sit down. The day had been entirely surreal and exhausting. What was ten more minutes?

'Life hasn't exactly been easy for me in the last few years,' said Ariadne, taking a large sip.

'No?' said Paul. He needed to go upstairs and check on Jude and Megan. Hopefully they had put themselves to sleep, but it was quite possible Jude was still on his screen, playing one of those apps that he had begged Sylvia to download. A skewer of guilt pierced his solar plexus. He was going through the motions, moving them around the place, keeping them alive, but he felt as if he was observing his children from behind a glass window in a police interview room. More than ever, he felt the lack of that emotional connection that Sylvia had had with them.

'I never married. No kids.' She looked at him ruefully. 'That's why Sylvia and I fell out, in the end. I was jealous. I wanted what she had. I couldn't accept that she had moved on, had new priorities.' Paul nodded tiredly.

'When I heard the news ...' Ariadne paused. Paul noticed her red lipstick was slightly crookedly applied. She had been a striking girl last time he had seen her. Now she was this. A portly woman whose disappointment was etched upon her face. But at least she was alive.

'I just felt terrible,' said Ariadne, with a rush. 'I felt stupid. That we had drifted apart for something as stupid as ... We had a row when she cancelled on coming out. And that was it. We never saw each other again.'

'These things happen,' said Paul. 'Don't beat yourself up about it too much. It's years ago. We were all so young.' He yawned, looked at the clock.

'I've also had health problems,' said Ariadne. 'Intermittent MS, you know.'

'I'm sorry,' said Paul. 'That's hard.'

'It is what it is,' said Ariadne. 'I try to make the best of it.' She sighed loudly, took another sip of wine. 'You know we used to make fun of you,' she said. 'Back in the day.' A smile played on her lips as she re-lived crueller, happier times. 'We thought you were so sensible and grown-up.'

Paul cleared his throat.

'We couldn't believe Sylvia ended up with someone like you. No offence.' Ariadne smiled at him. 'Ted! I can't believe he's still alive! I didn't see him earlier.' She stood, slightly drunkenly, and walked across the room towards the pug, scooping him into her arms. 'Come to mama. Do you re-member me looking after you? God, Sylvia used to love this dog. I can't believe he still exists.'

'He's pretty old,' said Paul. 'He's got diabetes.' He looked at the dog, whose fur was silvered with grey. There was a thudding of footsteps as Jude ran into the room.

'What's going on?' said Paul. 'It's bedtime. I thought Juju put you to bed.' Barbara had insisted on being called 'Juju' after Megan was born, rather than anything more biologically realistic.

'I can't get to sleep,' said Jude. His hair shone in the spotlights from overhead. 'Who is this?'

'I'm a friend of your mummy,' said Ariadne, teeth bared.

Barely, thought Paul. You never saw the best of her, the woman she became.

Ariadne bent, lowering herself to Jude's height. She looked like the witch from *Hansel and Gretel*, waiting to push the children into the oven, and even Jude, not easily scared, looked slightly unsure.

'God, you're gorgeous,' breathed Ariadne, as if she really was going to eat him up. 'Such a mixture of the two of you.' She looked at Paul. 'She really did have it all, didn't she?' She gestured her hand around the kitchen with its shiny appliances, finally halting with her hand extended towards the small boy.

'You need to sleep, Jude,' said Paul. 'It's nearly ten. I'll take you up.'

'No,' said Jude, dodging out of Paul's grasp as he went to catch him.

'Jude! Come back.' Paul felt the prickle of sweat that presaged performance parenting, the urgent need to prove to Ariadne that he could handle the situation. He finally caught his son's arm and half-dragged him upstairs.

Bloody Ariadne, sitting in his kitchen. Telling him how they used to mock him. On the very evening of Sylvia's funeral. As if he hadn't realised at the time. People like her had no self-control, no insight. All he wanted to do now was sleep. Or if he couldn't do that then perhaps re-read some of Sylvia's manual, imagine she was speaking the words. Enthralling as ever.

'Are you all right?' he said to Jude, who was finally in bed, staring at the ceiling. 'Today was hard.'

'I'm ok,' said Jude. 'Just a bit sad.'

'Me too,' said Paul, reaching for his son's hand.

'Do you think she can see us?' said Jude. 'Do you think she is watching down on us?'

'I do,' said Paul. 'I think she can see everything that you're doing. I think she'll always be watching. Like a star. Like we said.'

'But if she's always watching, how will she ever get a chance to rest?' said Jude. 'She is going to get really, really tired. And you know what Mummy was like when she was tired.' They looked at each other and smiled.

'I do,' said Paul. 'But she's at peace. I promise.' Even to himself, it sounded all wrong. Sylvia hated sitting still and was always moving. Laughing, scolding, dropping her keys as she slammed the front door. But Jude seemed consoled.

'I love you, Judey,' said Paul, Sylvia's expression ringing in his head. He seldom said those words out loud. Jude nodded, sleepily, and curled onto one side. Paul stood up gingerly and made his way downstairs.

He found Ariadne crying, messily, on the sofa. She looked

up at him as he entered and, with her flushed face, he caught a glimpse of the girl she had been.

'Sorry, sorry. This is your sad day and here I am, making a scene of myself,' said Ariadne, wiping her nose with her yellow satin sleeve. 'Sorry. I'm hopeless.'

'Don't worry about it,' Paul said, feeling an unexpected swell of sympathy as he sat down next to her. Perhaps it wasn't so bad that she was here after all, this envoy from their youth. Maybe it was even fitting. 'It's fucking awful. I just ... I just miss her so much.'

'Hug?' said Ariadne.

Paul paused and then submitted, finding himself enfolded in her large bosom, encased in its slippery fabric. Breasts, soft comfort, in his face. He felt a flicker of something that could have been desire or disgust. He pulled back.

'More wine?' said Ariadne. 'I think we deserve another drink.'

'We finished that bottle. But I think there's another one,' said Paul. Part of him didn't want to be alone either.

Ariadne stood and wobbled over towards the fridge. She rootled around inside and pulled out another bottle, triumphant.

'Bottle opener?' she asked, turning around, glancing up across the room as she did so.

'Um, in the drawer on the right-hand side,' said Paul, gesturing towards the pine dresser. A place Sylvia had often stood, scribbling things on the family calendar that was pinned on the adjacent wall. Reminders for Jude's karate lessons, Megan's endless sleepovers, glucose checks for Ted.

And, more latterly, the litany of her own hospital appointments. Somewhere, months back, was written the crucial one with Dr Z, which she had circled in purple pen, as if it were auspicious, but which had turned out to mean the end. The month left showing didn't have anything written on it. Sylvia had given up by that point, stopped projecting into the future and choreographing their family lives. Paul hadn't bothered turning the pages since, let alone recording anything. The calendar had been Sylvia's job.

'Great,' said Ariadne, spearing the cork and pulling it out with a damp pop. 'Glass?'

Paul held his aloft in response.

'You know I'm still in touch with Dane,' said Ariadne, sitting down heavily. 'Online. He's in Sydney and has five children. His poor wife.'

'I didn't know that,' said Paul, momentarily distracted by the thought of Dane-o, once unable even to successfully nurture a supermarket basil plant, now a father of five. 'I'm not really on social media.'

'It's mad how quickly things changed,' said Ariadne. She seemed closer to him on the sofa than he remembered.

'True,' said Paul, unnerved by her proximity, the quivering, hot pudding of her body, enveloped as it was.

'All those faces ... The same, just older. Sylvia's mother. She always terrified me. And her hippy sister and that boyfriend. I haven't seen them in such a long time. They used to come up and stay in our flatshare all the time. Before she met you.'

Paul looked at Ariadne, wondering how much she had

really known of Sylvia's life. What purchase she'd had on his wife.

'But we're all just the same, really, inside, I mean,' Ariadne continued. 'Aren't we? I don't feel any different from how I used to.'

Paul paused. He thought he intimated her message. He could just imagine what Sylvia would say.

'I feel different,' he said, finally, looking down at his drink. 'Listen, I really have got to call it a night. I'm broken.'

'Probably a good call,' said Ariadne, moving fractionally away. 'To Sylvia!' She raised her glass in a toast.

'To ... Sylvia,' said Paul, the name he had spoken so many times unwieldy on his tongue.

16

Sylvia's Manual

A note on Binky-bear. Megan doesn't know this and I'd prefer it if she never found out, but Binky has an identical twin (I call him Binky II) who occasionally gets swapped with his sibling. I started it in the days that Megan took Binky-bear out, when I was terrified she was going to lose him. There was that time she dropped him in the supermarket and we had that sleepless night, before going back in the next morning to find Binky propped by the scratch cards, looking as if he'd had a night on the tiles.

I rotate them so that they are equally love-worn and decrepit. One of those little tricks of motherhood, the pulling of strings from behind the scenes. So, if Binky ever goes missing, his doppelgänger lives in the loft, in a box in the far-right corner.

You need to wash both of them regularly. Use the hand-wash cycle and some fabric conditioner. Megan still likes to suck his limbs to fall asleep. Even now. If Eliza Jenkins could see Binky, knew how much he meant, Megan would die. She hides him before anyone comes round for a sleepover.

As a mother, you collect your children's frailties and their tiny flaws. You hold them tight. Motherhood is all about accepting the imperfect and for me that was a certain liberation. I realised that nothing and nobody is perfect.

I knew the exact location of Megan's birthmark on her left shoulder, the size of a five-pence piece. The dimple that appeared in her forehead when she smiled, as if it had migrated from her cheek.

I noted that strawberries give her red spots around her mouth. That she has a double crown, two tiny whorls spinning her shiny black hair in different directions.

I know that she is scared of ghosts, not burglars. That sitting in the back of the car makes her feel sick. That she will eat spinach or broccoli, but only if you douse them in butter.

That she talks in her sleep, suffers mild hay fever and loves white chocolate. That ibuprofen brings down her fevers better than paracetamol.

I know, before she says a word, exactly what kind of mood she is in at the school gate. The jut of her lower lip that tells me she is holding back tears. The zany mood she occasionally, rarely, gets in where she wants to put on music and dance around the room.

As for Jude, he doesn't have a single physical flaw that I can discern. Not one. And I've looked, closely, since the day he was born. Not a birthmark, or – miraculously, despite all the things he has climbed and jumped off – a scar. He looks almost uncannily perfect, with those round, blue eyes, that creamy skin. His flaw is internal, hidden, like my disease. It's in the way he can't process his emotions, can't find rest.

'Boys!' people say. But it's more than that. It's his cross to bear.

He skirts on the edge of hyperactivity, without being bad enough to warrant a label. But just when I think I can't bear it any more, he turns on a sixpence and becomes so charming it takes my breath away. See-sawing mood swings that wear me out, but also make every day exciting. You could never accuse him of being boring.

Even you, their loving father, don't have the breadth of knowledge that I do about our children. And I'm worried that it's going to die with me, all that information. That nobody else will ever be able to replace me, properly. Which is, I suppose, the reason that I'm writing so much of it down.

If I could find a way of making sure I didn't leave, I'd take it. Even if it meant hanging around in limbo, shut out from paradise. For – too late, I know – I realise that this is my heaven. You and the children. Even without Rosa. Even with a son that shreds my sanity. This is my earthly paradise, as good as anyone ever gets. I should have appreciated it more. Been mindful of what I had. But you know me, I loved to linger in the past and the future – those hinterlands of recrimination and possibility. I was terrible at staying in the everyday.

I want Megan to travel, to take a gap year. To go to Thailand and drink lurid fishbowl cocktails and puke out of the side of a rickshaw. I know how sensible you are but what I've learned is that you can't prevent disaster. It's never the thing you think. Look at me. This isn't what I expected at all.

And what I fear for Megan isn't early death or disgrace. She's far too sensible for that. Even as a toddler, she would always shun risk, looking askance at the children who misbehaved with her solemn brown eyes. No, what I fear is that she will be too careful. It's not that I want her to make my mistakes, far from it. But I want her to feel that vertiginous freedom of youth. The idea that anything is possible.

For Jude, I want the opposite. I want him to respect limits, to see the relief of order. I want him to find a way of not being over-whelmed by his emotions. Of not surrendering so easily to anger, or even to joy.

Essentially, for their best future success, our children need to learn lessons from each other. To watch closely and pick up tips on the areas of life they don't instinctively find easy. They are lucky to have the other one. Fortunate despite everything.

Do you remember proposing to me? I knew it was coming, after we'd had the ultrasound. Could feel you working up towards some-thing. Always your way to do things properly. I'd never considered myself the type for marriage, but with you, I loved the idea. So, I started to daydream. Maybe you'd do it at the top of that hill we climbed on our first date, by that same bench, the Gherkin and the Shard on the horizon, stolid witnesses to how far we'd come. Or perhaps you'd do it in our local. On the terrace, under the festoon lights. Ariadne gawping, my other friends ironically cheering.

But I should have known you wouldn't do it in a public place. In the end, when it came, it was less dramatic than my imaginings. But one of the better moments of my life.

I was lying in the bath, looking at my stomach, only just starting to change. You knocked on the door and came in, more bashful than I'd ever seen you, your cheeks already flushed. You kneeled down by the bath and, for what felt like forever, didn't say any-thing. As if you couldn't get the words out.

'Are you all right?' I finally asked you, smiling, encouraging. You shook your head, overcome.

Then finally – finally! – you brought forward the ring box which held that amethyst on a skinny silver band. Always intended as a holding ring, but I loved it – loved you – so much that I grew superstitious about changing it. Why upgrade something already ideal?

'Will you marry me, Sylv?' you asked, expression unsure. I paused. I wanted to suck every bit of joy from the moment that I could, to fix it in my memory forever. I slowly stood up, proud in my nakedness, sudsy water sloshing around my ankles. You rose too and I pulled you towards me, soaking your shirt, squeezing my breasts, our baby, against easy-iron cotton. 'Is that a yes?' you said, laughing.

'How could it ever be anything else?' I said, into your ear.

17

Then

Paul looked in the rear-view mirror. Sylvia was hunched over on the back seat. Her hair spilling forwards as she rocked. She made a noise like nothing he had heard from her before, but he recognised the register from other pregnant animals he had tended to.

'Oh God ...' she moaned. 'Paul, get me to the hospital. I can't take this.' She looked up, pleading. Her face changed by pain.

'We're going as fast as we can,' said Paul, cursing this part of the city on a Saturday lunchtime. People walking, infuriatingly slowly, towards coffee, brunch, maybe a picnic in the park. He watched a man with a child on his shoulders bouncing along the pavement. Fatherhood still seemed as remote as it ever had.

'We haven't got far to go now,' he said, trying to make his voice reassuring. And then, just like that, the contraction stopped.

'That was an intense one,' said Sylvia, almost cheerful. 'It's stopped now, for a minute. It's so weird, but in between you just feel completely ... normal.'

Paul swallowed. Normality didn't seem to come into this. He prayed Sylvia wouldn't notice how slowly they were moving. Cars clogging the road in front of him. Weekend drivers. He thought of the cat he had seen last week who had a litter of six kittens. The runt was obvious from the start. Smaller, uglier. It only lived until the morning.

'Do you think Ted will manage?' said Sylvia. 'I feel so bad at leaving him.' Paul and Sylvia both internally considered the little black dog, handed over to Ariadne the night before, when Sylvia first felt a twinge. Ariadne not the most reliable guardian, but in light of Barbara's attitude to pets, the only one they had.

'It's so exciting, Sylv,' she had said, leaning forwards to kiss her friend. 'You're going to be a mother. I still can't believe it.'

Sylvia had nodded, overcome. 'I can't either. It's mad.' She had kissed Ted on the nose. 'Be good,' she said, unaware that childbirth would irrevocably shift her attitude towards her adored pet. Now she looked out of the window at the sunshine. The smell of hot pavement and sweet, fetid rubbish drifted in through the open window. She felt the beginning of another wave.

'It's starting again,' she said.

'Just breathe,' said Paul. 'Remember the breath.' He couldn't remember exactly what it was supposed to be like. What had that NCT woman said? All these rules for humans. It was simpler for animals. He glanced in the mirror again.

Then out of the window to steady himself. There was a pub where he and Alice used to go when they first got to London. He remembered drinking lager at a corner table, her hand resting on his lap. A pebble of chewing gum in the corner of her cheek when they kissed.

'Aaarrrgh,' said Sylvia. 'Fuck! I can't do this. It huuuurrrrrts.' A concerto of agony. She was surprised by the pain. It was so pure and complete. It felt like something she was remembering.

Paul wished, for a moment, that she wouldn't be so dramatic in this, as in all other things. A twinge of fear about what kind of mother she was going to be. But childbirth was supposed to hurt, he told himself. This was normal. And she had been amazing since she discovered she was pregnant. Letting her body widen and change without appearing to mind.

'Nearly there,' he said. The traffic had cleared a little and the squat building of the hospital hove into view. He pulled 'up outside. They would just have to get a parking ticket.

Sylvia's contraction stopped and she was able to get out of the car, shuffle into the lobby, gripping onto Paul's arm.

'My wife ...' Paul stumbled over the strangeness of the word. 'I think she's ... I think she might be giving birth.' More strange words.

'Where is she, lovey?' said the receptionist, looking up from her computer.

'She's in the toilet,' said Paul. 'She seems to be ... pushing.' Another weird word. The thought of Sylvia's face, sweating and focused. Somewhere unreachable.

'We'll come and have a look at her.' The woman's tone was reassuring, but she didn't seem in a rush. She clicked through to something on her screen. Paul was certain he glimpsed a shoe. Was she ... shopping? How could she not understand the enormity of what was happening?

'I think someone needs to come now,' said Paul, getting desperate.

'Ok, ok.' She stood, a trace of annoyance in the way she pushed a pen into her top pocket. 'I'll get someone to take a look.'

Sylvia was found and guided into a room by a midwife who looked so young Paul felt like asking for someone else.

'There's another one coming,' said Sylvia. 'It hurts. I need something ...'

'Let's take a look at you,' said the midwife. 'Can you hop up onto the bed?'

Sylvia did as she was told. Took off her pants. She didn't care now. Something had taken over her body. A force as powerful and wild as a neap tide. And between contractions, her body was still, free from pain. The midwife nodded and smiled.

'Baby's coming right now,' she said. 'I can see the head.'

'What?' said Sylvia, who had been prepared for a first-time labour lasting for days. That was what she had been told was more than likely. The woman leading the NCT class had told them to ride it out at home for as long as possible or they would be sent home from hospital.

'No time for pain relief,' said the midwife. 'Unless you want a bit of gas and air. But it might slow things down.'

Sylvia shook her head. She hadn't realised that the finishing line was so near. She could do this. She felt a kiss of sweat spring onto her skin in response.

Paul smiled, amazed. Since falling pregnant, Sylvia kept impressing him in new ways. Acting on instinct, she had a newfound self-belief, more deep-seated than the brittle layer of confidence she normally demonstrated. Nonetheless, she had entreated him to stay only at the 'head end'.

'I don't want you thinking of me differently.'

But although Paul had agreed, he privately demurred. He had watched enough births in his life; there was no way he was going to miss his daughter's.

Yet, when it came to it, he was unprepared for the black head emerging from Sylvia. The blood and mucus. The slip of trunk and limbs. The cry, weak at first and then gaining strength.

'She's out!' said the midwife, as if she had caught a prize-winning trout. 'Baby is here!'

Paul stood, useless, overwhelmed. This wasn't the same as watching a dog or horse birth. Not at all. He felt tears rise at the back of his eyes.

'Our girl,' he managed, almost to himself, looking intently at the baby's body, curdled with vernix, scarlet-red. Sylvia lay back on the pillows, drained but euphoric, eyes shining from her mask of melasma.

'Do you want an injection to get the placenta out?' said the midwife. Sylvia nodded. Megan was checked and wiped on a table. From here, Paul could examine her face. She looked incontrovertibly like him. He tried to discern dominant maternal features – Sylvia's wide mouth and large eyes – but could only see his own pronounced jawline. She was wrapped in a thin, blue blanket and placed into Sylvia's waiting arms.

'Guide her to your nipple,' said the midwife. 'Let her feed.' But Sylvia didn't need to be told. She felt the little mouth fit on easily, like a jigsaw puzzle. Her baby.

'Look at that. She's a natural,' said the midwife. She didn't look quite so young now and Paul felt like hugging her.

* * *

The truth was, Sylvia was good at motherhood. At least to begin with. Birth and breastfeeding suited her, somewhat surprisingly. Barbara had been a resentful, uncommitted breastfeeder, abandoning it after a few days for the bottle. William didn't mind – if anything, he liked the opportunity to cradle Sylvia himself, to walk her to the end of the garden and stare out at the sea, talking to her about the different boats. And Tess, when she finally had Flora, struggled to produce enough milk, no matter how much fennel tea she drank. Not Sylvia. She was like a prize cow.

'Do you have a name for baby yet?'

Paul and Sylvia looked at each other.

'Megan,' said Sylvia, confidently. 'It means pearl.'

'Lovely,' said the midwife. 'I'll leave you three to get to know each other for a bit.'

18

Now

'I know Jude has been through a lot recently ...' Miss Willis, Jude's class teacher, spoke in a pantomime whisper. Paul nodded.

'I don't think it gets much worse,' he said, smiling bleakly. Miss Willis was all of twenty-six, her face still unformed, a spatter of acne on her chin.

'I understand the thinking was to get them back in their normal routine after the funeral, but, well ... we are having a bit of a difficult time with him in class,' said Miss Willis. 'He's been very angry ...' She paused, lowered her voice. 'He bit his friend today.'

Jude, in the book corner, looked over. He knew well enough not to smile obviously, but Paul saw amusement in the set of his son's mouth. A tiny curl of naughtiness, so like his mother's.

'That's not good,' said Paul, levelly. 'But that's not necessarily to do with what's happened. We both know that Jude has, um, always been a bit of a biter.'

'We can't have it,' said Miss Willis. 'I'm recommending Jude for some counselling. He needs an outlet for his ... grief. I know it was thought that keeping the children in school would be good for continuity, but I think he needs some recognition of what has happened. A ritual.'

'I understand,' said Paul. Although he didn't. The English loved counselling, it seemed, but he had never met a person who had been improved by it. He thought of the counselling Sylvia had. The CBT. The psychoanalysis. None of it scratched the surface, really. It had been like moving food around a plate, nothing more. He glanced around at the classroom. It was like the inside of a migraine. A riot of colours, spirals of tissue paper hanging from the ceiling.

'I know perhaps this isn't the time to mention it,' said Miss Willis, flushing. 'But he is also struggling with his phonics – still. You really need to keep up practising with the flash cards at home. Once things have settled down a bit.'

'Flash cards?' said Paul, blankly.

'I've got some more for you here,' said Miss Willis, passing him a plastic ziploc envelope filled with lettered cards.

Paul took it, wondering how he was going to manage to hold onto it. Since Sylvia had got ill, people kept giving him things that they expected him to retain, but they tended to disappear. Nobody had told him that being a parent required so much stuff. Sylvia had been the gatekeeper of it all. Since she hadn't been managing things, it was starting to mount up on all the surfaces. Permission forms. Clattery Calpol syringes. Plastic toys from magazines. Felt tip pens with their lids off.

'I'm just so sorry for your loss,' said Miss Willis. 'Sylvia was such a ... *great* ... mother and I can see how hard it is for the whole family.' Paul didn't bother nodding this time. He just wanted her to stop. 'It's actually hit me hard personally because my older sister has breast cancer at the minute,' said Miss Willis, head cocked to one side. 'She is having chemotherapy in Edinburgh. It's an epidemic. I think it must be the hormones in the drinking water.'

'I'm sorry,' said Paul. Since Sylvia's diagnosis, he found himself consoling more people than he would have thought possible.

'Thanks. I just can't imagine if she ...' said Miss Willis.

Paul couldn't take any more.

'Jude,' he called. 'We've got to go. Thanks for your input, Miss Willis.' The young woman's face fell. Clearly hoping for some kind of emotional catharsis, Paul thought grimly. Everyone wanted to use your tragedy to add piquancy to their own existence.

They picked up Megan by her classroom. She stood by the doorway, rucksack on her shoulders, hair neatly pulled back.

'Hi Daddy,' she said, offering her cheek for a kiss. 'How was your day?'

'Ok,' said Paul, cautiously. He was perhaps more worried about Megan than Jude. She seemed eerily composed since Sylvia's death, maturing at an alarming rate. He longed to hear her laugh, unguarded. 'How was yours?'

'We're not friends with Vita any more,' said Megan. 'Eliza says she's just a baby.'

'Right,' said Paul, as they started walking. Jude ran ahead, eddying in circles like a leaf caught on the wind. The boy skirted around a cluster of young Hasidic men, be-ringleted beneath their shtreimels. The Orthodox Jews of Stamford Hill, who lived in large numbers around the children's school, wore clothes from a different era. The women in the nylons and knotted headscarves of fifties housewives, the men always in black, flocks of crows on the pavements. Two communities, co-existing without interaction, phantoms to each other as they played out their different lives.

'Paul, hang on ...' It was Natalia P, a mother from the school and, unexpectedly, the most assiduous bringer of meals since Sylvia's death. 'How are you?' she said, reaching out a hand to briefly squeeze Paul's upper arm.

'Um ...' Paul glanced at Megan. Jude was still far ahead down the street. Natalia's son, Alvin, stood, sombre, by his mother's side. 'We are coping, just about. As best we can.'

'You just must let me know what I can do,' said Natalia. 'I mean, if there's anything ...' Paul thought of the meals she had delivered so far, to the doorstep. Each one different. An education in Polish cuisine. Cabbage leaves stuffed with mincemeat and rice. Ham hock. Borscht as pink as bubblegum. Meals prepared with the kind of attention that Sylvia had never managed. She had become a cleaner, but motherhood couldn't make her into a cook. She remained distrustful of food. They had lived on supermarket quiche and salad bags, salmon stir fry. Stuff she didn't need to touch but could snip from plastic and slide onto a plate.

'You've done so much already, Natalia. It's so kind of you ... You really don't need to do anything else.' He was still agog at the people who, in their crisis, had turned out to be the ones to offer practical support. This slim woman, neat in her tracksuit, had been delivering a meal a week since Sylvia's prognosis had been made public. Paul was ashamed to admit that he would have automatically considered her resources too meagre for such largesse.

Natalia bowed her head slightly, almost imperceptibly, acknowledgement of her contribution so far. 'I'm always at the end of the phone. You've got my number.'

'Thanks,' said Paul.

'I'd like to help you somehow,' said Natalia. 'With the kids. It must all be overwhelming. If you want me to take them after school sometimes. Or do some shopping … Cleaning, even. I could help.'

'That's really kind,' said Paul. But he was starting to feel frustrated with Natalia, with the weight of her sympathy and self-abasement. And he could hear Sylvia's voice in his head asking what this slight woman wanted from him, exactly.

'See?' he could picture Sylvia hissing. 'She wants you.' The thought of it made him consider Natalia briefly, shamefully, in a new light. Her neat body, the bleached hair she wore scraped back from her face. It had been so long. He shook his head, trying to dislodge the thought.

'Come, Alvin … We've got football.' She looked at Paul, her face a picture of distress, despite the changed register of her voice. 'I'm just so sorry for your loss.'

There it was again. That phrase. He could just imagine what Sylvia would say about it. 'How can you "lose" a person?' Quizzically, head on one side. As if he had misplaced her, along with his car keys. But perhaps they were right. Maybe she was just gathering lint behind the sofa, along with old crayons, and he would come upon her the next time he pushed it out.

'Thanks,' said Paul. For what other response was there? 'Thanks for thinking of us.' He put his arm around Megan's shoulder, squinted ahead for Jude.

'She was just so full of life ... before,' said Natalia, softly, then flushed guiltily. 'She – what you say? – she glowed. Syl-veee-aaa.' She drew out the syllables, her accent encompassing a sweep of freezing steppe, the castle in the heart of Krakow.

'She certainly did,' said Paul.

19

Sylvia's Manual

My body is a road map of my life. There's the obvious, of course. The recent car crash. The calamity that I thought I might be able to recover from, before I realised I'd have no such luck. The scars, expertly hidden under my armpits. Thin snail tracks that show I was cut and excavated.

My tattooed nipples, done by the very best at the job, convincing at first glance with their pinky-brown areolae, but flat as paper and completely without sensation. Lucky enough that I never much liked it in the days when you sucked my breasts, like a man-baby.

Yet, sitting here, with time to think, I see that there are other scars that form a kind of autobiography. Not so long ago I used to hate them, the flaws on my almost forty-year-old shell, but now I see them as something else. My story writ large upon my flesh, compelling and unique.

I would give anything now to inhabit that ageing body, marked by life but not yet by disease. If only I'd recognised, at each stage of my life, what I had when I had it.

As a young woman, I used to feel pure despair, trapped in my flesh, with no possibility of it ever changing. But what was I so bothered about? It's honestly hard to recall. I wanted slimmer hips. Like Tess. Bigger breasts. Again, like Tess. I didn't like my long torso. My knees. My short, square fingernails. My Roman nose. I had a list of flaws I'd obsessively check off, imagining that if only they weren't there, I'd feel free.

Yet looking at a picture of my younger self, I see how mad I was. So many precious minutes wasted on things that nobody else could see.

Another unexpected boon of breast cancer: no more thinking about losing weight. I may have kept shards of my vanity, but I've discarded that one, at least.

And strange that while I was bemoaning my ageing flesh, gently sagging like wax melting down the side of a candle, somewhere in my right breast the tumour must have already been growing. Slowly. Dr Z said it has probably been there for years. Funny, really. When I was doing the school run and fretting about my cellulite, I had a chip of kryptonite embedded in my bosom.

Anyway, I think you know most of my scars, if not their causes. But here's an audit, for you to remember, once I am gone.

There is the white thread from when I cut the ball of my foot on glass, aged eight. I was running ahead from William and Barbara on Sennen beach. Going fast, heading for the sea. A broken bottle, I think it was. Blood everywhere, surprising against sand. William and Barbara were grimly silent. Barbara covered it with a towel and drove us to the hospital, very fast. William sat on the back seat and held me, the towel wrapped tight. I had four stitches and a chocolate milkshake afterwards. They seemed such a unit, keeping me safe, but that was only six months before she left.

There are the stretch marks on my hips. Like striations in the sand left by a retreating tide. They're from the summer I was eighteen I think, when I tried to stop my nasty little habit before university and ended up gaining weight, my body splitting like an over-ripe peach. They're silvery and faded now, but that summer they were bright red, like the scribbles of crayon that Jude did on the wall of the downstairs toilet that time.

They made me feel so ashamed. Branded for life by my own weakness and greed. Nothing more than I deserved. It wasn't long until I started making myself sick again and lost the weight, but the stretch marks remained. You've got those bad boys for life.

Do you remember tracing your finger along them once? I told you to stop, that they were disgusting, but you smiled and said you liked them. You called them my 'lovelies'. If I hadn't already fallen in love with you, ten times over, I would have done so for that. Seeing my body through your eyes was such a relief.

Then there are the piercings. My upper ear done when I was fifteen. It got infected and I had to take it out, so it closed over. William hadn't stopped me doing it, but when I complained at how much it hurt, he gave me one of those looks he would only do from time to time. Where he really saw you. So much of the time he was in his head, thinking about quotas and tide patterns, where the shoals of expensive fish were most likely to be that week. It was almost worth it, just so that he would do that. And now I've got time to consider it, I can see how much of my need to be the centre of attention was about that feeling of longing that my father would notice me. That he would stop quietly going around his business and just devote himself to me, if only for a bit.

The navel I did with Tess not long afterwards. I had endlessly discussed it with her first. She was the loyal sounding board for my folly, always ready to listen to my latest plan. She came with me to hold my hand in that place near the train station, on the road that slopes towards the sea. I was shat on by a seagull as I came out of the piercing salon. Hot filth in my hair. How my little sister laughed at my misfortune. I made her hurry to get the bus before anyone could see me. Self-conscious, my tummy sore. On the journey back, Tess stopped giggling and became sober. She rooted in her bag for a tissue, before dabbing at the soiled patch on my hair and telling me how good the piercing looked, that it had been worth it. Soothing me, as only she could. I used to wear a little bar in it, with two blue plastic jewels on each end. I rued it after pregnancy, I can tell you. One of the many things that nobody tells you about having children is that your belly button will no longer ever be the same. It becomes cavernous and wide, irrevocably stretched, and the last thing you ever want to do is to draw attention to it. The piercing hole now only adds to the mess, but I suppose my crop-top days are long over.

There's my tattoo. At the base of my spine. A proper tramp stamp. Tess designed it. Did I ever tell you that? She sketched it on graph paper before I took it to the tattoo parlour in London. We were up staying with Barbara for half term and I was only sixteen. But nobody asked for ID. A jaunty mandala encircling a Sanskrit logo that was supposed to say 'Peace'. Years later, somebody told me that it didn't say that at all, but rather, 'Goat'. I never bothered to find out the truth.

That holiday was hard. Barbara was at the newspaper all day and she would take us out to smart restaurants for dinner in the evening, where we met her friends. I felt so guilty then, thinking of William in the house on his cliff, eating cheese on toast.

'My daughters,' Barbara would say, to whichever sharp-eyed, black-clad friend we were meeting. 'Sylvia is the brains and Tess the beauty.'

Then separately, to us alone, she would extol Tess's perfect figure, pillowy pneumatic but also lean, entreating her to try on particular items in her wardrobe, just so she could take pleasure in how she filled them. I, sitting on her bed as the audience, felt wide. It was the beginning of feeling trapped in my own skin. It was after that, that the illness, which had tentatively started to form as a possibility in my brain, really took hold. It increasingly seemed like the best option for someone as disgusting as me. Logic I now, far too late, see as flawed.

It was chiefly about control. From what I understand, it usually is. I couldn't make my mother come back to Cornwall, just as I couldn't make myself more like Tess. Similarly, I couldn't shrink the space between my hips, the size of my feet, the length of my femurs. My skeleton, like life itself, so intractable. So what else to do rather than try to marshall the soft, fleshy bits into some semblance of order?

Nobody really made me feel beautiful. Not my mother. Not the men that came before you. The one-night stands. The university boyfriend, Tom, who fancied himself as a DJ but now works as a tax accountant. He told me he was a 'legs man', but that I 'gave him the horn anyway', as if girls were cuts of meat in a restaurant, only there to be consumed.

There's my BCG scar on my arm. A keloid dent that was large enough for me to feel self-conscious wearing vests. We got them done at school, when we were young teenagers, but Megan and Jude had their TB injections when they were first born. Jude's healed with the tiniest whisper of a scar, but Megan's is a noticeable pock in her arm that she, too, will be aware of.

There's the white disc left by a particularly angry chicken pox on my right flank.

The crater under my left cheekbone from a zit that I dug at too furiously, digging into my epidermis. I knew that I was doing damage, but I was unable to stop myself. Like so many other times in my life.

The lump on my inner labia left from poor stitching after Jude's furious entrance to the world.

The purplish mark on my forearm from carelessly wielding a hot iron.

The appendectomy slit near my hip.

There are the pigmentation splatters emerging on the back of my hands and around the sides of my face. The veins on my thighs, like squiggling worms.

I'm a mass of marks and I expect that if you could cut me open, you would see more. Fatty deposits on my arteries, polyps in my colon. Perhaps the beginning of enlarged blood vessels in my brain. Another small consolation, at least, in this – I'm being spared William's fate. I'm still me, not being stripped away, day by day.

There's the rest of course. The stuff we know about. The cancer cells progressing up my spine and causing my vertebrae to shatter, mushrooming in my lungs. Their own eco-system overtaking my own. You don't need me to catalogue those, we've spent enough time thinking about them.

20

Then

At night, their bed was like a ship, bobbing on unchartered waters. The detritus of new parenthood weighing their craft down, the crumpled tissues, bottles of Infacol, doll-size nappies and milky squares of muslin.

They kept the night light on and the temperature tropical. Ted was banished to the kitchen. Sylvia woke every hour or two, responding to Megan's mewls, plugging her onto her nipple.

The exhaustion had a texture, like an object. Sometimes the desire to close her eyes, baby on breast, and just drift, away to sea, was almost overwhelming.

But Sylvia was vigilant, determined. She could do this.

The trick of getting a sleeping Megan from her into the Moses basket was a knack. And mostly Megan would wake again, demanding more comfort, skin on skin.

'Just bring her in with us,' said Paul, sleepily. But Sylvia pictured her baby's tiny nostrils being squashed, her breath stopped if one of them rolled onto her. Everywhere she looked was fresh peril. She worried about whether pushing the pram over cobbles could inflict brain damage. About the chemicals in the changing mat's plastic. About the air quality on their road.

Every time someone held Megan, she watched every movement, unembarrassed, only relaxing properly once Megan was back in her arms.

But within the confines of her constant anxiety, she felt more peaceful than she ever had. All her previous compulsions were crowded out by her new responsibility. Pulsing behind the routine of their days, carefully choreographed by Gina Ford, was a white euphoria. So, this was what it was all about.

And Megan made it easy for them. A sleeper who fed well and grew steadily along the ninetieth centile, already top of the class. She smiled when she was four weeks old, wryly, on her changing mat, prompting Sylvia to cry shaky tears of pure happiness.

'I don't deserve her,' she said to Paul, more than once.

'What are you talking about?' he said. 'You made her.' He shook his head. Motherhood suited Sylvia more than he could ever have expected. She was more solid than before, physically, but emotionally too. There were no empty wrappers glinting at the bottom of the bin. If she ate chocolate, she did so unapologetically, publicly. No big deal.

The only fly was Ted, who resented his new status and took to emptying his bowels behind the living-room sofa, then watching while Paul cleared it up.

'I'm sorry, mate,' Paul would say. 'It's not my fault.' Ted didn't believe him. Things had been better before.

Even Barbara was quite taken with the baby.

'I think she looks a bit like me,' she said, presented with her grandchild, newly washed, downy little head poking out of a snowy bodysuit embroidered with lambs. She looked down at Megan with a distant expression on her face. 'A bit like you, as a baby, too.'

'Yes, a bit,' said Sylvia, happiness making her softer. Privately, she thought Megan looked exactly like her father.

'So, how are you finding it?' said Barbara.

'It's … wonderful,' said Sylvia. 'I just didn't realise …' She trailed off. There was so much she hadn't realised. Behind the euphoria of her new love was growing a renewed anger for her mother.

Barbara nodded. 'Of course, you'll need to get back to work soon. It's so important to keep that sense of yourself.'

Sylvia smiled. Work was a distant realm of disenchantment. She couldn't imagine caring about any of that stuff. The success rates of the lab, Dr Vittorio's tedious ego, the new follicule-stimulating drug the industry was getting excited about, all those couples so desperate for what she now had – it all meant nothing to her.

Likewise, her former social life seemed unimportant. She had argued, grievously, with Ariadne only the night before when her friend had asked her out for a drink and she had refused. But she didn't mind. She had a new knowledge. It was all so trivial, at the end of the day. Nothing else mattered, but this.

As Megan grew, she steamed and pureed, washed and ironed. As each day went by and her baby's limbs grew sturdier, Sylvia drifted a little further away from the girl she had been.

It was Megan's decision to stop breastfeeding. She politely declined the nipple one day with a little shake of her head, shortly before her first birthday. Sylvia continued to try and force her for a few days, until it became clear than Megan had made a decision. She was ready to break the link.

Two months later, Sylvia was pregnant with Jude. This time there was no surprise. At least, not for her. She had known exactly what she was doing.

Mothering an infant, while exhausting and menial in so many ways, had given her a mental freedom she hadn't had in her adult life before. She was anxious about it ending. About having to juggle work and children. This was clearer cut. She had to let the lab know, of course. They were surprised, but less so when Sylvia, the new Sylvia, came in to talk to them. Sturdier, slower, distracted, with Megan on her hip and her stomach already stretching. Dr Vittorio, who had always had a special eye for Sylvia in her lab coat, could only raise his eyebrows and offer her another full maternity package to cover his dismay.

Paul was surprised. 'Wow ... That was quick.' He wasn't opposed to the idea, though. He, too, saw value in rooting Sylvia in the domestic. It was what Miriam had done, after all. A small part of him, one he was reluctant to admit even to himself, enjoyed the fruits of Sylvia being at home. He loved returning after a long day at surgery to see the lights on in the house, to think of Sylvia and Megan inside, waiting for him.

And Sylvia was safe like this, a defused bomb. No drunken regret, no agonised discussions about work, no running taps to hide the sound of retching. It's true, part of him missed the excitement of the old Sylvia, but he wouldn't trade this new motherly incarnation, not for anything in the world.

With Jude inside her, Sylvia was careful. She knew how much was at stake now, how precious her baby would be. She shunned paté and hot dogs, refused even a sip of wine. But pregnancy with a toddler in tow – even a sensible, calm one like Megan – was harder. The lifting, bending, wiping and sorting treadmill seemed endless. Sometimes she wistfully thought of being back in the wider world. On the tube, walking down the street unencumbered, meeting the eyes of men she would never see again. A person still with potential. But then she would smoosh Megan's chubby limbs, feel the baby fluttering in her stomach and remember she had everything she needed. Right there.

* * *

Jude started as he meant to go on. Arriving on a Tuesday, on the bathroom floor, just thirty minutes after Sylvia had her first contraction. Megan was still asleep in her pink bedroom, while Paul was by Sylvia's side, on the phone to the paramedics.

For ten precious minutes, it was just the three of them in the room. Jude gulped at the air like a landed fish. Looked quizzically at his parents. He was plump and red, rudely healthy. And unlike Megan, his mother's features were discernible.

'A boy!' said Sylvia, looking at Paul, delighted. She knew Paul had wanted a boy, despite his protestations to the contrary. And she felt pride at having delivered what he desired.

Paul was silent, overwhelmed with joy. His wife, his daughter and now his son. He felt a presentiment then, which he was to recall later – after Rosa and after Sylvia – that this was the peak of happiness. A twinge of fear in the middle of his joy, at having these gifts taken away from him. But he smiled and kissed Sylvia, wiped back her hair.

'You are amazing,' he said, softly.

Jude started to roar. His quiet beginning had been false. He was his sister's polar opposite in almost every way that counts.

The paramedics turned up, tense at first but then relaxing when they saw mother and baby both pink. Oxygenated and flooded with oxytocin.

'Looks like you didn't need our help,' said a grey-haired man, smiling. 'And seems like you've got a feisty one there.'

21

Now

'I saw Mummy last night,' Jude said, matter-of-factly. He was sitting in front of his bowl of cereal, the Weetabix congealing. 'She sat on the corner of my bed as I was falling asleep.'

Paul was standing at the kitchen counter, blearily squeezing a tea bag against the side of a mug. Like so many other nights since his wife had gone, he had eventually trudged upstairs the night before, re-read some pages of the manual, then taken his tablets and belly-flopped into unsettled sleep. He had dreamed of Sylvia and woken early, searching his sheets as if hoping for another of the bright filaments of her hair, but finding nothing. He ached for her presence. Her soft white skin, cool long fingers, knowing laugh. The hilarious, gently vicious way she dissected all social gatherings for his amusement. Part of him was still waiting for her verdict on her own funeral.

'That's not possible,' said Megan. She was eating and

reading at the same time, her hair brushed and her clothes clean. She didn't look motherless, far from it. If anything, since Sylvia's death, she had assumed an aggressive tidiness that was almost like a reproach.

Jude, in contrast, looked wilder than ever. His hair stuck out in all directions and there was a stripe of something brown – actual dirt – on one of his cheeks. His nostrils were plugged with snot.

'Mummy is dead. You know that.' She looked up from her book and softened her voice slightly. 'It's not possible, Jude.'

'But I definitely saw her,' said Jude. His bottom lip stuck out. 'I'm not making it up.'

'What happened?' said Paul, sitting down at the table. His tea was cold, a crinkly skin forming on the top of the liquid. He remembered Sylvia claiming that she had never had a truly hot drink after having children. That she was always busy, emptying things, signing permission slips, taking milk bottles out to the front step.

'She sat on the end of the bed and looked at me,' said Jude. 'She looked like she used to look, when she was still pretty, before she got sick. Her hair was long.' He stopped talking and looked defiantly at Megan.

'Jude …' Paul said, still searching for the right approach. His son's statement chimed queasily with his own longings and he tried to reach for the boy's grubby little hand. He hadn't realised how much grooming the children needed, like show ponies. More invisible work that Sylvia had undertaken, even after Rosa, when she was falling apart.

'Not possible,' said Megan, eyes flicking up from her book.

'You're imagining it. Probably because you are grieving. Isn't that right, Daddy? The mind can play tricks on us when we're in a state of shock, can't it?'

'Sometimes it can be hard to separate our imaginations from reality,' said Paul, slowly. 'We talked about it ourselves, didn't we, Megs?' He thought of his own longing for Sylvia's presence. The relics that he was shoring up as if they might bring her back. His most recent finds had been a trashy celebrity magazine, warped from being read in the bath, and a stud earring, crenellated fake diamonds. 'We all want Mummy to still be here, more than anything. It's not surprising that you dreamed about her. Especially last night, after we said goodbye.'

'It wasn't a dream,' said Jude, defiant. 'I really saw her. I was wide awake. I heard the door shut downstairs after that lady left. Then Mummy was there, looking at me. I swear it. Cross my heart and hope to die.'

'Jude,' said Paul. There was a warning note in his voice. He wanted his son to stop. The pain was more than he could bear.

'Don't believe me then,' said Jude, jumping out of his chair and running out of the room.

Megan raised her eyebrows and turned back to her book. Paul followed his son upstairs, past the wall of family photographs that Sylvia had organised. Her carefully curated life. There was a picture of the two of them in the park. In the early days. Before Sylvia fell pregnant. They were both smiling broadly, apparently carefree, Sylvia unthinkably pretty and unmarred. But those were the days when she had gorged near daily, like a snake swallowing a rat, and then went to the toilet and emptied her stomach. The days when she tore the skin around her nails off, like strips of satin, leaving raw flesh.

Then there was Jude, in his Moses basket, looking up and grinning at the camera. His limbs blurred, obviously moving, but his face tender. Megan sitting in a restaurant, in Rome, wearing a yellow sundress, with ragu smeared around her mouth and a single long strand of spaghetti hanging from her lips. Barbara when she was younger, in *Good Life* mode before she left, in dungarees, with chickens at her feet. William, on the cliff, in profile, Cornish sea in the background. And one of Tess and Sylvia together, arms linked, leaning in towards each other like a mirror image and laughing hard, as if at a hilarious joke.

In his room, Jude was lying face down on his bed, his body shuddering with sobs.

'I know what I saw,' he says, looking up at Paul. 'It was Mummy. She was here. You don't have to believe me. But it's bloody true.' He looked slightly shocked with himself for the swear word.

'Come here,' said Paul, whose own face was now wet with tears. 'I wish it was.' He would have given almost anything to actually see Sylvia, as she once had been. To remember how she was before all the tests, the trials, the needles and disappointment, in those days when anything was still possible. Unsullied and incandescent. When he believed she had already offered up all her secrets to him. He reached for his son and held his body tight in his arms, kissed the top of his curly head.

'I wasn't imagining it,' said Jude, but with less fight now. 'It was definitely, absolutely her.'

Paul didn't say anything. He rubbed his son's wiry back and glanced out of the window. The sky was a pitiless blue, hash-tagged with contrails.

And then he saw it. On Jude's Star Wars duvet cover. A single marmalade-coloured hair. He reached out and carefully pincered his fingers to pick it up, holding it up to the light, where it glinted.

* * *

Paul organised counselling for the children, with a woman that Barbara found, who came highly recommended, but whom he disliked on sight. Yet he continued to send them, because he felt he should.

His own therapist, the one he had seen in the weeks that Sylvia lay in the hospice, told him that 'should' didn't come into it.

'Grief is different for everybody,' she said. 'But like many human processes, it tends to follow the same stages.'

Ah yes, thought Paul. He'd heard about this, many times. Hadn't everyone? Denial. Anger. And then finally acceptance.

He seemed stuck in denial. Not just a river in Egypt, as Sylvia would have said. She always had found bad jokes hilarious.

But he couldn't imagine ever getting to the point of accepting that she had gone. He had never met anyone like Sylvia, let alone had anyone like her choose him. His girlfriends before had been like Alice. Sensible, healthy girls with good habits, like flossing and drinking eight glasses of water a day.

The wilder girls, the glamorous girls, the ones he tried to pretend he wasn't attracted to, found him too staid.

Even post-children, Sylvia shunned the recommended amount of water and vegetables. Left to her own devices and without the obligations of pregnancy, she would fall back on instant noodles and diet fizzy drinks, full of aspartame and caffeine.

His therapist, Sue, had told him to try journalling. Meditation. Thinking of Sylvia in happy times. She had told him that the grief would come in waves, washing in and out like a tide; some days would be harder than others. That he would never get over it, exactly, but the rest of life would come up to meet him again. Sensible enough, he had thought.

But then Sylvia died and he stopped going to see Sue. He couldn't see the value. After all, as Mick would have said, what was the point of sitting in a room and talking about it? His only conversation with his father, about the pancreatic cancer sweeping through his body, was when Mick said to him, as an afterthought at the end of a phone call, 'Not going to see the World Series next year, looks like.'

'Dad . . .' Paul had said. He had thought then of the distance between them. The sky and ocean. So vast and uncaring.

'Sink a tinny for me, right?' said Mick, moving on to talk of the possum in his back garden, gnawing the cables.

And there was the other reason too that he stopped. The first part of the manual Sue would have accepted. Liked, even. It would have excited all her kindly impulses. He could just imagine her eyes moistening, the wobble of her corned-beef arms. It was exactly the kind of thing a dying mother ought to do. But how to avoid discussing the less palatable side of Sylvia the document also revealed?

He couldn't trust himself to, so cancelled his sessions. But the children continued to go, to the other pointy-faced woman. Less kindly than Sue but, he hoped, possibly more effective.

They didn't speak of what they said to her and she didn't tell him, either. Sometimes, when he collected them afterwards, one of them would have sodden cheeks and the woman would look at him knowingly, as if she knew all his secrets. Then, as so often, he would reflect on how much easier it was with animals. They were so much more in touch with their instincts. They didn't need to frame everything with words, to articulate.

But despite the therapy, Jude still sometimes claimed he glimpsed Sylvia. Alone at bedtime, Paul would ask for more details as he tucked Jude in, hungry for them despite his better judgement. He was torn between wanting to stop his son's imaginings and a piercing jealousy. How he longed for his own mind to summon her so, to see her as she was. Sometimes, Jude would haltingly recount stories that Paul never realised Sylvia had told her son. Tales of their pre-parenthood life, that she had obviously whispered as she soothed him to sleep. A description of the pink, half-eroded shell Paul had found on a Breton beach and presented to

Sylvia as a gift, its inner workings exposed like an ear. She had thanked him for it profusely, before skimming it out to sea. Or the time he and Sylvia went to an outdoor cinema in fancy dress at Halloween. She a corseted zombie, he a particularly unthreatening, self-conscious vampire. The short-lived craze they had for oversweet mango juice from the cornershop. Their plan, kiboshed by pregnancy, to travel along a stage of the Silk Road.

Jude would present these snatches of their earlier lives verbatim and Paul would listen hungrily, catching Sylvia's intonation in his phrasing. Such testimony of their shared happiness helped soften the sting of the manual's divulgence, the surprise of which continued to catch him unawares, rising in his throat like heartburn. He just didn't know how to process it.

Meanwhile, he continued to shore up signs of Sylvia's former presence, like trophies. There were the strands of hair that he had found. So far, four sun-gold threads, like something out of a fairytale. He kept them wrapped in tissue paper in his bedside drawer, as if they might be able to summon her back, alongside a frayed toothbrush that she must have forgotten to throw away. Also, a well-used lip balm, worn down into a sickle shape.

It was one of the few places that Natalia wouldn't intrude, for after finally admitting the chaos in the house was becoming too much, he had tentatively asked her, one morning outside the school, if she might consider helping him out with it, just for a bit. He didn't use the word 'cleaning'. But Natalia was utterly unembarrassed.

'It's ok … Paul,' she said, donning rubber gloves on the first morning and heading for the cupboard under the sink. 'You need help, I help you.'

He didn't agree an hourly rate but left a sheaf of tenners in the fruit bowl on the days she came in, which were never discussed, but never there when he got back from the surgery. Privately he thrilled to the new domestic order, even if he still found the intimacy discomfiting.

Natalia started to assert her own domestic tics around the house – hanging the tea towels in a slightly different position, stacking the fridge in a new order, pouring a thick rim of toilet bleach around the bowl, using hangers to dry his damp shirts.

The butter, which Sylvia had always kept in a glass dish on the side, was firmly relegated to the fridge for health and safety reasons that Paul had to admit he sympathised with. Even when slender – especially when slender – Sylvia had been a butter fiend, chopping off chunks to stir into polenta or tile onto bread.

But he felt disloyal adhering to the new regime and would sometimes deliberately revert, draping tea towels on the counter as Sylvia had. Little tributes, indiscernible to anyone else.

* * *

'I wish I could have stayed for longer. To help you with the children,' said Miriam, on the phone.

'It's all right, Ma,' said Paul. He would never say anything else to his mother.

'How are the kiddos?'

'They're doing ... ok,' said Paul. 'As well as can be expected.' He thought of Megan's shuttered face, Jude's unsettling accounts of his mother visiting him. And his son's constant motion, which only seemed to be worse now that Sylvia was gone. The boy literally couldn't sit still for a moment. Even the digital cosh of the iPad was no longer completely effective. Paul had found him jumping off his bed, with the screen discarded, blaring away on the floor.

'Jude?'

'He's ok. Busy, you know.'

'That's boys for you,' said Miriam. 'You and Ed were the same. Terrors. You know you can always move out here and I'll help you as much as I can.'

Paul looked out at the evening and thought of his mother beginning her day in Australia. Her black coffee and Vegemite on sweet, white bread. Autumn drawing in for her, which meant maybe a jumper in the evening, but still meals outside, space. Maybe his home country would be the making of his son.

'I've got the practice ... They have friends. I can't just uproot them.'

'As long as you know.' His mother wouldn't say more.

'Are you ok?' he said. 'Your hip?'

'I'm ok. Your brother does what he can.'

'Right,' said Paul. 'That's good.' Ed, he knew, did nothing. Or rather, he mowed his mother's lawn occasionally, got one of his mechanics to regularly check her car, but without the faintest scintilla of emotional intimacy.

'Take care.'

'You too.'

He put down his phone and went upstairs. Megan was in her room reading. Jude finally asleep. Getting him down that evening had been a battle. They had been talking about Sylvia and something seemed to agitate Jude more than usual, so that he wriggled out of bed and danced around the room, asking for a snack with a glint in his eyes.

'No, Jude. You have been eating all evening. You had biscuits after dinner. And an apple.'

'I'm hungry.'

'Jude.' Paul felt desperate.

'I want a banana.'

'You had one already.'

'I want 'nother one.' Jude jutted out his chin, with its manly little cleft. Paul stared at his son and trudged downstairs looking for a banana. He came back upstairs to find Jude naked, his pyjamas tossed off in the middle of the bedroom floor. He was triumphant, chest puffed out, his willy dangling, shrimp-like and obscene.

'What are you doing?' Paul felt anger starting to rise. He found his son revolting in that moment, suddenly seeing his blue eyes as too far apart, his nose piggish.

'Nothing,' said Jude.

'Here's your banana. Put your clothes on.'

'I don't want a banana now,' said Jude. 'I want to play.'

'It's bedtime,' said Paul.

'Just five more minutes. Please.'

'No. No you cannot just have five more minutes,' shouted

Paul. 'You won't do a single bloody thing I tell you.' He gripped Jude's arms and shook him, ripe banana squashed between his hand and Jude's arm.

'Stop it, Daddy.' The knowing triumph had ebbed from Jude's eyes. He looked terrified, like the little boy that he was. Paul dropped his hands.

'I'm sorry.' He shook his head. He couldn't believe he had raised a hand to his son. The boy who had just watched his mother wither and die. 'I'm so sorry.'

Jude was silent, looking at Paul as if seeing him for the first time.

'Bedtime now,' said Paul. 'We're all tired.'

Jude put on his pyjamas without any more argument and climbed into bed.

'I hope Mummy comes tonight,' he said. 'To see me when I'm asleep.'

Paul nodded. Selfishly, he hoped for more recollections from their past, re-told through their child. He was starting to overly rely on these missives of their lost happiness.

'Why did you hurt me, Daddy?' said Jude. 'I was being silly, but you really hurt my arm.'

'I don't know, Jude. I'm sorry. I make mistakes too.'

Later, when Paul checked on his sleeping son, he saw him sweating, as usual. Running a race in his sleep. He reached out a hand to smooth his damp hair.

'I don't know if I can do this, Sylvia. Without you,' he said, aloud in the room. But it didn't feel as if she heard him.

22

Sylvia's Manual

A homebirth seemed the sensible option. The perfect birth for the perfect baby. I felt as if I owed it to her to make it so. I pictured candles, music, the umbilical cord pulsing until the blood ran still.

And you supported me, of course, as you always would. But your job lent you a confidence in staying away from hospital. You have seen life and death so many times, you weren't fazed. I was no different from a ewe in lambing season, a cat looking for a cupboard under the stairs. It was normal.

But I knew you hoped for a magical experience too. And I wanted to give it to you. To do that right. It was going to be the last time, we both knew that.

The midwives from the hospital's home birth team were similarly reassuring.

'Birth is a natural process,' said the older one, with the warm eyes and the salt-and-pepper hair.

'For third-time mothers the statistics suggest it's actually safer,' said the younger, tougher one. 'You're a pro at this by now!'

My previous births had been fairly unremarkable. Even Jude spooling out onto the bathroom floor. Remember that morning? I think it was the best of my life. Certainly, it stands out among all those other mornings of my life, now I'm taking stock.

So, there was nothing in my notes to suggest that a home birth wasn't a perfectly good idea. I was 'low risk' as they say, as if these things are predictable. As if those statistics mean anything on an individual level.

You can't go back. As you get older, everyone realises this. You can't slip back into being sixteen or decide to revisit twenty-eight. Now, in these four walls, I know that better than anyone. But if I could change anything, more than my diagnosis even, I would change my decision to have Rosa in our front room, in a deep pool of tepid water, next to the children's scooters and the piano.

I'd go back to that woman, myself, who thought she was already so seasoned, and counsel her to think again. To discard her rash, newfound self-confidence. To protect her newfound happiness fiercely, like a vicious dog. You made me feel like things were going to be all right, that I deserved contentment. But that was wrong.

When it came to it, you see, I longed for strip lighting, tabards, the sting of alcohol hand wash. The thrum of a huge hospital in full swing. Procedures, alarms, obstetricians.

It might still have happened, but I think I would have felt less culpable, less alone. And maybe you wouldn't have blamed me like you did.

You never said as much, thought you hid it carefully, but I saw it in your eyes. With one thing and another, I've got pretty good at sensing an undertow of blame in the last few years.

In terms of a manual, you might think there was nothing for

me to tell you about our third child. But you'd be mistaken. I had plans for Rosa, even after she was gone. I didn't stop being her mother. As time went by, that role seemed only to become more sharply defined for me, as if she was growing alongside my decline. A ghost child, getting more substantial as I started to fade away.

Sometimes I used to think I could hear her crying in the night, at home. I would wake up, the sound in my head, and climb out of bed, padding around in the darkness, looking for my lost one. I could never find her, of course. Not even in her room, which we turned back into the spare room, painting over the cheerful walls and getting rid of the cot, as if she had never been.

You have to be the one to keep her memory alive. Show her footprint picture to Jude and Megan. And that lock of her hair, in a box, in my bedside drawer.

There was no sign that anything was wrong, really, during the labour. The midwives were hands-off, as I asked them to be. A second thing I bitterly regret. Perhaps if I'd let them listen for Rosa's heartbeat towards the end, I would have realised that something was going awry earlier. But I didn't. I laboured on, unawares, grunting in the pool.

The kinder one kept asking to check, gently, but I thought it was going to interrupt my flow. Truth is, I wanted to be completely alone with my experience. I knew it was the last time I was going to give birth and I wanted to wring every sensation out of the process. To fully live it. So selfish.

Maybe if we went for hospital midwives, instead of hiring private ones, they would have insisted. As it was, we were paying them an enormous amount and ultimately, it seemed, we were in charge.

It wasn't until Rosa slipped from me and I saw her colour, that I realised. She was blue. Not the purplish colour of most newborns but an icier blue. Even when she was still underwater, I could see that something was terribly wrong. A presentiment of horror.

'Reach into the water and pick baby up,' said the midwife, who still hadn't realised anything was unusual. So, I did. Reached into the murky depths and fetched our baby. She broke the surface without a cry and I brought her to my chest. She was so beautiful and her hair, downy on her head, was already as red as mine. A coronet for our princess. But her fragile rib cage was still.

'She's not ... breathing,' I said, terror flooding me. Statement of the obvious.

'We need to just get her going,' said the harder midwife, more matter-of-fact, as if babies emerged not breathing all the time. But she was scared too and that's when the fear really started. They cut the cord immediately, not leaving it to beat as I had wanted. They took Rosa away, to the side of the room. I could only see their backs.

You came to the edge of the pool and kneeled, gripped my hand, murmured something. There was a flurry. They got the oxygen canister, the one that I'd assumed was just for show. I was still in the water and I couldn't see what was happening. Did you see more? I always wanted to ask you that, but never found the words.

I think, in that moment, I was still waiting for a cry. For relieved laughter and one of the midwives to say, 'You gave us a fright.'

But there was just silence. I'm sorry to make you revisit this memory, but I'm scared that if I don't write this down, you will gloss over it. Turns out this isn't just a manual – it's my testimony. So that when you do move on, without me, my version of events will still exist out there somewhere. Perhaps I'm even hoping that

Megan – or Jude – will come upon this one day. Will realise what happened. We couldn't tell them, properly. And then I got ill and Rosa's absence wasn't our biggest problem any more.

'We need to get you both into hospital,' said the younger midwife then. 'Baby seems to be having a bit of trouble breathing.'

She didn't say, 'Your baby is dead.' She couldn't, but I knew, I saw it in her eyes.

I stood out of the pool, a wobbly big-breasted sea-monster, gushing blood from deep inside myself.

'Give me my baby,' I cried. 'I want to hold my baby now.' The older midwife was coming off the phone. I think she rang the ambulance. But she was experienced enough to know there was nothing to be done. That what mattered then, in terms of whether the two of us would ever be able to recover, were the moments that immediately followed.

'Give her baby,' she said to the other midwife. 'The ambulance is on its way, but for now you should hold her.'

That's what we did. On the sofa. The placenta, that defective life-force, still shored up inside me. The last time we were properly together. A parody of the happiness of Jude's birth. She was wrapped in that blanket that I bought for her. The one with little ducks. And the matching hat.

She was so pretty. Your lips, my nose. The particular look of Megan and Jude on her features – the synthesis of our genes, our stamp. I kept waiting for her to stir.

We cried. Tears splashing onto her little face. It wasn't supposed to go like that. In that moment and in the months, years, since, I've been debilitated by the sense of sliding doors. If only it hadn't happened, we would have been sitting on the sofa waiting for a cup of tea, talking about her future. Changing her first meconium-filled nappy, exclaiming over sticky, black tar. Sweet normality presiding despite the magic of new life.

She should be here now, mourning me going, instead of the other way around. Helping Megan to look after you in your old age.

I don't know why I'm telling you all this. You were there. But I suppose the thing is that, my version of events is going to die along with me. And when it comes to Rosa, what I want you to do is to keep alive all the memories. Even if it hurts.

23

Now

'Daddy, Daddy, I found a photograph. A black-and-white one.'

Paul glanced at the digital clock on his bedside table. 6.20.

'Jude, it's still sleepy-time,' he said. 'Daddy's tired.' He had been dreaming of younger Sylvia, silky hair trailing on his torso like a lap dancer's, and he was reluctant to wake, to let reality reassert itself.

'But I found something, Daddy,' said Jude, his footsteps banging on the floor.

'What?' said Paul. He had remembered the night before. How he had gripped Jude, wanting to hurt him. He sat up. He had to be better than this. To be the father that Jude needed him to be.

'Look, a photograph. Of an old-fashioned lady.'

Paul looked at the photograph of an elegant woman with a moon-shaped face. It was actually sepia, a creamy brown. You couldn't tell the colour of her lipstick, but it was dark and

perfectly applied. He took it from Jude's hands and turned it
over, to see if there was anything written on the back.

Dorothea, 1942, was scrawled in spidery handwriting.

'That's your great-grandmother Dora,' said Paul to Jude.
'This must have been before Juju was born.'

'So, Juju's mummy?' said Jude.

'Yes,' said Paul. 'She looks a bit like you, actually. Around
the eyes.' That same wide-eyed, full-fat beauty. 'Why were
you going through those things? I hope you didn't make a
mess.' All the old photographs were kept in a battered leather
suitcase in the spare bedroom, which Sylvia grandly called
her 'office', as if a resumption of her career was ever imminent. Jude knew about the suitcase because Sylvia would
sometimes show him one or two of the photographs in it.
She had promised to go through them all with him when she
wasn't so busy, but the day had never come.

'I didn't!' The pitch and volume of Jude's voice shifted up
a notch. 'I just wanted to see if there were any pictures of
Mummy that I hadn't seen.'

'Don't worry, Jude, I believe you,' said Paul. Anything to
keep Jude on an even keel, to stop him segueing into a tantrum.

'What was Juju's mummy like?' said Jude, taking the picture again.

'I don't know. I never met her,' said Paul. 'I think she died
when Juju was quite little. I don't think Mummy ever met
her either.'

'Of cancer, like my mummy?' said Jude.

'Maybe,' said Paul. 'I don't really know. You'll have to ask
Juju herself. I've never really spoken to her about it.'

'Can I keep the picture?' said Jude. 'I'll look after it. Please.'

'Ok,' said Paul. 'But don't lose it.'

'Can I watch *Ninjago*?' said Jude, still clutching the photo-graph.

'Ok,' said Paul. Maybe he could sleep for another twenty minutes. The sheets were sweet, freshly laundered by Natalia, and he wanted to sink down into them and never wake up. But the sound of fighting from the iPad was too much and Jude squirmed in bed next to him, like a meaty eel. Eventually he gave in, accepted that the day was starting and sat up.

*   *   *

Barbara had come around to see the children and 'help' with bedtime. This meant sitting on the sofa drinking a large tumbler of whiskey and decompressing about her day in the office.

'It's the return of fascism,' she said to Paul, pointing a carmine-nailed finger. 'And social media has put us here. God knows why Sylvia was so addicted to it.'

Paul scanned his mother-in-law's face, wondering what she would have made of the secret her daughter had kept expertly hidden for so many years. Presumably she still had no idea?

'What, Jude?' Barbara said. Then let out an instinctive 'Sssh!' to her grandson, like a cough, wanting him to contain his energy.

'I found this picture of your mummy.' Jude was triumphant, waving it in front of her.

'He went through some of Sylvia's bits,' said Paul, not revealing Jude's quest to find unseen photographs of Sylvia. Barbara's sharp eyes had probably caught sight of the bruise on Jude's right arm, the hallmark of his poor parenting. If you looked closely it had obviously been made by fingers. She would think he wasn't coping. Not that she could lecture anybody on how to parent.

'Ah yes,' said Barbara, taking the picture from Jude's hand. 'This must have been just before she had me.' She turned the picture over and looked at the back. 'That's right, 1942.'

'She was very pretty,' said Megan.

'Yes,' said Barbara. 'I suppose she was. Didn't do her much good, sadly.'

'Why not?' said Megan, looking at the photograph.

'Well, she died when I was only eleven,' said Barbara.

'What from?' said Jude. 'Was it cancer like Mummy?'

'It was a bit vague,' said Barbara. 'It wasn't like nowadays. People used to just die and they couldn't really work out why. Children died all the time of things you get injections for nowadays. Measles … that kind of thing.'

Paul winced. He didn't like the direction this conversation was taking.

'There must have been some explanation,' said Megan, piqued. She disliked ambiguity.

'Hmmm,' said Barbara, handing the picture back to Jude, as if she were bored of the whole conversation. 'She was making pastry in the kitchen one day, kneading on the countertop, and then she fell to the ground. Just like that. Dead on the lino. I was the one that found her, actually.'

'Shit,' said Paul, looking at Barbara. 'I never knew that.'

'Yup,' said Barbara. 'Pretty grim. I remember holding her hand. It was all floury.' She was peering into her glass as if she might be able to summon more alcohol by looking.

'What was she like?' said Megan. 'I mean, before she died.'

'What was she like?' said Barbara. 'Well, my memories are a bit hazy, but she was a housewife, like most women were in those days. I mean … Well, she was my mother, so obviously … She loved baking. To this day I haven't tasted a Bakewell tart like the one she made. Not that I've ever tried making one myself.'

Jude was whirling around, with the picture in his hand.

'Watch it, Jude, you're going to knock into somebody,' said Paul.

'What was it like, when she died?' said Megan. 'I mean, you weren't that much older than us. I never realised that this happened to you too, Juju. You should have said.'

Barbara's eyes were unfocused and it seemed to take her a supreme effort of will to pull herself back into the room.

'Bloody awful,' she said. Then she looked at Jude. 'Stop that right now, young man!' Jude stilled.

'Mummy sometimes comes to visit me,' said Jude.

Paul's heart broke to watch his son's sincerity. The way he could unquestioningly believe in the impossible, seemed to find it a straightforward comfort.

'That's nonsense,' said Barbara. 'I don't want to hear you talking like that again.' Jude's eyes filled. 'Your mother is dead. Far too early. It's a tragedy.' Barbara stood. 'But you have to accept it and airy-fairy ideas about her visiting you aren't going to help anybody.' She plucked the photograph of her own mother from Jude's hand and contemplated it. 'Even mothers die,' she said.

24

Sylvia's Manual

I had done so well. Submitted to the yoke of motherhood, found myself even, under it.

I even convinced myself that I could pass muster as a decent human – you helped me do that for a while. Those happy years.

But what happened with Rosa undid me. It reminded me of my fundamental unworthiness.

The old habits came back swiftly. I went to the kitchen sink to vomit, leaving you sitting with her on the sofa, swaddled as if her tiny limbs were about to move. And then they took her away. God, they took her away. I shouldn't have wasted a second being sick, but it was as if my body didn't know how else to respond. I didn't even need to stick my fingers down my throat, I just retched at the horror of it.

The kids were due back from Barbara's. She still didn't know. Nobody knew. Who would I ring? Not my mother, Tess, or even Nush. There was nobody in my life I could bear to break that news to. Amid the horror, I remember feeling almost embarrassed. Such an inconvenience for everyone, expecting another little bundle instead of nuclear devastation.

I needed to go into hospital too, the midwife said. To get checked out. I promised I would, but instead I ignored advice and went upstairs to the nursery I had got ready for our little girl.

It was so perfect, down to the little mobile of floating stars above the bed. The changing tray waiting for another inhabitant. A wooden 'R' propped on the windowsill.

I had got too cocky, expecting good fortune. I should have known when I was preparing that nursery. I should have reminded myself of my past mistakes. Tess would call it karma. She knows all about that.

My stomach was huge, as if she was still safe inside. I sat on the nursing chair. The one that had already been through Megan and Jude. That had already absorbed spit-up, breastmilk, tears. I was leaking blood and amniotic fluid with its distinctive smell into one of those huge maternity pads. Motherhood so humiliating, at the best of times.

Eventually, you came and found me, led me down to the car, to the hospital. Where I should have been in the first place.

*　*　*

Later there was counselling, leaflets, discussions about the stillbirth problem in the UK. The highest number in the western world. Apparently, Rosa had always been measuring large for dates – why didn't anyone let me know? Why didn't anyone warn me this could happen? There was a network, for other parents like us. Special chat rooms, a bit like the ones I haunt now for my cancer.

I did try to engage. But the sadness of those other mothers was too much to take. Their excruciating disbelief at their fate didn't console me, only made me feel worse.

Just as the vomiting started, so too the bingeing. I needed something to bring up. Tunnock's tea cakes liberated from their shiny shells. Salt and vinegar crisps. Cheese strings washed down with fizzy pop. The kind of food I have rarely fed Jude and Megan.

I kept it hidden from them – and from you. Secrecy was back in style. Rubbish taken out early, mints sucked on the school run.

I hate to admit there was a comfort in it, my eating disorder, but there was. Magda welcomed me back, with a wink and a knowing, 'I knew I'd see you again.' So reliable, so consistent. A way to stop yawning nothingness from taking over. The baby weight fell off, although part of me wanted it to stay, as proof of Rosa's existence.

Everyone thought I was doing well. Even you, admit it. You were flailing yourself, but you thought I was being strong.

The other mums on the school run were trying to pity me, to be kind. Natalia P with her soft questions. Abigail Blackwood with her brisk sympathy.

But they grew weary of me, I saw it in their eyes. I was too hard, too unresponsive. I still wore my make-up, expertly applied like a mask. My face contoured into submission. I wore my hair out, doused my neck and wrists, the tender bits, in perfume. I still flirted with the male teachers, female ones too. I drank too much at any given opportunity.

I didn't fit their idea of what a grieving mother should look like. There was sympathy – it was their worst nightmare – but I was still me, at the end of the day.

Only Nush provided any succour. And even she was appalled by the awfulness of it, although she worked hard not to show it. She would squeeze my arm, saying 'I'm sorry' at pick-up.

But it didn't take long for people to forget either and that's what made me really angry. Every day began with the sickening slug to my stomach, every day I thought of her little eyelashes, those fingernails. I replayed the labour in my head, snagging on my errors, my selfishness.

How anyone could go around acting as if the world was still normal, I didn't know. Of course, I tried to hold it together for Jude and Megan. My other babies. They were my reason to keep going.

But they were getting so big, so much their own people, with their own strengths and drawbacks. They were no longer repositories of possibility. I couldn't take comfort in them the way you can a baby, nuzzling a downy head that smells of melon, feeling the satisfying weight in your arms.

I cooked up that mad plan to conceive again – do you remember? Even though Rosa had been an accident, I thought another baby would help.

But you put your foot down. Said you couldn't cope. So we stopped having sex, both too sad and fractured to consider it. Our sex life always so tied with procreation, even if we hadn't realised it.

Megan and Jude didn't really know what had happened. One minute I was pregnant and they were eagerly awaiting a little sister. Megan, in particular, was keen for girls to outnumber boys in our house. The next day, we had to explain that something had gone terribly wrong and Rosa had never properly woken up.

'Was she tired?' Megan said, a little frown between her eyebrows.

'She must have been,' I said, looking her full in the eyes.

Jude had made her a card, do you remember? It said, 'Hello baby. I hope you like *Ninjago*. Jude.' He had hidden it in his room, to produce when Rosa arrived. Instead, he ended up showing it to me that evening, when I was putting him to bed. I knew what it would have taken him, to make that card. He was so ambivalent about me having another baby and he hates writing anything, with such a passion, but had swallowed his pride to check the spelling with Megan.

He looked at me solemnly, as I held it between my trembling thumb and forefinger. I confess that I wept then, for the big brother he wasn't going to get the chance to be. For us. But most of all for Rosa, the bud that never bloomed.

25

Now

Sylvia's earthly remains were alarmingly copious. Paul had pictured a diminutive jam jar full of ash, ready to be neatly scattered. But the crematorium handed him a shiny paper bag containing a shoebox-sized vessel full to the brim, a parody of one of Sylvia's covert shopping sprees.

He didn't know where to put them. In the kitchen, near the food, seemed too macabre; the living room was too prominent. Eventually he settled for a spot on the top of the wardrobe in their bedroom. On bad nights – most nights – he would stare through the gloom at the box. Incomprehensible that his wife was dust.

To the casual observer, Paul looked like a man adapting to his new reality. He took the children to school in the mornings. He went to work. He sometimes asked Natalia to pick them up after school and give them supper, before he rushed home from the surgery.

On a Sunday night he washed Jude's hair, clipped his fingernails, soaped orange nuggets of wax out of his ears.

He remembered to shave. He did the grocery shop online, using Sylvia's log-in details and the shop she had saved for him. He didn't appear to grow sick of the same filled pasta and pre-made quiche.

He started a new box set. He even occasionally watched pornography, finding relief in foreign bodies, distant acts.

But, despite his best efforts, he was just going through the motions. Sometimes a memory of his wife would rear up, throwing him off course. The finality of it winding him until he managed to claw his panic back into its box. In a sense, it reminded him of his early days in London, before he met Sylvia, when his emotions had been subterranean, barely glimpsed, even by himself. Back then, he had assumed that was the best – safest – way to live, but she had shown him a different way of being. Of turning his face towards the sun. And now he couldn't forget.

The only time that he felt a glimmer of the man she had helped him to become were the twenty minutes that he spent tucking Jude into bed each night, when his voluble son would talk about his mother. Succour indistinguishable from sadness.

It had become like a game between them, a suspension of reality. Paul knew he should quash the boy's yearning, in the name of moving on. And yet, each day he found himself looking forward to that time spent lying on Jude's single bed, in the room lit softly by the orange nightlight, listening to his son.

In the tale of how he and Sylvia had met, Paul's heroism saving Ted came up, more than once. Paul was touched to realise how Sylvia had mythologised their beginnings for Jude, casting him in the hero's role. Jude also talked about his mother's habits, reminding Paul of things he had – inexplicably – already started to forget. The way she added salt to porridge ('Do you remember, Daddy? Disgusting!'), the way she cradled Ted, as if he were a baby, the way she always danced when doing the ironing, moving her hips while toiling on the mundane.

* * *

Sylvia had asked to be scattered at home. Her first home. On the cliffs near the house she had grown up in. William had been scattered there too. And despite all the years in London, her love of the city's thrum, she wanted to go back to where she came from, first of all.

Paul could understand the choice. To be swept up on a bit of sea air, washed out over the ocean, was an appealing prospect compared to the sickening wafts of nitrogen dioxide around their London home.

'The city is a place for life,' Sylvia had said. 'But if I can't live, I want my ashes to be blown out by the sea.'

But it meant a trip to Cornwall with the children and Barbara. It meant negotiating with Tess, who had gone back to her shed shortly after the funeral, to see if they could stay in William's house, which had been rented out for lucrative short-term lets since his death.

'I only wish I could come, but the shift pattern at work is a nightmare at the moment,' Nush said one afternoon as she dropped Ryan off for a sleepover with Jude. In the weeks since Sylvia's death, the boys' sleepovers had become a regular occurrence, a pocket of normality that Paul was increasingly reliant on. It wasn't just the fact that Ryan occupied Jude, but he also found himself looking forward to Nush's company, for the twenty minutes that she would stay and chat. She had known Sylvia, really known her, as so few people had.

'Don't worry,' he said. 'I understand.' But he, too, wished that Nush could be there. Her calm presence would be just the thing to help him cope with the maelstrom of Barbara, Tess and the children.

'You've been keeping the place nice,' said Nush, sniffing the air, which smelled of furniture polish, and glancing at the sofa cushions, each with a neat dent on the top where they had been chopped into submission.

'Ah, that's actually Natalia,' said Paul, guiltily. 'She's been helping me out a few times a week. I don't know if she needs the money but it's been helpful for me.'

'Natalia P? From school?' Nush raised her eyebrows. 'Alvin's mum?'

It occurred to Paul that he had never thought to ask Natalia about Alvin's whereabouts when she came to the house to clean for him, make soup, order his sock drawer.

'She suggested it herself,' said Paul. 'She seems fine with it.' He looked at Nush, pleadingly. How to explain how badly he had been struggling, how hard it was keeping on top of everything. The crucial items that had been slipping through his fingers.

'I know, Paul. I know. Maybe it's a good solution,' said Nush, reassuringly. Paul nodded.

'It's just for a bit,' he said.

Nush grinned at him and ran a hand through her silver tufts of hair. She was already in her green overalls, ready for a night's work.

'I've got to go soon. Shift starts in half an hour. Are you sure it's all right for Ryan to sleep over here?'

'Of course,' said Paul. 'Jude loves having him. We could all do with the company.'

'I wasn't going to mention it but I'm actually a bit worried about Jude,' she said. 'He just seems a bit different from usual. Even Ryan has noticed it. He gets tired really easily when they are playing tag and just doesn't seem like himself. It's to be expected, obviously, but …'

Paul cleared his throat. 'He's struggling,' said Paul. 'Sylvia was so good with him. He's cooked up this mad idea that she is coming to him. Watching over him at night.' He paused. 'We talk about her a lot.' He flushed with embarrassment and guilt, that he was indulging his bereaved son's fantasy. Poor parenting.

'Oh!' Nush's eyes glittered with something that Paul couldn't quite define. Maybe sadness. Empathy. Or amusement.

'The thing is … I know what he means,' said Paul. 'I know it can't ever happen, but part of me still keeps expecting to find her in the house. She was always here … Every corner reminds me of her.'

Nush looked at him, frowning. She glanced towards the stairs, down which the bleep of the iPad was emanating.

'Of course it does,' she said, scanning his face. 'This was your home. You built a life together. It's not surprising.'

Paul nodded.

'She said she had written something for you, in the hospice, and had it printed out. A kind of guidebook. She didn't want to hand it over herself so I put it in the car. Has it been … useful?'

Paul thought of the manual. Useful wasn't the word for it. That distillation of their lives.

'It's been … emotional,' he finally said. 'It's amazing to have something in her voice and she knew so much about us all. But it's been hard to read.' He thought of what Nush would think about Sylvia's secret. Whether she would have judged her friend harshly.

'Getting out of the city for a bit will be a good break. Useful for everyone,' said Nush.

Paul nodded, picturing the box on top of the wardrobe. Letting those bits of Sylvia fly off on the wind. Then there would be nothing left.

'I've got to go. Make Ryan clean his teeth. He's not that big on personal hygiene.'

'Well, he's certainly got company,' said Paul, sniffing his own armpit. Nush laughed then, picked up her keys.

'We all miss her,' she said, so quietly he almost missed it, before disappearing into the night.

26

Then

Sylvia ached for forgiveness. Exoneration. Since Tess had gone back to Cornwall after their terrible argument, she hadn't heard a word from her sister. It was the first time she could remember that they weren't regularly in touch. Every time that something occurred to her that she wanted to tell Tess, she would pick up the phone, before remembering.

Looking after Jude and Megan occupied her hands all day, but her thoughts were somewhere else, snagged in the distant past. She didn't recognise the girl she had once been. Sterilising bottles, hefting a bin bag full of soiled nappies out of the front door, it felt like a stranger's memories had been implanted into her brain. An unwelcome software update. For so long, she hadn't thought about these things that she had almost – almost – convinced herself they had never happened.

But her guilt also made her righteous. It had been so long ago. Ancient history. Surely Tess could understand that. She had been young and stupid. They all were.

Barbara didn't know what to make of their estrangement and neither of her daughters enlightened her as to its cause.

It was six weeks after the argument that Sylvia finally rang her sister, cradling the phone between her cheek and neck so that she could transfer Jude onto his play mat. He wasn't a baby who liked being put down and she knew it would be a matter of moments before he started to grizzle.

'Sylvia.' Tess's voice sounded like it came from the dark side of the moon. 'Thanks for calling. Listen ... You should know that I'm pregnant. I found out just after our trip to London.' Despite the tension between them, despite everything, Sylvia could discern the muted joy in her sister's voice, the lingering disbelief. Tess had wanted this for so long.

'Congratulations!' said Sylvia, her voice brittle with her own disbelief.

'Thanks,' said Tess.

'I'm so sorry, Tessy,' said Sylvia then.

'Honestly, forget it,' said Tess. 'I never want to talk about that again.'

* * *

'Well, at least you girls seem to have gotten over your silly disagreement,' said Barbara, who was spooning pea-green puree into Jude's mouth, carefully holding the spoon away from herself. She was dressed entirely in off-white silk, large stud earrings dragging down her lobes.

'Yes,' said Sylvia, carefully. In fact, the apparent rapprochement had only made her feel further apart from her sister.

Tess answered her calls, but remained distant, withholding the essence of herself. 'Wonderful news about the pregnancy.'

'True,' said Barbara. 'I think it's something she really wants and she's got the time down there in the valley to really devote herself to it. Not sure quite what else she's been doing. But what about you? Have the lab given you a start date for going back?'

Sylvia, standing at the sink with her back to her mother, and Megan hoisted on her hip, paused for a moment, before continuing to wash Megan's hands under the tap.

'Well, actually ...' said Sylvia, dabbing Megan's face.

'You are going back, aren't you?' Barbara smiled, an expression of polite bafflement on her face. Sylvia turned around and placed Megan on the ground. 'This ...' Barbara gestured around the kitchen. It smelled of pasta. The windows were slightly fogged and on the kitchen counter lay the shrapnel from lunch. A bottle of childhood vitamins that Sylvia had been given at the health centre. A rubber ring for Jude, who seemed to be perpetually teething, red-cheeked and angry. 'This won't be enough,' said Barbara. 'Trust me, I know. It's all-consuming right now, but you'll get to a point where you need something more again.'

Barbara thought then of her early days of motherhood. On the cliff. The happy moments – William's shy smile, the breeze that crept in through the open windows, Sylvia's stout little body slotted onto her left hip – offset by the sense that she was carrying a pail of acid on one shoulder, that at any moment might tip and slosh on her back, burning her. Nowadays they would have had a name for it. Back then, all she knew was that she missed the woman she had been. The career she had made. The blistering realisation that the gifts that had fallen into her lap weren't going to be enough for her, that she was going to end up letting them all down.

'A woman like you needs intellectual stimuli too. What will you do when Jude goes to nursery ... or school, even? They don't stay little forever, you know. What are you going to do with the rest of your life?'

Jude was trying to grab the spoon, to feed himself, like his mother let him. But Barbara held it just out of reach. Sylvia frowned.

'I can work that out then. The kids need me now. You're right – they won't stay little forever. And the lab wasn't prepared to offer me two days a week, so I think—'

'Two days!' said Barbara. 'You can't do a real job in two days. I can quite see why they couldn't offer you that. You should consider getting a live-in nanny and going back full-time.'

'I don't want to,' said Sylvia. 'This is my job now.'

'Is this Paul's decision – or yours? I mean, did you see his mother? At the wedding.'

'Of course.'

'Worn down by years of being a housewife ... For what?' Barbara frowned at Jude, who was still trying to grab the spoon and starting to shift and wriggle in his chair. Sylvia was silent. As usual, Barbara was going for the jugular.

She had never mentioned it to her mother, but Miriam's domestic template hovered over her and Paul's relationship. At least her husband had stopped saying, 'Mum thinks ...' or

'When I was a kid ...' He had learned not to compare. But Sylvia knew that she was never going to be able to compete with his mother, never going to achieve the same self-abnegation. And would she even want to, if she could? She thought of Miriam at the wedding, in her old dress, wrinkled and ignored, desperate for her son to look at her. All that love and effort poured into something that would one day casually walk away from you, flying halfway across the world. Even if you got it right – especially if you got it right – motherhood was based on diminishing returns.

'She raised two boys ...' said Sylvia. 'She did her best.' On the tip of her tongue, as bitter as an unswallowed aspirin, hovered the words, 'She stayed'.

'I know you think I was totally selfish and irresponsible,' said Barbara, as if she knew what Sylvia was thinking. 'But you don't fully understand ... I don't want you to get into a situation where you feel as trapped as I did, because then the whole thing falls apart.'

Sylvia shrugged. This was the fear that she carried around with herself.

'You know, my mother ...'

'What about her?' said Sylvia. She had never met her maternal grandmother, but Barbara often invoked Dora nonetheless, as a warning. Distrust between mother and daughter seemed to have been passed down the generations in their family, in lieu of cosy togetherness.

'At school she was brilliant at maths and science,' said Barbara. 'Top of the class for all that kind of stuff. But in those days ...' She grimaced. 'When I was growing up she used to do the accounts for the shop. It was something, to keep her brain active, but she could have been so much more.'

'I can't talk to you about this ...' said Sylvia. 'I'm going to have to take Jude upstairs for his nap.' She picked Jude roughly out of his highchair, not bothering to wipe the green meniscus around his mouth, and bundled him out of the room.

27

Sylvia's Manual

I'm getting sick of this place. We are all in a holding pattern here, circling. Of course, nobody in St Luke's says this. There is much emphasis on life. On freshly cut flowers, companionship, music. Moments thrown into sharp relief by shadow.

Stavroula, the Greek woman in the room next door, went yesterday. Ping. Time's up. Like the buzzer on a microwave.

She was younger than me, secondary breast cancer too. She used to be a pole dancer, she said. You could just about see the remnants of her beauty, amid the ruins. She had lived in London since she was eighteen and had never gone home but used to talk about the deserted beaches in Halkidiki. The monastery on the hill. The burning sun. Olive oil as green as grass.

She didn't have family come to visit her. Something had gone wrong there. No children either. So, she died alone. And this morning, when I was slowly processing to the lounge for coffee, I saw her bed was empty and freshly made.

Still incomprehensible – the before and after. Where do all those memories go? She used to talk about the clients she'd had, long ago, when she was desirable. How they would stare at her on the stage, hungrily, then try to touch her skin. She despised them a little, clearly, but loved them too. In a sense, they were the sons she never had.

Everybody is so kind here, all the time, it's starting to grate on my nerves. I need something to do. I'm sick of thinking things over. I never was one for self-reflection, but now it's been foisted upon me, like homework, at the end of a life.

Even this manual is becoming a chore. I'm so tired now that I'm struggling to order my thoughts. I'm starting to sink. I keep remembering things I should tell you but forgetting to write them down. Then they pop up again, taunting me, when I'm trying to rest. There's one thing that I can't forget though, which now I've started writing this, I've realised that I'm heading towards.

The nit lotion that works is Headstrong. Nothing else will kill those bastard twenty-first-century head lice, inured as they are to chemicals. Megan will submit and let you comb it through. Jude will wriggle and roar. You'll have to quell him with television and chocolate. Bribing Jude is a full-time job. Working out the most attractive treats and the best way to deploy them, like cluster bombs, across the days and years. In my experience, nothing motivates the boy better than Haribo sour snakes. My little gift to you, that one. Keep a packet in the top cupboard and only use in emergencies.

The problem is that it can start to feel like the emergencies are happening every day.

Funny to think, really, how far my parenting diverged from what I thought it would be like. Once I got used to the idea of having a child, I was so convinced I knew the right way to be a perfect mother. Every one of Barbara's faults was seared onto my brain. I pitied her, thought she was so pathetic in how she failed us. I simply never conceived that she was a person too.

I started out with wooden toys and organic vegetables, but it turns out this is how I end, encouraging you to motivate our wild, darling boy with jelly sweets.

But parenting is all about survival, it turns out. There are moments of euphoria, but there is also so much else. For me anyway, for us. Perhaps if both our children had been as docile as Megan, it wouldn't have been like that. And that's also what you realise. You're only as good a parent as your child, your little blank slate, will let you be.

Now that I'm here, I find my old job all the more incredible. We had so much power. We created life. It got claustrophobic in that lab, wearing our hair nets and masks, jostled together. But I never lost sight of the amazing thing that we were doing. Selecting the strongest sperm, the choicest eggs, to try and make the very best humans that we could.

Everything was sterile, perfect. It had to be. It was big business and we couldn't afford to make mistakes.

I wonder often if those couples that spent all their money having a baby were better parents because of it. We didn't even really try and our children fell into our laps. Did that make us complacent? If I'd had to spend desperate years waiting for motherhood, would I have been a better mother, when it came down to it? Has Tess been a better mother because Flora was harder to come by?

I wish it were as easy to beat cancer as it is to inject sperm into eggs in a petri dish. Science is so amazing, but it only takes us so far. I struggle with that. And with the idea that in ten years, or twenty, what I have might be curable. That I will have died of something antiquated, like bubonic plague, or polio. Of course, then it will be something else. All living things must have their predators, lurking in the wings.

When Megan got her first temperature, I remember the sheer panic. What if it became meningitis, or sepsis? Or any of those other things that you think will never happen to you, or those you love, until you have children of your own and suddenly mortality occurs to you?

It's been a burden, this realisation, since I became a mother. It sat on my chest, like a sleeping cat I was terrified of disturbing. And now it has finally climbed off me, and is stretching its spine in the sun, I can see how beautiful it was all that time and miss the warmth it created.

I'm now going to spend the rest of the day, until you come to see me, thinking of you. I wish I could talk about these things face to face, but I'm so tired and I've hurt you enough already, with all this, by dying.

I'm getting so familiar with the wall beside my bed. The fine fissures in it, spreading out like the branches of a tree. After I write this, I'm spent and I lie supine, staring at those cracks, wondering what it's all about.

I've been thinking a lot about the kind of life I want you and the children to have when I'm gone. One thing I keep coming back to is Tess. I want them to be close to their aunt. To bridge the distance that sprang up between me and her as we got older. We were different, yes. Chalk and cheese internally. But she looks like me, sounds like me, moves like I did. A living memorial.

When they're adults and they want to know how I would have

aged, they'll only need to look at her. Oh, she's more beautiful than I ever was, I know. But still we were cut from the same cloth.

And she remembers things that nobody else knows about me. About how we used to stay in the sea until our lips turned blue with cold. How we 'camped' on the front lawn in summer under those endless stars. And later, how we hoodwinked William into letting us go into town to meet boys and drink cider at the bus station.

Before you, she was the chronicler of my existence. She's the only one who knows exactly what our childhood was like. The minutes and hours that made us who we are. The day that Barbara told us, with a brief phone call, that she wasn't ever coming back, Tess found me trashing my bedroom, ripping my books off the shelves and pulling the duvet off the bed. She didn't say anything but took me by the hand and led me out of the house. She was wearing a rucksack on her back and she pulled me to our favourite spot on the headland, where the bouncy tufts of thrift formed al fresco furniture. Inside her bag, she had all our old dolls, the ones I had already started to shun by then, and she lined them up in a row. Cloth princesses.

She laid out the toy tea set and absorbed me in a long game. Until I forgot about Barbara.

It was almost dusk when William found us, frantic with worry. 'I thought I'd lost you,' he shouted at us, he who so rarely raised his voice. 'I thought you'd gone too.'

28

Then

Sylvia assumed that she couldn't make friends with other mothers. That she was somehow deficient, missing the necessary willingness to agonise about secondary school entrance exams while Megan was still in reception, or to subtly insinuate how useless her husband was. The truth was, Paul was her best friend.

Her daughter was one of the most popular girls in her class, but none of the other parents became more than acquaintances. Sure, she would sometimes go for coffee or drinks. But she always felt like her younger self, unable to discern precisely what the terms of engagement were. At a karaoke night she overdressed and drank far too much, hogging the microphone all night. The next morning she lay in bed groaning, remembering the tight smile on Abigail Blackwood's face.

But everything changed when Jude started pre-school. He didn't much like sitting on the carpet for circle time, her son, or sharing poster paints at the easel. But, from the first week, he made firm friends with another little boy called Ryan.

'Is this your son?' said Sylvia, to the woman standing near Ryan at pick-up time one afternoon. It was so busy that Sylvia had edged in sideways, shielding her growing bump from the crush of other parents, exclaiming and holding their children's artwork aloft.

'Yes,' said Nush, smiling a wonderfully warm, slow smile. 'You must be Jude's mum. Ryan talks about him all the time.'

'Mummy, I am not wearing my coat,' Jude interjected, glaring at Nush. Ryan was already in his, zipped up to his chin.

'But it's so nippy out there,' said Sylvia, offering Jude his jacket. She hated these moments, the sudden urgent need to prove to other adults that she was in control when she was fairly sure she wasn't. 'Come on, Jude, not now.'

'Ah, I wouldn't worry about it,' said Nush, putting her hand on Sylvia's forearm. 'If he's really cold, he'll wear it.'

Sylvia looked at her gratefully. She was used to other parents staying silent at times like that, pretending they weren't watching.

From that first meeting Nush always made her feel comfortable, good enough. Within weeks, they had a regular coffee date on a Wednesday lunchtime when pre-school finished early, Nush's shift-schedule allowing. The progress of their own friendship mirrored that of their sons, tentative to start with but then rushing forwards with unbuttoned relief. For Sylvia, who had felt progressively lonelier after it became clear her relationship with Tess would never be the same, it was a consolation. Nush, in turn, liked this nervy, red-headed woman and her energetic son. So many of the other parents were closed books. It was a desirable school, the kind that people lied to get into, renting nearby. She was lucky to live in the catchment, she knew. It was good for Ryan, for his future, but she hadn't necessarily expected to make any real friends.

There was something touchingly vulnerable about Sylvia. Her face still open. Despite her house, her husband, the two children and her hugely pregnant stomach, there was still a whiff of girlhood about her, of possibility.

*　*　*

Sylvia exhaled in relief as she sat down. 'God, it feels good to take the weight off.'

'How are you feeling?' asked Nush, glancing at Sylvia's bump. It was so big, it looked like a prosthesis tacked on to help her play a part.

'Pretty good,' said Sylvia, turning her face to Nush. 'I mean, keeping up with Jude isn't easy, at the best of times, but the pregnancy has been fine.'

'Are you going into Homerton?' said Nush, thinking of the hospital that her ambulance drove into. The bewildering extent of human need that she encountered on each shift. She loved her work, but it drained her. The fragility of human life writ large in every sixty-five-year-old with emphysema struggling to breathe, every five-year-old with a head injury, every surprised middle-aged woman having a coronary.

'No. Having a home birth!' said Sylvia. 'I've been working up to it and third time round, I think I'm ready.' Nush smiled, but Sylvia could tell she didn't approve. That was the thing she liked about Nush, her feelings were obvious, not buried under layers of courteous passive-aggression. And yet, still, she felt an urgent need to convince her of the merits of her decision.

'They just tend to medicalise things in hospital,' said Sylvia, defensive. 'I've done so much reading about it and you're much more likely to end up with intervention. Birth is a natural process.'

Nush was silent, glancing outside at Jude and Ryan, jumping in unison on the trampoline and laughing.

'It feels a bit like she's doing a somersault in there. Here, feel ...' Sylvia reached out and took Nush's hand, placing it on her stomach.

'Wow, gosh ... she's a wriggler!' said Nush, relieved at the change of subject. She had at least one homebirth mother a month in the ambulance with complications.

'She certainly is,' said Sylvia. 'I hope she's not going to be quite as active as Jude, though ... But apparently Paul was the same as a boy and he's fine now, so ...'

'Jude's great,' said Nush, who could see the concern that Sylvia had for her son. She read it in the way that she looked at him, the anxious frown and fiercely whispered, 'No, Jude. Not now.' But although Jude was loud and constantly on the go, he had a kind heart, it was clear to see.

'Do you see much of Ryan's father?' said Sylvia. Nush was a single mother, not an unusual thing any more, but something that marked her out as different at their particular school. But when the women met, they never discussed Ryan's father. Nush, so open about most things, had always been closed on the subject.

'Well, actually ...' Nush cleared her throat and laughed. 'I don't really talk about it, but I had Ryan on my own. Used a sperm donor.'

'That's brilliant,' said Sylvia, clumsily trying to transmit nonchalant acceptance through over-enthusiasm.

'It's not something I broadcast at school,' said Nush. 'I've always figured it's on a need-to-know basis. After I left Sandeep, I thought I had thrown my chance of having children away. But then I got to forty and decided to take matters into my own hands.'

Sylvia glanced down at her stomach. What would it be like, she wondered, to have a baby with somebody you had never met? To go into labour, without somebody by your side holding the hospital bag. Someone you could berate but would still remain devoted. She couldn't imagine it and felt sorry then for Nush, as well as awed by her bravery. She knew what Barbara meant now, when she talked about motherhood being a lottery – you just never knew – and to buy that ticket on your own seemed incredibly courageous.

'All I know is that he's Italian. From the Amalfi Coast. An engineer who likes listening to Jay-Z,' said Nush.

'Jay-Z?' said Sylvia, laughing. The detail struck her as so incongruous.

'Ryan can contact him when he's eighteen,' said Nush, looking out the window instinctively towards her son. He was neatly constructed, fine-boned and with a shock of shiny, blue-black hair, his skin the colour of iced coffee. Contrasted with Jude's milky blondness, they looked like catalogue models for an expensive children's clothing company.

'Does Ryan know?'

'Of course! I've been reading him books about it since he was born,' said Nush. 'There's lots of support out there. My family don't approve.' She jutted her chin out slightly. 'They've met Ryan a few times, but they struggle to accept the situation. We don't see them that regularly now.'

'Families are tricky things,' said Sylvia, resting her hand on her stomach and thinking of Tess, whose congratulations on the third pregnancy had been politely enthusiastic, but who still felt so far away. Sylvia had hoped that the arrival of Tess's own daughter, Flora, would usher in renewed closeness, as they bonded over motherhood. But if anything, the gap seemed only to widen, Tess's fervent attachment parenting serving to further underline their differences in approach.

29

Now

'We're only going for the weekend, so if you don't mind having Ted, that would be amazing,' said Paul. 'He's got so used to you now.' He laughed nervously. He wasn't sure if he was exploiting Natalia. She seemed to do an awful lot of work for the money he paid her, but he was starting to find it hard to imagine how he'd cope without her quiet ministrations.

'Where are you going to scatter the ashes?' said Natalia.

'Where Sylvia's from,' said Paul. 'By the sea where she grew up.'

'I see,' said Natalia, coolly, and he couldn't tell if she approved. Perhaps where she came from, they wouldn't do such a thing.

He still hadn't worked out how old she was. Initially he had thought much younger than he and Sylvia, but as the weeks had gone on, he had noticed the fine furrows around her eyes, one or two greys pulled back into her ponytail. She semaphored youth, but he was starting to suspect she was not much younger than him.

'Say goodbye from me,' said Natalia.

'I will.'

*　*　*

The journey to William's house took eight endless hours. They left at 6 a.m., in a vain attempt to beat the traffic, Sylvia's ashes wedged into the boot alongside their bags and Jude's football. Barbara installed in the passenger seat, Jude and Megan in the back.

Paul couldn't help but remember all the other times they had made that journey, Sylvia asking him a stream of random questions as he tried to concentrate on the road, resting her feet on the glove compartment. The snacks she passed into the back for the children, the endless music changes, the ironic whoop she always gave as they crossed the boundary into Cornwall. This journey was much quieter; even Jude didn't bother querying when they were going to get there.

As they passed Bristol, heading further west, it started to rain, great splodges on the windscreen. Paul felt the pathetic fallacy keenly. He was carrying out Sylvia's last wishes, just as instructed, but he felt foreboding. The anger he had felt at the manual's revelation had thus far been overlaid by grief, by necessity. He missed her so much, he would have forgiven anything. But heading to Cornwall, he felt it sputtering into life. How dare she?

'Look at this weather,' said Barbara, frowning. 'At least

Tess is going to have set up the house for us. Can't believe I'm finally going to see it after all these years.'

Barbara never did get down to see William when he was ill, something had always held her back. Paul knew it angered Sylvia, but after Rosa, his wife's own efforts to see her father, to support Tess in advocating for him, had dwindled. She managed once a month and would return home sozzled and subdued from drinking canned cocktails on the train. 'That place is hell on earth,' was all she would say of the specialist dementia home. 'Shoot me before I *ever* have to go somewhere like that.'

Paul had last been to the cliff house shortly before William was moved, finally rendered completely incapable by a cloudburst in his brain. He remembered the house then as a testament to the old man's decline, with piles of paper and rubbish on every surface and yellowing sheets on the bed.

So it was a surprise to see it in its incarnation as a holiday let, neutrally decorated, with kitchen cupboards stocked with instant coffee and salt, as well as bossy little signs pinned up around the place exhorting guests not to smoke or put anything other than loo roll down the toilet.

'How was the journey?' said Tess, who had let them in and was busying around turning on switches. Flora, a dreamy, biddable child, shadowed her, clutching a corner of her mother's skirt. Barbara was standing on the front lawn, looking out to sea, heels sinking into grass, overcome, while Jude and Megan, uncooped, buzzed around the garden.

'Nightmarish,' said Paul, curtly. His anger was seeping out towards Tess too, now. She had known and never told him.

They had all known and he had been the unsuspecting idiot.

'What time tomorrow are you thinking of, to scatter the ashes?' said Tess, her poker face not revealing if she had registered the unusual tone in Paul's voice. Paul, always so equable.

'She wanted sunset,' said Paul. What Sylvia wanted, she usually got.

'Bring the kids down to Brean in the morning for a bit then,' said Tess. 'They can play in Flora's treehouse.'

'All right,' said Paul.

After Tess left, he wandered out to find the others. He came across them, sitting on William's bench, looking out at the sea. Barbara was talking to the children, recalling their grandfather, and Paul stood and watched them for a while, before they noticed. He moved closer. On the back of the bench was the inscription Sylvia and Tess had chosen for their father.

> *We are such stuff,*
> *As dreams are made on, and our little life*
> *Is rounded with a sleep.*

* * *

William's cliff was industrious, for fishermen and farmers, set by the seasons. A place for cutting cauliflowers under a slate sky. In contrast, Brean Valley, where Tess had lived since leaving school, had been, for decades, a known hippy enclave. A hamlet of flimsy chalets and tents occupied by a motley intergenerational tribe, united in their alternative views. Wind chimes tinkled in the breeze and rumours swirled about the LSD factory somewhere out the back. The parties were infamous. Revellers daubed in UV paint. Sound systems hauled into the trees, pulsing music under fierce stars.

Paul had been to one, shortly after he first met Tess and Danny. Cornwall had surprised and thrilled him. It was so different from where he came from, the landscape so much more cluttered and Lilliputian, the sea so freezing it stung his skin when he tried to swim. But the state William was in shocked him, as it did Sylvia.

'He's got so much ... older,' she had whispered, when her father, who had greeted Paul as if he had already met him, presented them with a scant lunch of hard-boiled eggs, without accompaniment, blasted until they were like rubber balls. 'My dad was never like this.'

Despite the sadness, the nagging realisation of William's new vulnerability, they still went to the party in the valley. Hope and desire rising ruthlessly in the face of decay. He remembered dancing until dawn, before sneaking back to the chalet with Sylvia to spoon, still wide-eyed, on Tess's sofa.

Now, so many years later, he made his way down the ribbon of footpath to the valley, bracken dying back on either side, Jude and Megan following him. Barbara had stayed in the house, her laptop ajar and a glint in her eye. She was probably filing a piece about the whole experience, Paul thought, bitterly. Barbara clung to the idea that everything was copy.

As he emerged from the footpath into the base of the valley, he saw that Brean was largely unchanged. A few more tents, perhaps, extra vehicles rusting, overgrown with ivy, but nothing more. After the cliff it was notably windless, the placid air sweet as ice cream. He made his way to where he remembered Tess and Danny's chalet to be and, sure enough, stuck into the earth outside the verandah, so it pointed towards the sky, was a turquoise surfboard with a neon barracuda on it.

'That's the one that I became a world champion on,' Danny had told him once. 'I keep her there lest we ever forget.'

Looking at it now, protruding upwards like a thumb, Paul felt sick. In London, Sylvia's secret could be ignored, squashed down, if not dismissed. But here, it was all around him, insinuating itself like smoke from a nearby bonfire.

30

Sylvia's Manual

I think it's time I told you something important. Once I thought it was a secret I'd take to my grave but since I've started writing this, chronicling our lives, I've realised how wrong that would be. You'll only truly understand why Tess and I grew apart if you know. And for the children to have their auntie, you need to do that.

Tess will never tell you herself. She might have cut me out of her life in the last few years, but she is still too fiercely loyal to me – and Danny – to ever do that.

It wasn't Tess's fault, you see. It was mine. I told you I wasn't a good person. I have known that about myself, all my life. My fundamental unworthiness has dogged me. I think I was born that way. Motherhood taught me that nature, not nurture, is the important bit and I think I simply came out dissatisfied, selfish, competitive about all the wrong things.

And there was no one I competed with more fiercely than my sister. She never reciprocated, but I always wanted everything she had, starting with our wooden alphabet bricks and dolls, before moving on to more important things.

Danny was always Tess's and never mine. Childhood sweethearts. He was in my year but would never have looked at me. Tess was the catch. She was the Helen of Troy of our wind-blown comprehensive, incandescence shining through mild acne.

They got together on the school bus and announced they were 'going out'. It was innocent, at first. They held hands at break time and spoke on the phone, sometimes snogged at the bottom of the playing field. She wore his army jacket. William didn't know what to make of it. She was only fourteen. He grumbled about it a bit, but then moved his attention back towards the sea, like he always did. But Barbara was thrilled when she heard.

'You're like me,' she said to Tess. 'The boys are going to love you, darling. A red-blooded woman.'

I was predictably jealous. Overshadowed, as usual, by my younger sister. At my school, at that age, being academic gave you no status at all. It was about the snogging, the fingering, how big your boobs were. Tess won on all counts. And she was so calm about the relationship. Those were the days of Danny's pomp. He was one of the most desired boys in the school, already had two surf brands sponsoring him for competitions, but she acted as if it were no big deal.

But my treachery wasn't only down to that. With my current vantage point, I can see that I was angry with the way that Tess forgave our parents. She didn't rail against Barbara's selfishness, or the fact that William could never afford to buy us new clothes. She somehow managed to get the best out of both of them, without even seeming to try. I tried so hard but never could.

197

So, there was that, but also – listen to me make excuses – her happiness in her own skin. Since I could remember, I had itched to be someone else, somewhere else. Adolescence had only heightened my dissatisfaction with myself. It must have been written all over my face. But she was content with what she had. Despite the fact she struggled with schoolwork and bumped along in the bottom sets at school, she had an ease in herself that people responded to.

So, I borrowed him sometimes. Danny, that is. Like a top or a lipstick. With the casual cruelty of an older sister. I justified it to myself in all sorts of ways. I still am, as you can see.

It wasn't hard, to make him want me. A teenage boy. Not hard at all. In that sense, he was the vulnerable one, in thrall to his testosterone.

'You know you could be twins,' he said to me the first time. We were in the woods at the back of Brean Valley, just above where they live now. I feel sick writing this, but I don't know if he and Tess had even slept together at that point yet. I was on the ground among the ivy. Mud on my legs, leaf shrapnel in my hair. 'Except you're so different.'

'Different how?' I asked, self-harming.

'She's fitter,' he said. 'But you want it more.'

His words should have pulled me up short, made me stop before I started. But the truth was, that in confirming my sense of myself, his careless comment made me feel seen. Understood. It provided a warped self-justification, not enough to stop the searing guilt I felt as I climbed the footpath home afterwards. The sense that things could never be the same again. It should never have hap-pened and once it had, it should have stopped straight away, but somehow the thing with Danny grew legs. Like a scary sex-spider that terrified me. It happened again. Then regularly before I went to London for university. Each occasion branded onto my memory. So many things about that summer stick in my mind. Until I met you, it defined me. Even here, if I shut my eyes, it comes rushing back. Youth. The cuff of friendship bracelets on my arm, the endless sun, which brought out all my freckles, long days on the beach, salty skin, the sickening thrill of my own treachery.

Tess never had a clue. I've always had a knack for keeping secrets and it turned out that Danny did too. Or maybe he was just too stoned to give the game away.

After I left home, I did my best to kill the affair. To starve it of oxygen. But I think I revelled in the sense of power it gave me. An occasional drunken fumble if I was visiting William, when Tess went to bed early. The time that Danny came to London without her and ended up outside my halls of residence. He had bought me a present, he said, before presenting me with a tiny box. It contained that opal ring I mentioned. A black stone, shot through with iridescence, like a thwarted rainbow. Perfectly symbolic. I told him I could never wear it, but he said it didn't matter, that I could look at it sometimes and think of him. I'd love to say I never did.

I got together with Tom not long after that. A fellow student with a commitment to blurry nights, our relationship should have ended what I had with Danny for good. But it didn't. I still craved that sense of power that only sleeping with my sister's boyfriend gave me.

But once you and I got together I didn't need Danny any more. I never even thought of it. I didn't need to prove that I was the more desirable sister, the winner, because I had you. You made me feel good and worthy of something better, for the first time.

199

Danny didn't want it to end. He told me in a thousand glances that it wasn't over. But I was so sure, once I met you. I was going to be a different person. You gave me that option and I was ready to take it. My bad habits were over, those secrets that dogged me.

But he kept trying, kept pushing. Wouldn't let it drop. Even after he and Tess decided they wanted a baby. Even after I had Megan.

Then when Jude arrived, he and Tess came to visit us. To see the new baby. I was flush with happiness at my son and thought – hoped – it was all water under the bridge. I was a mother-of-two, a grown woman and I couldn't have cared less about Daniel Clemens.

I don't know what on earth he was thinking. I was still wobbly and undefined in renewed motherhood, hardly hot to trot. My stitches still burning, my nipples shielded in plastic, seeping milk.

Yet still, he thought he could resume things, somehow. He came up behind me in the kitchen when I was making tea, after you'd gone to work and Tess was in the shower. Kissed the curve of my neck as if he owned me. Such an idiot. I had been up every hour throughout the night and was so exhausted that I could hardly see straight.

I lost my temper with him, told him to leave me alone. I was so worked up, you know how I can get, that I didn't realise Tess had come outside the kitchen door, that she heard every word. If I'd just been a bit quieter, perhaps I could have kept my dirty secret. I'll never forget the look on her face. The confusion. Then she screamed at me for five minutes, in a way I'd never seen her scream, before sitting down sobbing quietly. She made me tell her everything. When it first happened, how long it lasted. If anyone else knew. I obliged with the details – I felt as though I owed her honesty. But Danny was silent throughout, staring out of the window. After what felt like hours Tess finally said she had heard enough. She got her things together, looked at Danny, asked him if he was coming too. She seems calm, Tess, mild even, but she's tough. Then they walked out of the door.

Still, I don't know for sure that she would have stayed with Danny, after that, if it wasn't for Flora. She must have been pregnant on that trip, but I had no idea and I don't think Danny did either.

There's the fact Tess loves Danny, too. She always has. And despite what I'm telling you, he's not all bad, Danny. Led by his desires certainly, but not malicious. A pleasure merchant who wants everyone to have a good time. When it came to William, he showed his best side. It was Danny who helped her wash him, before they got a carer. It was Danny who used to take William's boat out when he was no longer able, bringing in sheaves of sparkly, fresh mackerel, to make our father smile. And it was Danny – not me – who was in the ambulance when William was finally transferred into the home.

In contrast, I failed our father when it counted most. Sure, I went to see him occasionally, but my centre of gravity remained with you and the children in the city. Then, after Rosa, I lost the stomach for any more misery. In some ways, I said goodbye to him before he had actually gone.

So now you know. My albatross. I'm sorry I couldn't tell you in person. I could never find the words and then I got too weak, too tired. I don't want our final days together to be marred by this thing. It was never something that mattered to us, I didn't want to give it that significance when we had so little time left.

But I want Megan and Jude to have a relationship with Tess and

I see now that that will never happen unless you understand what happened between us. There was a reason for her distance – it wasn't just casual cruelty. As for Danny, he's weak and stupid, like a pet cat that just seeks enjoyment, thoughtlessly, where it can, belly exposed in a square of sunshine.

Please forgive me for keeping it quiet for all those years. I so nearly told you when we first got together, that afternoon when we supposedly confessed our secrets. Wiped our slates clean. When you said you'd once been involved with your best friend's girlfriend, I could hardly believe it. For a minute, I thought we weren't so different after all. But then you admitted how quickly you'd been forgiven, how casual it was. I realised we weren't the same at all. What I did was so much worse because Danny meant everything to Tess. And as time went on and you got to know them both, it got even harder to tell you. I worried you'd see me differently. A person capable of betraying the people she loved the most. I still worry about that. All the best things in my life came from you.

31

Then

'I think it's time we got you home ...' Nush put her hand on Sylvia's arm.

'No ... One more drink.' Sylvia's eyes sparkled and two spots of high colour sat on each cheek. A half-cut Aunt Sally.

'Getting pissed ... it's not such a good idea,' said Nush. She herself had nursed a single drink, while Sylvia had drunk three large glasses of wine. Oaky, pub Chardonnay as yellow as a urine sample.

'Why not?' said Sylvia. 'Nothing else works.' The pain sat in her chest, like a stone. Each day she had to get up, to get the children to school, clear up the breakfast things, keep the show on the road. But thoughts of Rosa's tiny hands were just out of sight, behind each thought. Getting so drunk she could hardly see, concealed them for a bit, until she woke at 3 a.m. and all she could see were tiny digits, reaching out to her.

'What about Paul?' said Nush. 'He needs you tomorrow. The kids do. You can't do this.'

'You don't get to decide,' said Sylvia, pulling back her arm. She was thin again now, like she used to be. All clavicles and ribs, clothes hanging off her. But she wasn't young any more and when she caught a glimpse of herself in the mirror behind the bar, she could see incipient jowls despite the soft lighting, agony etched on her features. She was becoming one of those women she had always sworn she wasn't going to be, worn down by life and circumstance.

'Let's go and get something to eat, at least,' said Nush. 'I've got to be back by ten for the babysitter.'

'Paul's probably asleep,' said Sylvia. She giggled. 'That's all he does. Work and sleep. Sleep and work.'

'He is suffering, too,' said Nush, quietly. 'And the children. But you ... falling apart. This is only going to make things worse for everyone.'

Sylvia turned to her friend then, jabbing her finger in the air. 'This isn't me falling apart,' she said. 'This is who I really am. This is who I was before I met Paul. Before we got married. I'm just returning to how I used to be ...'

'This isn't who you are,' Nush muttered. 'I don't recognise this person.'

'You don't really know me at all,' said Sylvia.

'That's not true,' said Nush. 'Don't say that.'

Sylvia motioned to the bartender, a younger man who watched her cautiously, as though she were a grenade that might explode at any moment.

'Another ... what was it ... Chardonnay, please?'

He nodded, mutely, fetched another large wine glass.

'It's rank but it does the job,' Sylvia muttered, under her

breath. The cheaper the alcohol, the more like self-abuse it felt.

The pub was their local. A place where you could take the children for fish and chips at tea-time, watch sport on huge screens, or drink yourself into oblivion. A hall for all comers.

'I was stupid to think I could ever really be happy,' said Sylvia then, almost to herself. 'I thought I could handle it. Life. But I couldn't. I can't.'

'Life is tough,' said Nush. She had sat down again, pulled her phone out and was texting her babysitter. 'For everyone, Sylv. I'm so sorry about what happened but you can't just … give up.'

'She was perfect,' said Sylvia. Tears had clustered now at the corners of her eyes. It felt like she never stopped crying, these days. All day, every day, they dribbled out ceaselessly. The corners of her eyes were red raw and she had taken to wearing sunglasses, almost continually. 'She was as perfect as I knew she would be. The perfect baby.'

Nush looked stricken.

'It was my fault. I just keep replaying it. If I'd had her in hospital. If I'd let them listen to the heartbeat more regularly … It was my own stupid fault. I'm like a murderer. I murdered my own baby.'

'That's not true,' said Nush. 'These things happen sometimes.'

'Don't pretend,' said Sylvia. 'You thought it was a terrible idea to have a home birth. I should have listened to you.'

'You weren't to know,' said Nush. 'There was no way of knowing.' She, too, had replayed her conversation with Sylvia about the birth. That one they'd had when she had tried so hard not to reveal her concern about the idea.

'Pshhttt.' Sylvia pushed Nush away and reached in her wallet for money. 'Here.' She gave it to the bartender and took a large sip of wine.

'After this, I'm taking you home,' said Nush, quietly.

'I'm not going home,' said Sylvia. 'I don't belong there. The children would be better off without me. I'm only going to let them down, to ruin their lives. I thought I could be good enough for them, but it turns out that I can't. It's impossible ... I'm guilty. They would be better off with just Paul ...'

Nush shook her head.

'He's such a good person, Nush. So good. He just loves me and loves the children. There is nothing complicated. It's all so easy for him. He just gets on with it and does the right thing without thinking about it ... All the time.'

'You're a good person too,' said Nush. 'One of the best. You have got to stop blaming yourself for what happened. You're torturing yourself and you're only going to tear up what you've got. It's awful, what happened was awful. But it's self-indulgent if you let it ruin everything else. Also, Paul is not a saint. It's not fair on him to constantly pretend that he is.'

Sylvia put her head in her hands.

'You have to go home and you have to be there tomorrow, for Jude and Megan. And Paul.'

'I just ... can't. I don't know if I can do it ...' Sylvia stood. 'I'm going out for a cigarette. She started to walk to the door, weaving her away across the bar, and stepped out into the night, lighting up in a smooth motion and inhaling. Since Rosa she smoked all the time, even in the house in front of the children. At first they had stared at her, appalled, but they had swiftly grown used to it.

'Sylvia?' It was Natalia, hurrying along the road, her thin shoulders bolstered by a puffa jacket. 'I was just coming back from work.'

'Oh,' said Sylvia. Something about this woman always made her feel guilty. She was so sober, so industrious, so tidy, in her cheap clothes.

'I'm sorry, Sylvia,' said Natalia. 'When I heard about the baby, I couldn't believe it. If there's anything we can do, anything at all. You simply have to let me know.'

'Thanks,' said Sylvia. She was starting to feel sick. And thoughts of fairy limbs, tiny fingernails and soft lips like a tiny, organic socket were starting to intrude again. Rosa had existed, with all her genetic information just there, ready to unfurl. She was never going to discover what kind of person her youngest daughter would have been. A girly girl who wanted to dress like a princess, or a tomboy, who loved climbing trees. But it was all there already, waiting.

'We are supposed to plant a tree for her tomorrow,' she blurted out. 'A holly tree, at the edge of the crematorium garden.'

'That's beautiful,' said Natalia.

'It was my fault,' said Sylvia, conversationally. 'So, I don't know if I can go. To the planting, that is. I don't know if I can bear it.'

'Your children will need you,' said Natalia, a whisper of reprove in her voice. 'And Paul.'

'Yes, thanks,' said Sylvia, sarcastically. She didn't want to be judged by this watchful woman.

'Sylvia . . .' Natalia paused, stepping forwards. 'I just wanted to say you aren't alone. I also—'

'I can't just now, Natalia,' said Sylvia, raising her hand and showing Natalia the flat of her palm. 'Sorry, but I just can't hear whatever it is you're about to say.'

Natalia flinched and stood back. 'Bye then,' she said. 'Good luck for tomorrow.' And she hurried off into the night, Sylvia watching her retreating form.

'Who was that you were talking to?' said Nush, once she went back inside.

'Natalia from school,' said Sylvia, winding her scarf around her neck. 'I think you're right, I'd better get home.'

But she didn't go back to the house where Paul and the children lay slumbering, preparing themselves for the next day. Instead, once she was sure Nush had walked down the street, she slipped back into the pub. To chase her wine with vodka.

32

Now

The skin on Danny's chest was the colour of a teak bench, his muscles sinewy from surfing. He was cutting wood, raising the axe above his head and bringing it down with a thump. Paul stood, at the edge of the clearing, watching. The other man's controlled, easy violence made Paul's blood thrum.

Jude and Megan had disappeared with Flora, to see her treehouse, which was built in a larger ash tree, somewhere among the saplings, a grown-up in a crowd of teenagers. Dutch elm disease had ravaged the valley's elm stock in the eighties, the newly planted sycamore only just finding their feet. Tess was somewhere inside, making tea, doubtless that straw-coloured herbal concoction she favoured.

'So, are you coming later?' said Paul, while Danny took a break, wiping sweat off his forehead with the T-shirt he had discarded on a nearby tree stump. It was a cloudy morning and Paul had found the stripping off unnecessary. But Danny was proud of his physique, he knew. Even now, after all these years.

'Not sure, mate. Kind of felt like I said my goodbyes at the funeral. Think I might just leave it for immediate family.' Danny threw his T-shirt back down and looked Paul in the eyes. 'If that's all right with you?' Something about the casual gesture, combined with Danny's peacocking, infuriated Paul. The nub of anger in his chest, which he had been trying to ignore for so long, since he read Sylvia's confession, swelled.

'What do you care about what's all right with me?' he said, standing and walking over to where Danny stood. 'What the fuck do you care?'

'I don't know what you mean.' said Danny. But the look in his eyes said that he did, that he knew exactly what Paul was talking about. For a dizzying moment, Paul itched to pick up the axe on the ground, to drive it into Danny's bare chest. Alarmed, his ears ringing, he turned on his heel and walked back to the chalet.

'Everything all right?' Tess was standing at the stove, stirring something with her bony white arms. Her dreads were pulled back into a thick ponytail with something that looked like twine.

'Not really,' said Paul, leaning against the flimsy wall. He wanted to get out, to do the job he had come to Cornwall to do and go, never returning. He looked outwards to the chalet's verandah, where wind chimes tinkled incessantly in the breeze.

'What is it?' Tess had moved closer now, was standing in front of him. So like Sylvia and so not. Those distinctive irises, one brown and one blue. Heterochromia. Sylvia had always said how stunning it was, but Paul found it creepy. Sylvia's had been the clear blue of an August afternoon.

'I know about Sylvia and Danny,' said Paul. 'She wrote me this manual for looking after the children after she was gone and, towards the end of it, she admitted that they'd had something. For a long time.'

'Oh.' Tess took a step backwards but continued to look at him.

'I just don't understand it,' said Paul, scratching his forehead. It felt as if something was beetling inside his brain.

'She never betrayed you ... Sylvia. It was all before she met you,' said Tess. 'I know that for sure.'

'I know. But still ... How could she keep it hidden for so long? We used to all hang out together. She treated me like a fool. And how could she and Danny have done it to you?'

'I don't know.' Tess inhaled sharply. She looked as if she might cry. 'She could be extremely selfish. You know that as well as I do. And as for Danny, well ...'

'How could you ever forgive them?' said Paul, thinking of Danny and his easy grace. But just as Tess was about to answer, the children ran in. Megan and Flora and Jude, in a pink-cheeked, breathless gang, talking about the treehouse and the game they had been playing, demanding biscuits and water. Flora reached for her mother and Tess reached down and swung her daughter up, then held her close, looking over her head at Paul. He read the message in her eyes. This is how. This is why.

They gathered on Hella Point at 6 p.m. Sylvia's little family. The promontory above the cove, covered in a patchwork of gorse and heather. It was windy, the sea the multi-toned grey of an expensive paint chart, and Paul clasped the cardboard box to his chest. This wasn't what he imagined. At this rate there wouldn't be much scattering going on – the ashes would be whipped away as soon as he opened the lid.

Danny hadn't come. Paul knew it was for his benefit and he was glad he wouldn't have to stare at that handsome, weathered face. He had left the valley with Jude and Megan after his talk with Tess, not wanting to take things further. He wasn't looking for anyone's penitence, or to talk about it. It was over now. He just wanted to get on with the job of saying goodbye to his wife.

'Shall we begin?' said Barbara, assuming the role of adult. Paul and Tess nodded. They had agreed that they were all going to share a memory of Sylvia. 'I remember Sylvia in the bath when she was about four, asking me what happened when you die,' Barbara said. 'I told her that I didn't know, but that I imagined it might be a bit like a really good night's sleep. I hope that's what this is, darling girl.' She tottered forwards and Paul opened the lid of the box. Barbara grabbed a handful of ashes and tossed them into the westerly wind, so that they were blown out across the sea.

'My turn,' said Jude. Paul lowered the box so that it was at Jude's level.

'Um,' said Jude, looking around at the assembled faces. 'I remember Mummy telling me stories about dinosaurs,' he said, slowly. 'And I remember her being kind when I scribbled on the wall downstairs.' He flung his ash in the wrong direction, so that it blew back onto his chest, and he looked crestfallen, but Paul smiled, reassuringly, before looking at Megan. The girl's face was white, her eyes already streaming.

'I remember Mummy making paper dolls when I was little,' she said. 'She would do it with me almost every day.'

Paul remembered those chains of paper dolls, Megan meticulously colouring in their faces with different features, their interlinked arms. They had a string stuck up in the window for a while, it got so faded from the sun that it started to disintegrate.

Megan neatly tossed her ashes out over the sea. 'Goodbye, Mummy,' she said. 'I love you.'

Tess stood forward then. She was crying hard but silently. 'I remember we used to sometimes play dead when we were little,' she said. Barbara nodded in agreement. 'Sylvia could never lie still long enough. She couldn't stop moving or laughing.' She reached forwards then, for a bit of Sylvia, holding a handful of dust clawed in her hand for a moment, as if reluctant to let go. Finally, after a couple of minutes, she simply opened her palm, face up, and the wind whisked the ash away, in a hurry to reclaim the fragments of organic matter. 'I'm sorry, Sylv,' she said.

Paul cleared his throat. 'I remember,' he said, finally, 'the night that Jude was born. He was asleep on Sylvia's chest and Megan was sitting on the sofa next to us. We watched the evening news and ordered a takeaway. She was so exhausted but we were so happy. I had never felt so complete before in my life. That wasn't so long ago. I never imagined how much could change so quickly, but nobody made me as happy as she did.' He paused. 'Despite what a pain she could be sometimes.'

Everyone giggled, relieved for the change of tone. Paul opened the jaws of the box wide, so that all that was left of Sylvia was torn away, across the ocean, into the endless grey.

Later, he and Jude were the last to walk down from the headland, the day waning. The boy seemed reluctant to return to the house.

'Come on, Jude,' Paul said, reaching out his hand. 'The others will be waiting for us.'

'I'm just … just looking,' said Jude, scanning the sky. Paul realised then what his son was seeking. He scanned the sky and then pointed with relief.

'There it is. Jude – look!'

'Mummy's star,' said Jude, with satisfaction. 'It's there.'

They stared up at the night's first discernible star, a faint pulse of fire from the distant past. Paul wasn't sure how long they stood there, hand in hand, but by the time they eventually started to walk back to the cliff house, many others had come out too. Innumerable sparkles cluttering the sky like crumbs. Hard to fathom that the murky opacity they knew in London wasn't the reality. That the stars were always there, whether they could see them or not.

33

Sylvia's Manual

You all visited me in here today. I kept up a good face for the children. I played with Jude and his motley assortment of preferred toys for almost an hour. Some complicated game where Yoda and a brachiosaurus had to save a Lego knight from certain doom. Then I read to them both – *The Lion, the Witch and the Wardrobe* – while they rested on either side of me in the high bed and you sat in the chair and looked at us.

It reminded me of so many other times before, at home, in our king-size bed, where so much of our family life was carried out. Like a non-X-rated Tracey Emin sculpture, our bed saw all the action. It was where we read endless stories to the children, while they sucked down beakers of warm milk. Where we lay, spooning, drifting off to sleep, joked, or argued. It's where I sat with my laptop warming my thighs, buying clothes I couldn't really justify, sipping on white wine. Or watched endless box sets, disappearing down the rabbit hole of pretend worlds. We could never agree on the same ones.

You liked violence, Vikings throwing axes and slicing throats. I liked glossy dramas where people emoted in stylish outfits.

You looked tired, I thought. I got a glimpse of the man you'll be when I'm gone. Still good to look at, but older, scarred by life. I'm so sorry to be doing that to you. You probably wish you had never met me, the amount of stuff I've put you through. You probably wish I had never brought Ted in to see you that day.

She was called Alice, wasn't she? That girl you had just split up with, when we met. I think she hoped for a reconciliation but I plucked you away from her with the confidence of someone taking what is rightfully theirs. Sometimes I think how much easier your life would have been if you'd just stayed with her. A couple of children, a home in Australia with a swimming pool in the back yard. Barbecues on the deck, surfing after work with Ed, Miriam a more useful grandmother than Barbara could ever be.

Jude was irritating you a bit, I could tell. You barked at him when he got down from my bed and started using the chair as a climbing frame. But I didn't mind. I've told you. Jude's energy is so precious to me now, I don't know why I ever took it for granted. He radiates a life force, like the Jedi he is convinced he is. If only he could transfuse it to me. I'm getting so tired, you see. This is taking all the effort I have. I feel as if I'm reaching the end of something, drawing in like fog across water.

There was a moment, when the children went to the vending machine for drinks, that we were alone. I craved having you all to myself, but it was too much. Just too freighted with love and sadness, for both of us, and we ended up chatting like strangers, about swimming lessons and the new mini supermarket on the high street. Anything to keep it light and breezy.

I'm doing it your way, when I see you. But this, this thing I'm writing for you, is my way. All the drama and emotion spilled out, for you to hold and dip into, when you can face it. There was so much I wanted to say to your face. I wanted to talk about Danny. To tell you that it never mattered to me. That you were the only one.

I longed to reminisce about those good times, at the beginning. That day I got us locked out of my flat and it started raining. When we walked back to yours and got soaked through. I still remember the yellowish light of that afternoon, the smell of rained-on pavement. It was fun, rather than annoying, because we were together. An everyday magic.

I wanted to talk about Megan being born. And Jude. Rosa, too. The good and bad things that made up our marriage, made us who we are. But I could tell that you couldn't bear it. Fully fledged emotion makes you jumpy, even now. So, I keep it as bright as I can.

Barbara came in after you had left. On her way to dinner, naturally. Even with her eldest daughter slipping away, she still has an active social life. I've come to understand that it's her coping mechanism. We all need our ways of getting by. I think we are closer now. I'll never find her easy, but I'm getting there on forgiving her. All our lives are curate's eggs, after all. Good and bad sitting side by side. I can't imagine a life lived where that wasn't the case, so maybe she isn't as much to blame as I thought.

I wanted to convey that I understand her better now than I ever have. That dying has given me a perspective, knocked me off my moral high horse, the one I had no right to ever sit on in the first place. I told her I was sorry, for not forgiving her sooner. For constantly holding her to account. I could have sworn she welled up, for a second, but then she leaned down and pulled me close, so I couldn't see her face. The kind of embrace that we must – surely – have shared when I was Jude's age, but which I can scarcely recall. It was strange, being so physically close to this person on whom I've always blamed so much. To anyone else, just an elderly woman. To me, some kind of invulnerable being. And yet her smell so familiar – Elnett hairspray, the ink from her fountain pen, a top note of Shalimar.

'You don't have to say that,' she said, fiercely, into my hair. 'You have made me so proud.' It was a while before she could safely pull away, by which point her eyeliner had descended into the filigree of lines beneath her eyes.

Nush visited me today too. I find her visits easier than yours, I have to confess. Every time I see you and the children, I remember all I've got to lose. But with Nush, it's different. We are just in the moment. She tells me about her most recent shift at work and I find all the drama soothing. Blue lighting, schizophrenics, drunks, coronaries, strokes. Vomit, blood, piss. Life lived at the margins, or about to be. It makes the days, minutes, hours that I have left feel more credible. We are all just potentially moments away from death, after all. I'm not so very different from everyone else.

And she brings me things. Bars of chocolate. A pebble she picked up from her trip at the weekend with Ryan. A trashy magazine.

Sometimes we drink wine in plastic cups and we talk about her love life. The woman is a liability. She just cannot find a good man. She attracts spongers and weasels. But I admire her for sticking at it, her optimism. Despite all that has happened to her, despite being on her own with Ryan, she still believes in love. Is it hideously mean to say that a part of me thrills to the fact that she can't find it?

She is looking for what we have. I see that now. She is hunting for the sense of peace I found as soon as I met you. That sense of ease, of a jigsaw piece slotting into place. I suppose that some people never find it and so I'm grateful that I did. Even though I'm dying, I got to experience that and I'm forever grateful.

I talked to her today about sorting out my things. All the fun stuff. My dresses and rings and shoes. All those fripperies I loved so much, in the 'pre' days. I took pleasure in looking nice, you know that. In making heads turn. I still could, after the children. And sometimes, with them running ahead of me, I felt a sense of pride. A mother, but still desirable. After Rosa, cranking it out took more time. More eyeliner, more perfume. And when I looked in the mirror I saw a facsimile of myself, but with sadder eyes, like someone who has seen too much.

Anyway, I imagine that you might want to leave the contents of my wardrobe untouched. To remember me. But I don't want you to. I think you need to move on. And the idea of all those pieces of clothing mouldering away makes my heart ache. I want someone else to wear them, to dance in them, eat delicious food and sit in a sunny park.

So, I asked Nush today if she would help you to sort them out. She'll have a better idea of what to do with it all. What can be sold on eBay and what needs to be taken to the charity shop. She won't want to keep any items, I don't think. It's not really her style. But she will know where to take them. And I've told her the dress to keep aside for Megan, as well as any other pieces she thinks our girl will want.

I've also asked her to put this somewhere you can find it, once I've finished writing it and Khadija has printed it out. Somewhere you can't miss.

34

Then

Newly built, the surgery had already acquired a gentle under-tow of desperation. It emanated from the wipe-down lino, the blinded windows, the smell of alcohol hand gel and sweat.

On the wall was a screen to show appointments, but also a series of plaintive health messages. 'Do you know as little as 20 minutes of brisk exercise three times a week can drastically improve your health?' 'Eat 5 a day!' 'If you cough for more than three weeks, make sure you tell your GP.'

The doctor was running late. Very late. And Sylvia had an urge to just walk out of there, into the autumn sunshine. It was only an hour until she needed to collect the children from school. This was probably nothing. Why was she here, looking for trouble?

Since Rosa, she wanted to keep all contact with doctors to a minimum. She no longer had a belief in their ability to keep anyone safe.

She glanced around the room. As a sample of humanity,

it could hardly be more diverse, from the young mother in a burqa, baby on her lap, to the elderly Caribbean man, with his walking stick, and the middle-aged Turkish woman, with long purple, acrylic fingernails. The thought of all the people, all the rank need in the room, was overwhelming.

Eventually, there it was, her name flashing up on the screen. 'Mrs Clarke, Room 8.'

She stood up and went to the room, unsure of who she was going to meet. She never saw the same doctor twice at this large, inner-city surgery. The care was almost always irreproachable, but it was like starting from scratch each time she went in. This time, the girl looked about twenty-five but had the brisk air of someone much older.

'Sit down, please.' She glanced at Sylvia, then carried on tapping something into her screen. 'Now, how can I help you today?' She turned to fully face Sylvia, who noticed she had a piercing in her upper ear cartilage. A hint of another life beyond this wipe-down room, with its sink and examination bench. A young person's life of parties and kisses and possibility.

'I found a lump in my, um, right breast. When I was in the shower.'

'Were you doing a self-examination?' said the girl.

'No, just lathering up,' said Sylvia. 'Shower gel, you know. The tingly mint stuff that makes your bits ...'

'Ah right. I see.' The girl was emotionless. 'I'll need to have a look. I'll just ask my colleague in for safeguarding purposes.' She disappeared from the room for a second and came back with an older woman, who introduced herself as Dr Pointer.

Sylvia shrugged off her cardigan and started to lower her vest strap.

'If you could just come and sit up here and take off your bra and top,' said the girl-doctor. Sylvia did as she was told. She was wearing a lacy pink bra – she had always loved fancy lingerie and her underwear drawer was like an aviary of exotic birds. She draped the embarrassing garment self-consciously on the bench. Despite the expensive bra, what lay underneath disappointed her. Since her third pregnancy her boobs had shrunk. They had been expecting to be swollen for longer, fuller, and now they were reduced, like empty pockets, never to be full again. They were no longer breasts that could reduce a grown man to almost agonised focus.

'Can you show me?' said the girl-doctor. Sylvia guided her to the lump. No bigger than a pea, really, but fixed in her flesh, not like the glands she sometimes felt under her armpit, that shot across like billiard balls.

'That's it,' said Sylvia. 'Just there.'

'Ah, yes, I see.' Girl-doctor's hands were cool and dry. Sylvia wondered who else she touched with them. Girls? Boys?

'I couldn't feel anything else,' said Sylvia, hopefully, still waiting for the younger woman to dismiss her, to tell her to put her clothes on and leave. She was aware of stale booze on her breath. This girl was probably close enough to smell it. She felt as if it was seeping out of her pores. Every day, she told herself she would have a night off, but then six o'clock came around and the lure of a glass of white wine was too much. Then one became another, until she had drunk two bottles.

Instead of dismissing her, the doctor started examining Sylvia's breasts, both of them, in more detail. Pressing her fingers into flesh and radiating outwards.

'Could you lift up your arms, please?' She started pressing into Sylvia's armpits, the older woman watching dispassionately.

'Right, if you could just pop your clothes on ... Thanks, Dr Pointer. I don't think it's anything,' continued the girl-doctor. 'Probably a cyst. You're young. But I think we should probably get it checked out anyway, just to be on the safe side.'

Sylvia nodded. She realised that she knew. That she had known since she first felt it in the shower, soaping herself furiously while Jude hammered on the door to ask her where his toy ankylosaurus was. It wasn't a cyst. She was struck with pristine clarity in that moment.

'Do you have a family history of breast cancer?'

Sylvia thought of Barbara. Her large, firm bosom, often jacketed. Her cleavage lined and freckled by the sun. Tess's breasts were similarly proportioned, the size of babies' heads, her own far humbler.

'I don't think so,' she said. 'Certainly my mum is fine and I think her mum ... She died quite young, but it wasn't cancer, as far as I know.'

'What about on your father's side?' said the girl-doctor.

'Nothing as far as I'm aware,' said Sylvia.

'No prostate stuff?'

'No, not that I know.'

'Ok. We'll just organise an ultrasound to check it out. Like

I say, I'm sure it's probably nothing, but it pays to be sensible.'

'Is alcohol a risk factor for breast cancer?' said Sylvia. 'Drinking?'

'Well, yes,' said the girl-doctor. 'Drinking raises your risk of certain cancers. It's a good idea not to surpass your weekly limits.'

Sylvia thought of her drinks the night before, drunk in the kitchen while she sat on her laptop and Paul watched sport in the front room. The rum chaser after the wine had run out. Dropping down the rabbit hole of booze every night after the children were asleep. Those precious hours when the anxiety stopped for a bit. The thoughts of Rosa became muffled and she didn't feel the urge to binge and then vomit.

At the planting of Rosa's holly tree, she had been so hung-over she'd had to find a corner to throw up, retching acid shame out until she could face Paul again.

'Try not to worry too much. I see things like this all the time and it's almost always nothing,' said the young doctor.

Sylvia nodded but didn't smile. She knew this wasn't nothing.

* * *

Outside, hurrying towards school, Sylvia felt a wave of panic. She had left the lump for seven days, to make sure it wasn't going to disappear on its own. Each day, she prayed not to feel it but each day it was there, inescapable.

She pulled out her phone to ring Paul. He knew she was coming to have it checked out. He had offered to feel it himself but she had declined.

'I've been referred,' she said, without saying hello.

'Oh ...' said Paul. A whoosh of terrified surprise.

'It's cancer, I know it.' She let out the sob that she had been holding in since she was in the GP's airless room.

'You can't go thinking like that,' said Paul. 'This will just be a precaution. You need to keep positive.' He clung quickly to his usual tenets, the belief system that had always served him well.

'It's my punishment,' said Sylvia. 'For what happened to Rosa.'

'You're not making sense,' said Paul. 'This is ridiculous. You've got to stop being so hard on yourself.'

Sylvia started to cry then. In the street outside the school. She didn't care who saw her. She didn't care if anyone thought she was an unfit mother.

'It's just too hard ...' she said. 'I can't ...'

'You are going to be fine,' said Paul, his voice reassuring as ever, deliberately shot through with sunshine. 'We've got this. Even in the unlikely event that it is cancer. They cure that these days, you know.'

'It's not going to be fine, Paul. It never was fine.' She was hit by a sense of the impossibility of everything. She had always been fundamentally wrong; how had she ever thought otherwise? And now this.

'We'll get through it,' he said, his voice projecting the confidence he was reaching for himself. Sylvia marvelled afresh at her husband's ability not to get bogged down by misfortune, to look on the bright side. It was what she had so loved about him, first of all. But it wearied her now.

'I'd better go, I'm at the school gates,' she said.

'Ok, love you,' said Paul.

'Love you,' said Sylvia, mechanically.

Jude barrelled into her arms. 'Mummy!' he shouted. Miss Willis stood at the door, arms crossed.

'He had a good day, today,' she said. 'Did some good sharing and a bit of writing. Didn't you, Jude?'

Jude's bad days hung in the air and Sylvia could only manage a small smile at Miss Willis.

Jude looked at Miss Willis and grinned, before pushing into the classroom door to make it swing.

'Don't do that,' said Sylvia, automatically. 'Come on, let's go.'

Megan was doing her violin lesson and this was her time with Jude. The pocket in the week when it was just the two of them. She both looked forward to it and dreaded it. She enjoyed having him all to herself – drinking in his stubborn features and kissing his head until he said, 'Oi, Mum, stop,' and pulled away. But she was also on edge, following the steps to a complicated dance that nobody had ever taught her. The one that would stop Jude having a meltdown about something. Refusing him chocolate or another ten minutes on the trampoline might result in twenty minutes of solid screaming, hammering his fists on the floor.

What was good was that keeping up with his demands meant that she couldn't think too much about the lump in her right breast. The cells buried in her flesh, that might unpick her life, or might turn out to be nothing.

35

Now

'She wanted you to have this,' said Paul, offering Tess the envelope, a paperclip still clinging to its right-hand corner like a parasite.

'Sylvia?' There was a note of incredulity in Tess's voice. 'She wrote something for me?'

Paul nodded. He was standing by the driver's door to the car; the children and Barbara were already stapled inside. He had put off giving Tess the letter for long enough.

'She wrote me a kind of ... guide, for when she had gone. Letters, too. For the people she loved.'

Tess shook her head wonderingly, but reached out her hand.

'Typical bloody Sylvia,' she said, but her tone was fond. 'She always did have to wring every last bit of drama she could out of a situation.' Paul smiled. 'You know, when we were kids she used to rope me into endless shows on the front lawn. Every time, she was the star – Cinderella or Princess

228

Leia or Little Red Riding Hood. I got to be the wolf, or an Ugly Sister ...' She laughed. 'Chewbacca if I was lucky.' She looked at the envelope. 'Drama queen.' At that her face crumpled. 'I just miss her, I miss her so bloody much.'

'I do too,' said Paul, reaching out for Tess, a confusing embrace, his wife's sister's milk-bottle skin, her pale eyebrows, the flash of her one blue eye, so similar to Sylvia's. Tess smelled good, like sunbaked earth, but he longed for the heady thwack of Sylvia's scent.

'Why?' said Tess, pulling back. 'Why did it have to happen? I should have ... I should never have ... I just assumed that one day we'd be ... back where we were.'

Paul didn't say anything. There wasn't an answer, as far as he could see. Barbara was looking at them questioningly from the passenger seat.

'We'd better get moving,' said Paul. 'I hope it's ... helpful in some way.' The words sounded lame, even to himself. He climbed into the car and as they reversed down the drive. Tess stood on the front path of the cliff house, her face blotchy, waving the hand that clutched the envelope, like a white flag.

'Did you only just give her Sylvia's letter?' Barbara said to Paul. She had been silent on the contents of her own.

'I was just waiting for the right moment,' said Paul. 'It took me a while to realise it would never come.'

* * *

It was one of those modern, unseasonably warm autumn days, Londoners still unsheathed in flip-flops and scanty clothes, music spilling from open car windows. Bare earth showed through parched grass like skin on a balding scalp.

They had been back from Cornwall for a few days, in their usual routine but with a slight sense of disbelief that all the official steps of saying goodbye to Sylvia had been performed. All that was left was the yawning emptiness of life without her in it.

The house had been fragrant with inhabitation when they returned. And as Paul moved around the kitchen, warming up the food Natalia had left, following the instructions she had written on a Post-it note, he could feel Barbara watching him, an idea forming in her mind.

'So, are you ... Is there anything happening with this woman?' she asked, finally, nodding in the direction of the stew.

'She's just a mother from the school. She's been helping me out a bit with the cleaning. A bit of cooking. And no, we aren't ... there's nothing going on.'

'Well, she's a much better cook than Sylvia at any rate,' said Barbara, lightly. 'I suppose it must have been hard to cope.'

Paul looked at her.

'I know that men tend to ...' Barbara coughed. 'To move on more quickly.'

'Honestly, it's not ...' said Paul.

'I just want you to know that I wouldn't judge you if you did,' said Barbara, watching him carefully.

Her words stayed in Paul's mind during the next day's surgery, a routine neutering. He felt a flicker of sympathy for a young Siamese tom, whose potency he plucked away so easily. His next patient was a kitten with a hernia. A deep bulge in the velvet of its stomach. Her owner was a woman in her twenties with a sweet face and a mane of blonde hair. Thoughts of Alice came unbidden into his mind. One of those straightforward girls he had always been involved with before he met Sylvia and realised he hankered after something else. Like developing a craving for bitter chocolate when you've spent your life eating Milky Bars.

Alice had contacted him after she heard the news about Sylvia. She was married now, of course, with sons of her own, but he knew her condolences were utterly sincere. That's how it was with someone like her. Like him. Everything out in the open.

As the girl reached into her bag for her phone, her hair falling forwards, he felt his libido sputter into life in a way it hadn't for a long time. Since Sylvia's diagnosis, his desire, once so reliable, had shrunk. He had been scared of hurting his wife, both physically and emotionally. And then after the mastectomy, things were never quite the same again. They both knew it.

He was too careful, too restrained, never again to be overcome simply by proximity to her body. When had the last time been? Sometime after Dr Z gave them the terminal diagnosis. Maybe after one of those sessions where they both lay on their double bed crying, holding each other tight. It had probably been slow and loving, familiar but unfamiliar, comforting in a way but steeped in sadness.

For so long, desire to him had meant Sylvia. She had

231

always set the pace, she still was. But perhaps he needed to decisively move on. Maybe with someone like this girl. She might do.

'She'll need a little op, but she'll be fine,' he said, standing up straighter. His eyes dropped from her face to her chest for a split-second, but long enough for her to notice.

'I had no idea that kittens could have this kind of thing,' she said, quickly. 'I just bought him off Gumtree last week. The woman said he was fine. I just didn't realise.'

Paul saw girls like her all the time. In their late twenties, craving a bundle to look after but not in a position to have a baby. Opting for a pet without realising for a second what they were getting into by acquiring life. Probably, by the time this kitten finally died, this pretty girl would be wrinkled and jowled, all those unexpected responsibilities leaving their mark.

'It's not an unusual condition,' said Paul. 'She'll be perfectly fine.' He stroked the kitten along her spine. 'You can leave her in tonight and collect her in the morning. I'll give her a flea treatment while you're here.'

'Oh good,' said the girl, smiling, revealing a row of white teeth, unscarred enamel. 'How often will she need those?'

'Once a month. You put it here on the back of the neck.' Paul anointed the little tabby.

'Gosh. So much to learn,' said the girl. 'I can hardly re-member to feed myself sometimes. I'm going to have to get myself together!' She pushed back her hair, flirtatiously.

He smiled in response but was tiring of her selfish in-nocence now. He wasn't sure he had the energy. And the thought of having to watch a young woman like this grow disenchanted did not appeal.

'So, shall I just leave her with you?' she asked.

'Yes,' said Paul. 'Pick up her tomorrow after ten a.m.'

'So nice to meet you,' she said, extending a hand.

'My pleasure,' said Paul.

He watched her leave and thought of Sylvia, a decade before leaving the very same room, her fiery hair down her back. The ache he had felt as she went, the understanding that she meant something important to him. However difficult he found the manual's revelation that she had never been completely honest with him, he remained convinced he could never feel like that about anybody ever again.

36

Sylvia's Manual

With all this time to think, I find that William keeps coming into my head. After Danny, the crack in the wall presents him to me. Exhibit B of my selfishness.

For as well as stealing her boyfriend that fateful summer, I failed Tess in that regard. I let her mop up our father's illness. She was the one who pleaded for the community psychiatric nurse to visit him and later took him to the consultant. She was the one who made sure he ate. Who lit the fire in the cliff house so that he didn't freeze to death. Who arranged the driving assessment to see if he was still safe on the road.

And later, when he had that stroke that pushed him into true incapacity, it was Tess – and Danny, bloody Danny – who sat with him in the ambulance on the way to hospital and held his hand.

It's clear to me now how badly I let him down. My father who was always there for me. I tried, I really did, but after Rosa I couldn't bear to look his disease in the face. I couldn't handle any more reminders of mortality. It felt like death was everywhere, waiting in the wings. Everything I had always cared about seemed pointless. And I'd started to drink. It helped stopped me thinking about Rosa, but it also blurred my sense of responsibility towards William.

I should have moved down there, to look after him, when his mind started to fray at the edges. I should have forced you to relocate to the cliff house, pulled the children out of school and taken them with me if I had to. I should have done everything I could for him.

He did that for me, once upon a time. When Barbara left and he was a single father. He did everything he possibly could with the knowledge he had. It wasn't his fault that he didn't have a clue. What man of his generation did? Let alone a crabber, used to long hours at sea, the company of men, hauling pots from their watery hiding places.

He used to make our school packed lunches the night before. Granary bread, ham, cherry tomatoes wrapped in clingfilm. Always the same, the bread faintly acquiring the taste of plastic. I hated those lunches, but now I'm a parent myself, I can appreciate the effort. He kept going, after she had gone. He took care of us when many men like him wouldn't.

He wasn't a reader. Nobody had ever expected him to be. He left the village school at fourteen, to work on the boat with his dad. But he read to us, at night. Sometimes stumbling over the words in books like *Tom's Midnight Garden*. His horizons expanding as ours did. That's why I love those stories so much now. They make me feel closer to him.

It wasn't easy to feel that intimacy with him. Like you, he wasn't a talker, or a hugger. He hadn't been taught how. And a part of him was always out at sea, lost to the waves, thinking about the tide, where to take the boat, whether he could catch enough. But he was always there for us, when we needed him. On summer evenings, I used to look out of my bedroom window and watch him downstairs, on the bench in the garden, smoking his pipe in the dark. His face in the half-light as weathered as the granite boulders that littered the ground around our cottage.

But when he needed me, really needed me, I didn't do enough. Sure, I can make excuses about the state I was in. About Rosa. But the plain truth is that I couldn't bear it. The visceral horror of the locked ward where he lived, the shouting and smell of bleach barely concealing the smell of piss. William was always so particular about what he wore. Despite the chaos of the house, his clothes – our clothes – were always relatively clean. He had a fresh smock every day, the fabric faded purplish-blue by sun and repeated washing, ready to receive a new influx of fish scales and smears of blood. And I almost never saw him without his black cap over his grey curls. A stereotypical Cornish fisherman. If you look at a picture of him by the boat, it could have been from a hundred years ago and he was proud of that fact.

But towards the end, he wore the same kind of things that I'm wearing now. Invalids' clothes. Modern, ugly elasticated garments that can't rub or snag. His spindly legs were encased in tracksuit bottoms. Practical, but almost unbearable to witness, he would have hated it so much. His head uncovered, his crown of thinning grey curls exposed.

William met Megan when she was a plump, watchful baby. He hoisted her into the air above his head, where she surveyed him calmly. But he was too far gone to realise I was pregnant with Jude. He barely glanced at my swollen stomach.

Megan couldn't understand it. She knew he was her grandfather, so why was he staring into space, jaw slack? You know Megan, she wants people to play by the rules and William categorically wasn't. I explained that he was poorly, in his head, but she was too little to comprehend. I spoon-fed him his lunch that day. Although his body was withering away, his appetite seemed heartier than ever. He ate gargantuan portions of soggy meat and treacle pudding, mouth opening for more, like a terrifying baby bird. I didn't want Megan to see him like that. I didn't want to see him like that myself.

But there are so many things that I want our children to know about him. Things you have to tell them, or they will be lost forever.

He usually cut his face shaving and would use tiny fragments of tissue paper on the cuts and lashings of Brut Original on his neck.

He couldn't cook and so we ate crisps, Kit Kats, Dairylea triangles, tangerines, endless rounds of sandwiches. Catering in the Cliff House was like being on a permanent 1980s picnic.

He could read the sea like no one else. Knew when there was a rip tide in a particular patch of water, where the dolphins liked to show themselves, the exact route around the Runnel Stone, through the dangerous rocks.

Despite his seriousness, he had a loony sense of humour, which only showed itself on some occasions. At those times, he would get the giggles and be unable to stop himself, clutching his stomach. Tess and I always loved seeing him like that, unable to get the words out.

As a young man he was handsome. Surprisingly so. It's what snared Barbara, after all, as well as the sheer novelty of a romance with a fisherman. And she wasn't the only acolyte. As well as his broad shoulders and dark hair, I think those previous girlfriends must have been drawn to his remoteness, filling in the silences with their own fantasies.

In truth, he was a true ascetic, his appetites minimal. So unlike Barbara's. It's impossible for me to imagine them together and happy, but by accounts they were, for a time. Both madly in love with their idea of the other person.

37

Then

'Well, the bad news is that it is cancerous,' said Dr Z. 'But it's just one tiny spot. It should be eminently treatable.'

Sylvia was looking at his face. It was quite incredible – the man literally had no visible pores. He looked as if someone had airbrushed his skin, as if he bathed in a vat of coconut oil every evening.

'It's cancer?' she said. She felt Paul's hand grip her knee but she didn't turn to look at him.

'I'm so sorry, but yes.' Dr Z, a stranger to them then, kept his gaze on her face, his expression empathetic but controlled.

'But I have two children,' said Sylvia. 'Jude and Megan. They're in primary school.' Pointless information offered, as if it was some kind of protection.

'I understand this is difficult news,' said Dr Z, his eyes darting between the two of them, 'but cancer is much more treatable now than it was in the past. And we've caught this in good time.'

Sylvia nodded.

'You are going to need a mastectomy, though, as it's quite an aggressive form. And chemotherapy.'

'A mastectomy?' Sylvia frowned and looked instinctively at her right breast. Her breasts had always disappointed her. Too small in relation to Tess's. Modest little things that she felt self-conscious of. But the idea of not having one of them at all – now that she couldn't comprehend.

'Just on one side?' she said.

'That's what I'd recommend,' said Dr Z. 'There is no raised risk of the cancer developing on the left side.'

'Right,' said Sylvia. She had entered a new world now, of risks and probabilities and best outcomes. She would never again take sweet normality for granted, she realised in that moment. Just as you don't truly appreciate your freedom before having a child. One of those pivots in life between one phase and another.

'Listen, it's a lot to take in. There's a nurse who will come to talk to you about the next step.' Dr Z had finally moved his gaze from Sylvia's face. He must have been trained how best to deliver this kind of news, thought Sylvia, bitterly. He must do this all the time.

She nodded again, numbly, and stood. They had to fetch Jude and Megan from school.

Outside, they cut across the hospital car park. They hadn't been able to park in it and had to find a spot in a street several minutes away. It was a warm afternoon. She longed to be in a garden somewhere, with a beer, wearing a silly strappy dress and flip-flops.

'I'm sorry, Sylv,' said Paul, trying not to convey his own fear.

'Well, it's not exactly your fault, is it?' She felt like being cruel to Paul then. She couldn't carry the weight of his devotion for another second.

'Of course not. Listen, we're going to get through this together.' He reached for her hand. She felt like pulling it away, but she let him hold it. 'You heard what the man said. It's just one tiny spot.'

* * *

One tiny spot. In the weeks after the cancer diagnosis, that was what Sylvia and Paul found themselves clinging to.

There were other phrases they preferred not to dwell on. Like 'Grade II' and 'ductal hormonal carcinoma'. But 'one tiny spot' sounded like a pasta sauce stain on a white shirt, easily removable with the right washing powder, or the right treatment. Which meant chemotherapy, radiotherapy and a mastectomy.

'It's relatively aggressive,' said Dr Z. 'We want to maximise our chances.'

Sylvia resented the use of the collective pronoun. Dr Z looked so fresh and calm, it was impossible to imagine him facing something like this, staring into the abyss. Sylvia imagined him treating the sick and dying, but with a forcefield keeping himself safe at all times, like one of the superheroes that Jude was so obsessed with. Cancer Man: superpower – immortality.

241

His radiant good health seemed in direct contrast with the hospital itself, with its teeming reception, incessant beeps and general sense of suppressed chaos. Sylvia hated hospitals. The trips to A & E with Jude, over sprained wrists and bumped heads, had been torture enough, as if she had known, deep down, that someday she herself would be the patient, would be beholden to whatever the building had to offer.

Paul wasn't a googler. 'What's the point?' he would say. 'Dr Z is one of the leading breast cancer experts in the world. That's good enough for me. We just have to put our faith in his hands and hope for the best.'

Sylvia couldn't understand this perspective. Part of her wanted him to take it off her hands, the internet research. A corner of her wished that he would question things more, look into the different options internationally. But instead it was she who got sucked into the quicksand of studies and different treatment options. Of chatrooms and podcasts.

'I might not need chemotherapy,' she said. 'There's a genetic test in California, which can tell you whether it will actually increase your chances, based on your own DNA.'

'Do you really want to risk *that*?' said Paul, who was secretly, guiltily wondering if Sylvia wanted to avoid the physical indignities of chemotherapy. The hair loss, the puffy steroid face. He knew she was putting on a brave face with all the make-up after Rosa's death, but privately he wished that she would let her grief shine through. It would be more natural. 'Surely you just want to throw whatever we can at it?'

'It's not about taking a risk ... It actually tells you if it's necessary,' said Sylvia. But they couldn't afford it and there was a value in simply surrendering to what Dr Z had to offer. The fighting, the struggling, the squinting at cancer cells on internet pages late at night wasn't doing Sylvia any good.

'It's just one spot.' She broke the news to Barbara four days after she found out, over the telephone, a gin and tonic cradled in her lap on Ted's head. She hadn't breathed a word to anybody but Paul until that point.

'Cancer?' said Barbara, who was of an age where the word had dimensions. She had already started to lose friends fairly regularly. 'What sort and how bad? And darling, why on earth didn't you tell me sooner?'

'My chances are good. It's pretty normal these days,' said Sylvia, trying to put on a brave face, but in the end failing and starting to cry, hopelessly, over the phone. 'So many women my age get cancer nowadays.'

'Oh darling,' said Barbara. 'I don't know what to say.'

'It's going to be all right,' said Sylvia. 'They seem to have caught it quite early.'

'Oh Sylvia,' said Barbara. 'I'm so sorry.'

'Don't be sorry, Mum,' said Sylvia, rigid with the impossibility of it all. 'I'm going to be all right, I've just got to get through this.'

'But after William and your baby ... This is just too much,' said Barbara, as if complaining to a hotel manager about shoddy service.

'Bad things come in threes,' said Sylvia weakly. 'I'm sure this will be our family's bad patch over for a bit.'

'You must let me know what I can do,' said her mother. 'I can help with the children. Are you going to need a, um ...?'

'Mastectomy?' said Sylvia. 'Yes. On the right side.' Bye-bye right breast, she thought. The one that both Megan and Jude had favoured when breastfeeding, its teat shaped slightly more pleasingly.

'Just one side?' said Barbara, presenting Sylvia with a vision of herself as single-breasted, like some lopsided Greek goddess.

'I'll have a reconstruction, once my body is over the treatment,' said Sylvia.

'Oh darling,' said Barbara. Sylvia could hear ice chinking in the background, being sucked towards a mouth.

* * *

One tiny spot. That was the title of the email that Sylvia sent to Tess. Inside she explained her predicament but kept the tone upbeat. That was how things were between them, since Tess had found out about Danny. They were in touch and civil, but it never went further, as if they were afraid of what would be unleashed if they scratched the surface.

Tess was distraught, reading the email out from her phone to Danny, whose own face turned grey beneath its tan.

'What if she gets really ill?' Tess's voice was small. She reached down to press her face into Flora's hair. 'I thought we still had plenty of time to get back to how things used to be.'

'Maybe you should send her a link to that documentary about that guy who cured his bowel cancer with a juice cleanse,' said Danny, who had stood and was pacing the chalet. 'There's that guy in Penzance who followed it and he's doing great. Total remission. Healthier than ever.'

Tess shook her head. She knew that Sylvia and Paul mocked her and Danny's way of life. Their homeopathy, veganism, belief in the healing powers of marijuana. They would take it as a rebuke. Danny meant well, but he struggled to see anyone else's perspective, or to discern their scorn.

The distance that had grown between the sisters meant that Sylvia didn't know Flora was unvaccinated but she could just imagine what her older sister, the scientist, would say if she knew.

'I can't believe it,' said Tess. She had always assumed that Sylvia was invulnerable.

* * *

'It's just one tiny spot,' said Sylvia to Nush. Ryan and Jude were on the iPad playing a game in which they entered another world, constructing houses and building tunnels. Jude was stilled, for once, falling inside the screen while Ryan watched.

'Woah. That's cool,' said Ryan, good-naturedly. He was always so sunny, that boy. Born that way, said Nush, proudly, once confiding how he had smiled at her in the hospital, just hours old, as if greeting an old friend. Sylvia had tried not to feel jealous, thinking of Jude's unabated screaming, which had only been soothed by constant feeding. One of the biggest unspoken truths about parenthood – some people just have it easier than others.

'Oh god, I'm so sorry,' said Nush. She came around the island to hug Sylvia. They rarely touched and Sylvia wasn't sure how to respond to the embrace but Nush's solidity was comforting.

'It's ok,' she said, finally, drawing back reluctantly. 'I think they have caught it pretty early. My chances are good.' She glanced at Jude. Chances. Of survival. That she should be discussing these things in the room where she habitually heated spaghetti hoops and poured glasses of wine, chided Jude and helped Megan with her homework, struck her. She was normally so consumed in the everyday and so bogged down by what happened with Rosa, that she didn't consider her own mortality. Her own finite time left on earth, hours and minutes and seconds counting down, like the timer on a bomb in an Eighties action film.

After Rosa, she had been increasingly aware of the fragility of her other children. She would slyly watch the purple veins at their temples, the inhale-exhale of their breaths. When Jude first got a temperature after Rosa's death, she felt a greasy panic, undercut with a sense of being utterly alone. It reminded her of how she had felt when he and Megan got ill as babies. What if it was meningitis? Or blood poisoning?

She watched him vigilantly as he lay on the sofa. Jude was always easier to manage and more loveable when he got ill. He stopped jumping, shouting and asking questions, accepting his incapacity with a stoicism she found endearing.

He was all right by the morning and she could breathe easily again. But all that time, she hadn't considered that it might be her that was next. Rather than Paul, or one of her other children.

Nush was silent, looking at Sylvia with those surprisingly pale brown eyes that were witness to so much.

'It's shitty,' she said, finally. 'I'm sorry. Let me know what I can do.'

'I will,' promised Sylvia. She reached in the fridge for wine. 'I should probably cut down my drinking,' she said to Nush. 'But wine makes everything better.'

'You've just got to look after yourself,' said Nush. 'Whatever that means. Have a glass, but don't go overboard.'

Sylvia thought of that night in the pub with Nush before she found the lump, when Natalia had appeared. The shame of the next day, hiding her bloodshot eyes with sunglasses, as the children had turns digging the hole for Rosa's holly tree to be planted.

'Easier said than done,' she said, but smiled reassuringly at her friend. That was the thing about cancer, she found. Even with someone as self-reliant and sane as Nush, you, as cancer victim, had to proffer succour. To show that you weren't going to let it break you. No one liked to be reminded of the bad stuff, after all.

38

Now

'You're still here.' Paul was surprised, coming in after work to find Natalia stirring something at the hob.

'I'm making vegetable soup. Nice and healthy,' she said. 'I told Barbara I could stay instead tonight.'

'The kids?'

'Upstairs. They've had a wash. Alvin is at a club.'

'Thanks so much for bringing them back at such short notice, Natalia,' said Paul.

'You can call me Talia,' said the woman. 'And it's no trouble.'

'But you're spending so much time away from Alvin?' Paul put his leather bag on the floor.

'It's ok. Alvin is a happy boy,' she said, putting the wooden spoon down on the counter in a fluid motion, so it didn't spill a drop of soup.

'Daddy, Daddy, it's saying no charge.' Jude ran into the room, waving the iPad. 'Daddy, sort it out.'

'Hello to you, too, Jude,' said Paul.

'Oh, hello, Daddy,' said Jude, carelessly, looking at the dark screen.

'Say hello to Natalia too,' said Paul. 'She's made us some amazing soup for supper.' He looked across at her, realising how his words relegated her to charwoman. 'Do you want to stay and eat it with us ... Talia?'

'Ok,' she said, quietly but with a certain satisfaction, moving towards the saucepan. 'I'll put it in bowls.'

'Megan, dinner time!' called Paul, up the stairs. If the children were surprised to find Natalia eating with them, they didn't mention it. They, too, had grown used to her in the house.

'This is good soup,' said Jude, who usually only liked the neon kind that came out of a can.

'Yes,' said Megan. 'Can I have more bread?'

Natalia buttered a slice and handed it over to the girl. Paul looked around. The evenings were closing in and the light from above the kitchen table spilled over all of them. For someone with their face pressed against the window, they would look like a perfect nuclear family. Nobody would ever guess the truth.

The children were politer than they would have been for their own mother. They took their soup bowls to the dishwasher, tidied away the napkins.

'Thanks, Natalia,' said Jude, unprompted, before following Megan upstairs.

'What have you done to him?' said Paul, laughing and looking at Natalia questioningly. She smiled, inscrutable.

'Seriously, though, we're so grateful for everything you've been doing. I don't know if I would have been able to cope without you.' He thought of what Sylvia had said about Natalia, as if she had predicted all along how this woman would slide into her house, gently rearranging things. His wife hadn't wanted that to happen. But why did she always get to decide everything? She had never been completely honest with him, after all.

'I'm just trying to help ... and you're helping me too. The extra money is coming in useful.'

'Well, thank you,' said Paul. At this, as if seeing something different in his eyes, Natalia moved closer towards him.

'You still look so sad, Paul,' she said. 'So unhappy. I just wish I could rub away some of this pain. You need to smile again.' She touched the righthand corner of his mouth, where the tender skin shifted into stubble. Paul remembered the girl in the surgery, the desire he had forgotten he could feel. How easy it would be to let Natalia slip into his bed. She was already changing the sheets, after all.

*　　*　　*

Sylvia's hospice clothes had depressed both her and Paul, although he battled not to show it. It was so far from the person she had been, someone who minded about what she wore. A woman unafraid of white jeans, silk shirts and string bikinis. One on first-name terms with the local dry-cleaner, even after motherhood.

Paul consciously avoided her old garments, the painful

reminder of the former her. He kept the door shut on the high heels with their scarlet soles, the skinny leather belts, the handbag made of suede as soft and pale as clotted cream.

Instead he would nip into Marks and Spencer and just buy new things for her. Track suits and wide T-shirts. That way they could both maintain the fiction that one day she would be standing in front of her closet again, fingers trailing over fabrics, complaining, 'But I haven't got a single thing to wear!'

Now, with Nush standing in the background and the children asleep, including Ryan, on cushions on Jude's floor, Paul opened the cupboard tentatively. He hadn't mentioned the incident with Natalia earlier in the evening. Nothing had happened after all. She had dropped her hand and busied around looking for her things, before leaving to collect Alvin. But he knew something between them had changed. He was going to have to make a decision.

The wardrobe smelled fusty and sweet. And the familiar garments – the bodice that had once pushed her breasts into satisfying curves, the sheepskin gilet, the palette of Sylvia-colours, heavy on the pink despite her hair colour – made him groan audibly.

'People think that red-heads can't wear pink, but they're wrong,' she had told him on one of their early dates, with characteristic self-obsession. 'It's actually an extremely good idea, providing you get the right shade.'

Why was she making him get rid of these things? And so soon? It was typical Sylvia. She had to still be involved, pulling his strings like a puppet-master.

'We don't have to do this now,' said Nush, looking at his face. 'It can wait, you know.'

Paul turned to her. She looked tired, her sleepy eyelids at half-mast. She had just come off shift and was still in her uniform.

'She said in her manual ...' he said.

'Oh, screw the manual,' said Nush. 'Sylvia's gone. She's not going to know.'

Paul frowned, uncertain. He knew she had technically gone. He had seen her corpse, released her ashes to the Cornish wind, but she was still everywhere around him, pervading his life. He couldn't shake the thought of what she would say about Natalia's discreet attentions to their home.

'Listen, I loved her too,' said Nush. 'I'm not being disrespectful. All I'm saying is that this doesn't have to happen tonight. She's only been gone six weeks. There's no rush here.'

'She wanted to feel like her clothes were being worn, not stuck in this cupboard,' said Paul. 'It was really important to her.'

'I'm sure. Clothes always were,' said Nush, her tone fondly sarcastic. 'I'm not saying you shouldn't have a clear-out eventually, but only that it doesn't have to be now.'

'Let's make a start,' said Paul. 'You're here. I don't think I can do this alone.'

'Ok, well then, a pile for charity, a pile for Megan and a pile of stuff we could sell online for more,' said Nush. 'If we're really going to do this, we may as well get on with it.'

They started to sort through the garments, sliding them off hangers and checking their labels. Despite her own profound lack of interest in what she wore, Nush had an eye for the labels that might earn money.

'Oooh, that looks expensive ... Is that the one she wanted to give Megan?' said Nush, as Paul pulled a green dress out of the wardrobe.

'Yes. This is the one,' he said, holding it up in mid-air. It was a garment for a mermaid, low-cut and full-length, made of heavy satin that changed colour slightly as it moved.

'It's beautiful,' said Nush, reaching out a hand to feel the fabric. 'I don't think I ever saw her wear that.'

'I remember one night she did,' said Paul. 'We were so wasted.' He thought then of that evening. When they were still new to each other and just being together was intoxicating, never mind whatever they had drunk, whatever they had taken. Ariadne was there and Tess, up from Cornwall. Danny, too.

Danny had mocked Sylvia's dress, Paul remembered. 'Are you going to a ball or something, Cinderella?' he had said, staring at her, with what Paul now realised, in retrospect, was bitterness.

Sylvia had only smiled, always assured about what she wore, about standing out. But those were the days when she was making herself sick daily, the confidence only skin-deep after all.

'She was so beautiful,' said Paul. 'Back then.' He felt embarrassed.

'She was beautiful at the end, too,' said Nush, softly. 'She was lovely on the inside as well and that shone through.'

'I know she was ...' He flushed, guiltily. 'She could be amazing, but ...'

'I realise she could be a bit self-centred at times, but her heart was in the right place,' said Nush.

Paul wondered what Nush would think of her best friend if she knew what she was capable of, what she had done to her own sister. Tears clustered at the back of his throat and he blinked hard, trying to stop them. Nush noticed and smiled, sadly.

'Paul, mate ...' Nush held her palms up in apology. 'I don't know why you married such a handful.'

'More than just a handful,' said Paul. 'You know the manual ...' He dropped the item of clothing he was holding and crossed the room to the double bed, where the document was tucked under his pillow, where he had taken to keeping it. He pulled it out, shaking the pages. 'She makes this confession at the end. Something she had never told me ...' He shook his head, the concealment striking him afresh.

Nush was silent. She wouldn't push him. Paul hesitated. Despite everything, he still wanted Nush to like Sylvia as much as she always had. Their friendship had been so important for his wife. Redeeming.

'She had an affair with Tess's boyfriend, Danny. It went on for years,' said Paul, finally, succumbing to the vertiginous pull of the confession. 'Right up until she met me.'

'Shit.' Nush's mouth a perfect 'o', like the letter on Jude's alphabet poster, illustrated by oranges, octagons, an octopus. 'No wonder they weren't close.'

'They were once,' said Paul. 'When we first got together, before Tess found out, we saw her all the time. Then one day it all stopped and Sylvia never explained why. I thought I knew everything about her, that we were each other's grand love affair. I miss her so bloody much but it turns out she was hiding something from me all along.'

'Come here,' said Nush. He was comforted by her flat Brummie vowels, her solidity. Nush was exactly the person you would want descending out of an ambulance as you lay prostate on a pavement. 'Why don't you put this away for a bit?' She placed the manual on a pile of folded pashminas at the base of the wardrobe. 'And madam's clothes can wait.'

39

Sylvia's Manual

Ok, I'm changing the subject now. From my transgressions. Short attention span, you know me. But I'm bored of feeling guilty and in these pages, at least, I get to call the shots. So, it's back to the domestic sphere for more tips. Specifically, on children's parties.

Of all the jobs of being a parent, birthday parties were the bit I most loathed. You start enthusiastic, but as the years go by and you realise that they aren't going to stop happening, boredom sets in.

The cakes. The balloons. The small talk with other exhausted, middle-aged people. Everyone so nice, but only really interested, deep-down, in their own child, with that projected selfishness of parenthood that masquerades as altruism.

At your own children's you are wired, like an event manager on their biggest day of the year. At other people's children's you are bored, or at least I was.

At least with Megan, you can drop her now and beat a hasty retreat, but Jude is still of an age where people expect you to stay for proceedings. For pass-the-parcel and singing 'Happy Birthday'. Or maybe that's just because Jude is how he is — the other mothers wanted to make sure I was there in case he bit somebody or had a meltdown.

As Jude's mother, I was always on high alert. But actually, he's always been pretty good at large gatherings. The other children are so over-excited it stills some frantic part of him, they meet halfway. He's usually content to jump around and so I got to sit for an hour or so, drinking horrible tea or warm prosecco.

You will be expected to continue the parties and I want you to. I don't want Jude or Megan missing out because I won't be there to do it myself. You will need to bake. Barbara won't do it and shop-bought won't do. In time, if you find another woman, she can do it for you. But until then, you will have to do it yourself.

Jude likes banana cake. No icing. Megan goes for anything with chocolate.

The pans and bowls are in the bottom drawer to the right of the cooker. My domain. I have to admit that part of me thrills to the thought of you creaming butter and sugar or cutting out circles of greaseproof paper. Baking isn't like other cooking. You can't cut corners, you have to follow the rules.

I don't like regulations in many settings, but when it comes to making muffins, I'm all for them. It's really the only kind of cooking I enjoy. There is something so soothing about creaming butter and the smell of sugar perfumed with a vanilla pod. Getting the rise on a sponge cake just right affords a certain kind of smug pleasure.

I find the preponderance of cupcakes in the world of cancer perplexing, nonetheless. I get it, cake is comforting. But only good cake and those fundraisers with sloppily iced, shop-bought muffins do nothing for the spirit. They remind me too much of those days of cornershop madeleines, which barely touched the sides before coming back up again, into the toilet bowl.

Also, as a general rule, most women with breast cancer are trying to shirk sugar. To avoid getting even fatter or more strung out on the stuff than they already were. To stop the cancer cells gobbling up the sweet stuff. So, to continually remind them of what they are trying to avoid seems cruel. A pantomime of good cheer. There should be green juice coffee mornings instead. Made properly, that stuff is delicious.

I want you to sing 'Happy Birthday' to the children for the rest of your life. It doesn't matter if they're in their twenties. I want them to squirm with embarrassment for it and you'll know that I'm just there alongside you.

The fabric for the golden throne is in my wardrobe, at the back. It's just a strip of glittery gold lamé that I found in a fabric shop on Berwick Street. The end of a roll. You need to drape it on the birthday girl or boy's chair the night before, so they wake up and come downstairs to a throne for breakfast.

Make pancakes. As well as the cake that comes later. Stick a candle in them and douse them in syrup. Tie their presents with ribbons and pile them up so that their eyes pop. I want them both to have birthdays to remember, even if I'm not there to facilitate them.

That goes for Rosa, too. I don't want the 17th June to be a day of mourning each year. Or worse still, forgotten or glossed over. I want you three to talk about her, to turn around the few facts we knew about her, so that they glint in the light. She had red hair and a determined chin. Her middle name was Barbara. She had the long fingers and crescent moon fingernails of a concert pianist.

We lived that day, her birthday, even if she didn't. And it needs to be recalled. For all of our sakes. Hell, bring out the golden throne if you feel like it, make the children write cards. Get them to talk about their little sister, to keep her memory alive.

Same goes for me. I don't wish to be mawkish, but I want you to celebrate my birthday each year too. I like a black forest gateau, personally. A bit retro for some tastes, I know, but life offers one too few opportunities to eat cherries. It might be a bit challenging the first time you make it, but you'll improve.

I'd like you to get out old pictures of me when I still looked good. That one where I'm wearing the yellow bikini on the beach in Spain, the denim hot pants at Ariadne's party, where my pupils are dilated and my skin sweaty, but my hair fell just so.

And the family pictures, as well. The newborn ones where I'm puffy and shell-shocked. The family holidays. Bring those out. Talk about me. Discuss my flaws, if you like, but just keep talking.

And in the evening, when the children have gone to bed, or out, drink a glass of red wine and toast me. Even if your new woman is curled up like a fat prawn on the sofa next to you. Make her talk about me too. I won't be forgotten. I won't just fade into the background.

You can find someone else, but I'd like to think that I'll always be in there in spirit, somehow, like some kind of phantom ménage à trois. She will probably hate me, but make sure she has to live with me, on birthdays at least.

40

Then

Everything ached. Her head, her stomach, her limbs, but most of all, the site where her breast had been. The pain-killers they had given her were nauseatingly strong, but as they started to wear off, the pain reared its head.

She hadn't been able to look yet. She knew there were staples in her skin, crudely gathering it back together.

Paul was tender, the children subdued. And she was re-lieved, so relieved, to be back at home, away from the strip lighting, the constant temperature-taking, the buzzing of alarms. How anyone could work in a hospital, she had no idea. She had never felt such gratitude for her house, in all its normality. She could even sit on the sofa without itching to pick up the pieces of Jude's Lego strewn across the floor.

'I can't look,' she had said to Paul, when he brought her sugared tea in bed. 'You're going to have to look for me.'

She saw him quail then. He was trying so hard. He had always been better than she, but he didn't want to admit this new reality. That wasn't Paul's way. He would have preferred her just to get the reconstruction out of the way and never take her bra off again, she knew.

'If that's what you want,' was what he said.

'Yes,' she said. She wanted him to know how reduced she was. She wanted to see it in his eyes.

It was later on, when Jude and Megan were asleep, that she raised her top. She winced. It was still painful to lift her arms.

'Does it hurt?' said Paul. Sylvia nodded.

'We don't have to do this now,' he said. 'You heard what they said. It's going to take weeks for the swelling to go down.'

'I just want you to look for me,' she said. 'I need you to see.'

He nodded and as he looked, he kept his expression studiedly neutral. She was a specimen now, a patient. She had seen this expression on his face when he looked at Ted's scabs, the ones he still sometimes got on his stomach, around the scar that showed where Paul had saved him so long ago.

'What does it look like?' she said, keeping her own eyes on his face. She didn't know if she personally would ever look down there, at her own chest. If she would ever be brave enough.

'It looks ...' He was silent.

'Come on!'

'It looks ...'

'Paul ...'

'Well, it looks fucking awful, if I'm being honest.'

261

Sylvia glanced at her husband. That hadn't been what she was expecting at all. She smiled and let her top drop down. Something in his words felt like a release. She felt a bubble of hilarity rise up inside. Such a relief, after all the fear.

'Fucking awful?' she repeated, but with a smile on her lips. 'Fucking awful?'

Paul sensed the change in her mood. 'Yes. Fucking awful, I'm afraid. Like a car crash, actually.' They both giggled then at the horror, the sheer impossibility of it all.

'Well, thanks,' said Sylvia. 'Nice to know you're being honest.'

'I'm sure that after the reconstruction it will—'

'It'll probably still be fucking awful,' said Sylvia. 'Be sure to tell me, won't you?'

'I will,' said Paul, smiling and reaching for her hand. 'You know whatever it looks like, it won't stop me loving you.'

And Sylvia did know that. Felt it afresh. After Rosa, she had started to think that maybe the love between them had dried up, but there it was again, welling up from somewhere. A surprise.

'Thank you,' she said then, squeezing his hand with both of hers. 'Thanks for everything. You are more than I ever deserved.'

* * *

Megan was circumspect about Sylvia's new body. Yet Sylvia caught her glancing at her chest. The girl knew that her sickness had been sited there, at her core.

'Do you want to ask me anything about my operation?' she said, aiming for casual, as she shuffled fish fingers from the baking tray onto melamine plates.

Jude was still upstairs. He had ignored her shouting at him to come and wash his hands. On a normal evening, she would have felt the anger rising, like cola spurting out of a shaken can. But one advantage of cancer was that she didn't seem to find her son as irritating as she previously had. Of all the silver linings, this was perhaps the sweetest.

'Did it hurt?' said Megan. She glanced at Sylvia.

'Yes,' said Sylvia, honestly. 'It really hurt. But it's the thing that is going to make Mummy better.'

'Are you going to die?' said Megan. She was looking at the table as she said that and her face reddened slightly. Sylvia realised that this was the question that her daughter had longed to ask her, all along, in those other careful chats she had orchestrated since the diagnosis.

What to say? She put down the baking tray and went over to squeeze Megan's shoulders. Her daughter had shot up recently and become more substantial. Her shoulders felt almost like those of a young woman.

'We're all going to die, Megs,' said Sylvia, softly. 'But now I've had this operation – and with the other treatment – I should live as long as everyone else, as long as I would have done before. But none of us know for certain what will happen.'

Megan nodded, satisfied. It was all she wanted to hear. But Sylvia spent the evening replaying the conversation in her mind. She was torn between the desire to offer maternal reassurance and the impossibility now of ever truly doing so.

Jude was also fascinated by what she had undergone. Unlike Megan, he begged to see where she had had her operation.

'No, Jude!' she said. 'I wouldn't show you my booby before and I'm not going to show you my non-booby now.'

'Please, Mum?' said Jude. 'I just want to look.'

Sylvia shook her head. She wasn't going to play to her son's sense of the macabre, always so finely honed. Instead of cars, or houses, or suns with smiling faces, Jude drew monsters with razor-jaws and distended eyeballs. It was as if he had an innate connection with the grotesque, but perhaps that was just small boys.

'Pleeeease?' said Jude. 'I just want to see what it's like.'

'No way!' She had stopped getting undressed before the children when she got pregnant with Rosa. Their scrutiny had started to get to her. She had felt enormous, like a huge hippo, and their beady witness made her self-conscious. But she remembered doing the same to Barbara. Staring, both fascinated and repulsed by her breasts, the bronze fur between her legs.

She didn't want to be assessed by her children or to be found wanting. She loved the way they had always taken her body as an extension of their own, little colonialists unaware of their privilege. Jude had annexed her right breast, now gone forever, as his dominion. To be separate, to be criticised, was distressing.

If Jude had found her gently sagging breasts amusing before, it was hard to know what he would make of the new battle scene on her chest. He would probably just shrug, insouciantly, but she worried that the image would stay with him forever, buried deep in his subconscious, knitted into his idea of adult womanhood. No, she wouldn't do that to him.

* * *

'I'm feeling much better, thanks,' she said to Natalia. She had avoided doing the school runs so far, but Paul had had to go in early that morning and so it was unavoidable. Natalia had determinedly made her way over to find her at drop-off.

'I'm just so terribly sorry for you,' said Natalia. 'After everything you went through with the baby ... This is the last thing you need.'

'Yes,' said Sylvia. 'It's certainly been, um, tricky.'

'I don't know how you are coping. But life is hard. I've been wanting to tell you that I lost a baby too. A girl. She came at twenty-two weeks.' Natalia stood stiffly. She had clearly screwed herself up to impart the information.

'Oh god, I'm sorry,' said Sylvia. This was what Natalia had tried to tell her outside the pub. She had known that night it was going to be something like this. Personal tragedy, she was learning, was like a magnet for other people's suffering, sucking all the horror towards you.

'She was breathing,' said Natalia, quietly. 'But they wouldn't do anything for her. Too young. They said she didn't have a single chance. So, they left her and after a while, she just stopped.'

'I'm so sorry,' said Sylvia, willing herself not to show her distress. She couldn't cope with this right now.

'Sometimes, I think . . .' Natalia paused. 'Well, you know . . . everything happens for a reason.'

Pow. There it was. The platitude that Sylvia found most grating. Along with 'What doesn't kill you makes you stronger.'

'Do you really think that?' she said, unable to stop herself. 'Do you really think that your baby died for a reason? Or my baby? You can't possibly think,' said Sylvia, unable to stop herself, 'that I've had my right breast cut off *for a reason*? Or are you just saying it, Natalia, for something to say, because it doesn't make me feel better, you know.'

'I was just trying to say that sometimes there can be good things that come out of bad,' muttered Natalia. She had coloured, her cheeks flushing a deep puce. 'I was only trying to be kind. To share.'

'There is no reason for most of what happens in life,' said Sylvia. 'I'm certain of it. So please don't offer me that bullshit.'

'You think you're better than me, don't you?' said Natalia. 'But you aren't. We are just the same. Just people.'

'You think I don't realise that?' said Sylvia. 'It doesn't mean that I want to hear every little detail of your life.'

Natalia recoiled, as if she had been hit. She shook her head slightly and then turned around, melting into the crowd of other mothers. The minute she was gone, Sylvia felt searing guilt. There was something so submissive about Natalia, it brought out her mean streak. The thought of what Megan would have said, if she had witnessed the scene, was like acid in her stomach. She pulled out her phone and rang Nush.

'I just gave Natalia P a bollocking,' she said.

'What for?'

'She told me that everything happens for a reason.'

'Oh god, she didn't? Well, she deserved everything she got then. Clearly,' said Nush.

'But she also told me that she had a premature baby who died. A little girl.' Sylvia's voice broke.

'Shit,' said Nush. 'But she was trying to be kind.'

'She wanted us to bond over our dead babies,' said Sylvia. 'Like we're part of some kind of club. I can't do it, Nush. I know it makes me a monster, but I just can't ...'

'Sssh,' said Nush. 'Don't beat yourself up. Get through this and you'll have the time and energy to be kind to Natalia P one day, I promise.'

41

Now

'Daddy!' Jude thundered in, as usual, shortly after 6 a.m. Paul had only been asleep for four hours. After they had abandoned the clothes and the manual, Nush had suggested they open a bottle of wine instead and they had stayed up for hours talking. About Sylvia, yes, but also about the children, Nush's family, Ryan, then music, politics, their conversation radiating out from the personal, the tragic, to their place in the world. As if they were meeting for the first time.

'What's Ryan's mum doing in yours and Mummy's bed?' said Jude, quizzical. Paul pushed himself up, confused, before remembering. At 3 a.m., he had realised that there weren't sheets on the spare bed and had suggested that Nush sleep in with him. There had been no ulterior motive. But part of him hadn't wanted to be back in the bedroom on his own, the wardrobe still open and Sylvia's clothes, like discarded snakeskins, in piles on the floor. Nush had paused, but then cheerfully agreed, 'Why not?' And now there she was, fast asleep, but identifiable by her cropped helmet of silver hair. 'Is it a girl or a boy?' he briefly pictured Dane-o snickering. Unlike Sylvia, she was a still sleeper and had hardly moved since they had passed out. He had woken once, but the regularity of Nush's breath had sent him back to sleep.

'We had a sleepover,' he whispered to Jude. 'Sometimes grown-ups do too. It got late and we were talking, so she fell asleep there. Shall we go downstairs and I'll put the television on?'

Jude narrowed his eyes and glanced again at Nush, but then acquiesced, letting Paul shepherd him out of the room, hand between his little shoulder blades.

'Is Ryan awake yet?' he said.

'No, Ryan always sleeps for ages,' grumbled Jude. 'It's boring.'

Paul wondered what it would be like to have a child who didn't wake first thing. He hadn't slept pass 6 a.m. since Jude was born. For a long time, it had been 4.30 a.m., every morning, which had almost broken Sylvia.

'Juice?' Paul himself drained a slug out of the carton of orange juice. It was still dark outside and the kitchen floor felt icy. Ted lifted his head from his bed wearily in greeting. Nobody apart from Jude wanted to be up at this hour of the day.

'Yes,' said Jude. 'I'm thirsty.' He looked as if he had been wrestling in the night; his hair was pasted to his forehead.

'Why are you so sweaty?' said Paul, passing Jude a glass.

'I don't know, Daddy,' said Jude, draining the plastic beaker. 'I get hot.'

'Hmm,' said Paul, glancing at his son. He reached out a hand to feel his forehead, which was in fact clammily cool. Despite his job, it had always been one of Sylvia's tasks to check the children's temperatures, to administer the medicine, to take them to the doctor's surgery. He felt a sudden stab of terror at this other facet of his newfound responsibility. But Jude seemed fine, humming to himself, jiggling in his seat. His stomach was still rounded, like the baby he had been just five minutes before, but his limbs were lengthening. He was starting to look even more like Sylvia, with those puppetty arms, rubbery lips and carrotty hair.

'Can you turn on Netflix yourself?' said Paul.

Jude nodded. Since Sylvia's death he had got scarily proficient with the remote controls. It was so tempting just to let him gorge himself on the screens, to keep him quiet, to still him, to forget for a while that he even existed at all. He ran from the room and Paul sighed.

'Morning,' said Nush, entering the room.

'Hi,' said Paul, carefully, standing up from where he had been bent over the dishwasher, aware of his boxer shorts, his skinny torso and the scarcity of his chest hair. Nush wore her clothes from the previous day and her face was creased with sleep. She looked younger than usual, less butch.

'Hey,' said Nush. 'Well, this is an early start.'

'It's actually not too bad for Jude,' said Paul. 'Thanks for staying. It was great to talk.'

'It was, wasn't it?' said Nush, smiling broadly. 'Are you making coffee?'

* * *

Later, after Nush and Ryan had left, Paul tidied up Sylvia's clothes. He wasn't ready to let them go yet, these reminders of who his wife had been. No matter her instructions. The slight thrill of realising he didn't have to do exactly what he was told after all. Cursing at the fiddliness of narrow-necked blouses, trousers to be folded along precise pleats, accessories to be inserted in monogrammed dust bags, he slowly got the job done.

He left the manual where Nush had placed it, on top of a pile of cashmere scarves. Then he glanced at the top shelf in the wardrobe. There was the shoebox Sylvia had mentioned. He brought it down, sitting on the armchair with it on his lap.

It was full of photographs he hadn't seen before. Teenage Sylvia in a Nirvana T-shirt and baggy jeans, heavy brown lip liner belying her short-lived attempt at grunge. She and Tess on the beach, arm in arm. One of her smoking on a park bench, breathtakingly thin.

There was also a collection of beer mats with numbers scribbled on them, the scalps of her conquests.

Then sheaves of letters. Many from Tess when Sylvia first went to university. Full of outlandish spellings and crossings out, the first insight Paul had had into his sister-in-law's dyslexia. Postcards from Tom, Sylvia's university boyfriend. A Valentine's card – *'To sexy Sylvia. You turn me on. Love from?'* The question mark a challenge. Then, squashed down at the bottom, a clutch of notes from Danny. In the rounded, childish bubble-writing of the Valentine's card and full of protestations of eternal love. Of needing to see her again. Of wanting her more than anyone else ever would. Queasy, Paul piled everything back into the box and put it back where it had been.

The hoard revealed Sylvia's romantic hinterland in a new light. There was Tom, of course, but aside from that, despite the many flings, it had only ever really been Danny – until she had met him. She had always seemed so worldly, but in fact her little secret had stunted her relationships, skewing her sense of herself.

42

Sylvia's Manual

I'm coming to an end. Of this, and of everything. I think I've said it all. You are as equipped as I can possibly leave you in the domestic minutiae of our lives. For the rest, you'll have to find your own way.

And yet, and yet. I still don't want to say goodbye to you, to us. I sleep for hours and I scarcely dream, but last night, I did. Of us. We were walking through mature trees, following a path into the forest, like a superannuated Hansel and Gretel. But Jude and Megan skipped ahead of us. Not quarrelling for once but laughing.

I don't know if I made it clear enough, but I never met anyone as good as you. There was no hidden agenda, you helped me – and everyone else – because you wanted to. You instinctively understood that it was the true route to happiness, whereas I spent so much time wrapped up in myself. You surprised me with your virtue. Your steadfast support of me and our children. It reminded me of William.

You showed me what it is to live in the present, to focus on what you have. A lesson I struggled to learn, but never tired of watching you teach.

I couldn't have chosen a better father and I know you're going to be ok. That's why I'm writing this really, I think. To say that it's all right to be ok. Don't feel guilty, even when you're in someone else's embrace. Remember me, but move on, decisively, up life's escalator.

I've decided that I'll probably be there, anyway. At the back of the church when Megan gets married (Megan is so conventional she will definitely choose a church). I'll be wearing a large hat and drawing attention to myself. Megan may be annoyed.

I'll be at the sidelines at sports' day, putting on an unseemly display of triumph when Jude wins a race. I'll be lurking behind the blue curtain on Jude's inevitable trips to A & E.

I'm going to be there, somehow, if I can swing it. I'm going to watch you get old, the lines in your dear face deepening, while I stay forever like this. Or no, actually, since I get to decide, I think I'll choose to be forever in my early thirties. After Megan and Jude were born. I was happiest with myself – my body and my mind – then. And it was thanks to you.

Hold the children tight. Tell them you love them. I know you find it hard to say, but you must. Whisper it into their cheeks at bedtime, mention it casually as you pour milk on cornflakes, toss it away as a greeting as you leave them at school. I want the words to be so familiar to them, they take them for granted.

I was the emotional one, the hugger, the shouter. But you need to take on that role now. It'll get easier as it becomes a habit. Everything does. Life is just the accumulation of habits, good and bad.

I know you won't smack Jude. You're far too patient for that. But you might want to, I'm afraid to say. There might come that time when he pushes you to the ragged edge of reason and you feel like jumping off.

I still remember the four occasions I did, burned into my memory with shame. The hot-headed hand on the back of his leg at the end of a torturous afternoon, when he refused to get into his bed and I could picture in my mind the gin and tonic waiting for me downstairs. I'm not proud of it. I wasn't perfect. But nobody ever loved that boy more than I did. Nobody understands him like I do. He has frequently driven me crazy, but the tenderness was always there.

As for Megan, she'll never drive you to the edge in the same way, but make sure that doesn't mean she drifts away. That she looks to someone other than you — Eliza Jenkins, heaven forbid — for emotional support. You need to keep her close, to tuck her under your wing like the baby bird she still is, until she can fly off on her own.

I've been thinking and I've decided I'm going to write letters for the children. For them to open on their eighteenth birthdays. For when I'm gone. I'd dismissed it as a simpering cliché, but I think I have to shy away from my lifelong tendency towards scepticism. After all, Jude will only have the vaguest memories of me when he's grown up. Megan will have more, but Jude's will be snatches, fragments open to interpretation.

A letter in my handwriting is a concrete thing. Nobody can take that away from him. I'm not going to type them up, just write them out when I've got a burst of strength. In that loopy longhand I use so seldom now, which makes my hands ache. Maybe ones for

Tess and Barbara, too, if I can find the strength. There's so much I assumed I'd still have time to say. If I tuck them in the back of this, will you hand them over? When it's time.

I know you will. I could always rely on you.

One last thing. It's taken all these words I've written to understand how important it is that I say this to you clearly. With a straight face. No snarking, for once. If you get the chance of happiness with someone else, please take it. Grab it hard and hold it close. Don't worry what anyone else says, know you have my blessing. You deserve it, my darling. You deserve everything good.

43

Then

'You need to do it. Grade one all over.' Sylvia brandished the clippers at Nush.

'Are you sure?'

'Completely sure. Open the Champagne and get on with it.'

'If you insist.' Nush popped the cork out of the dusty bottle. It was a vintage one that Sylvia and Paul had been given at their wedding, which had resided in the cellar ever since.

'I was saving it for a special occasion,' said Sylvia. 'This seems as special as anything else.'

Nush poured the acidic fizzy liquid into the two waiting glasses.

'Why are you having wine?' Ryan had appeared, solemn-eyed.

'It's just juice for mummies,' said Sylvia, matter-of-factly.

She had found a lock of her red hair on her pillow that morning. She had hidden it from Paul. She couldn't bear his face. He had always loved her hair.

'That's right,' said Nush.

'Jude won't let me have a go on Minecraft,' said Ryan. Jude was selfish with his toys and his computer games, but he was normally better at sharing with Ryan than anyone else. But in her years of being his mother, Sylvia had realised that Jude sniffed out tension like a bloodhound and started to act up, even when it was carefully concealed like the lock of hair she flushed down the toilet that morning. His intransigence with Ryan would be because of what was happening to her, she was certain of it.

'That's not true,' Jude barrelled into the room, indignant. 'I was just building this really cool church and Ryan is so rubbish he was going to ruin it.'

'Let him have a go,' said Sylvia reflexively. She wanted the boys out of the room, safely sequestered behind their digital babysitter. Megan was at Eliza Jenkins's house. This was her window to do this. She needed to be shorn before Paul got home.

'No,' said Jude, rudely.

'You can have crisps,' said Sylvia, reaching into the snack drawer and tossing packets at the boys. Their eyes lit up. 'But go away. And Jude – share!'

As they left the room Sylvia felt the need to apologise to Nush for her son and her lackadaisical parenting.

'I'm sorry. I just wanted some peace. I know I'm a terrible mother.'

'Don't worry,' said Nush. 'It's a hard time for everyone. A few snacks aren't going to hurt anyone ...'

'But Jude, he ...'

'Jude's fine,' Nush reassured her. 'Now chin-chin.'

They both took a swig of Champagne. Sylvia thought of the last time she had drunk it, in her red dress with Megan inside her, expectant in every sense and happier than she had ever believed possible.

'Mmm. The good stuff,' she said. 'I'm only drinking this from now on.'

'It could get to be an expensive habit,' said Nush, eyeing Sylvia draining her glass.

'I haven't got time to waste on cheap alternatives,' said Sylvia. This was a philosophy she was applying in other areas. Since her diagnosis, she had gone on a spending spree, buying foundations, concealers, sparkly primers, lipsticks the colour of watermelon and coral. She had bought impractical studded jeans, a ruinously expensive handbag and a pair of chunky heels, which still sat in their box, encased in tissue paper. Paul was going to freak when he saw the credit card bill. But she wasn't going to hold back now. Who knew how much time she had left and shopping soothed her like nothing else.

'Don't say that,' said Nush, evenly, but she didn't look at Sylvia. 'Shall we do this?'

Sylvia nodded. Nush started at the back, moving the clippers up around Sylvia's scalp. A hank of hair, the colour of a ginger-nut biscuit, fell onto the kitchen floor.

Sylvia held her breath. She had no idea who she was going to be without her hair. It had defined her and Tess from her earliest memories. From the rude comments ('Oi, ginge!') to the men who fondled it, incredulous, confessing their fantasies.

'You all right?' said Nush.

'I'm ok. It's just weird ... that's all.'

'I actually think this could look really good,' said Nush, kindly. Sylvia swallowed.

'I'm just not waiting for it all to come out in my hands,' she said. 'I couldn't bear that.'

'Quite right,' said Nush. 'I like a short crop myself, as you know. More distinguished. You're never going to look back.'

'You'll look after them, won't you? If I'm not here,' said Sylvia, not turning her face around. Nush looked down at her friend's head, half shaven and half still long.

'Ssssh,' she said.

'I mean it,' said Sylvia. 'Promise you will.' She turned around then and gripped Nush's arm.

'Ok,' said Nush. 'I promise.'

Sylvia sighed with relief and turned back. Nush continued the job in silence, until it was all gone, Sylvia's hair, spilling like so much orange paint onto the wooden floor.

'I had no idea there was so much of it,' said Sylvia, sadly. So many things she had taken for granted. 'You know Rosa had red hair?' she said to Nush, then. It had struck her afresh. That connection she had had to her baby girl.

Nush placed the clippers down. 'Yes,' she said. 'You told me that. I'll sweep this up.'

'Do you think she would have looked like me when she grew up?' said Sylvia, grimacing a little.

'She would have been lucky if she did,' said Nush, levelly.

'Wait. I want to keep it,' said Sylvia, reaching out to stay Nush's hand as she moved towards the bin with the full dustpan and brush.

'Do you think that's a good idea?' said Nush. 'What are you going to do with it?'

'Sit in a darkened room and mourn my lost beauty, of course,' said Sylvia.

'All right, boss,' said Nush. 'Whatever you say.'

* * *

Later, after Nush had taken Ryan home, Sylvia had looked at herself properly in the mirror.

It didn't look deliberate. She didn't look like some hip girl trying to look edgy. She looked vulnerable and weak. A victim. There was nothing to distract from the pale translucence of her skin and she noticed afresh a fine fretwork of veins at the corner of her temples. Green under white flesh.

'Cool!' Jude had said when he saw her. 'Your hair is even shorter than mine.'

But Megan had been horrified after she collected her from Eliza's house.

'Mummy! You should have told me,' she said in the car home. 'What do you think Eliza's mummy thought?'

'I don't really care what Eliza's mummy thought,' said Sylvia. But it was a lie. Carly Jenkins was a big, slow-moving woman with a mane of shiny black hair. She had gestured to Sylvia's skinhead.

'Wow!'

'I know,' Sylvia had said, running her hand over her scalp. 'Nush did it this afternoon. It was going to go anyway.'

'It looks great,' said Carly. But Sylvia could see the pity in her eyes. Carly was a nice, but deeply conventional, woman. It was a mystery as to how she had produced a child such as Eliza, and she was, as a result, blind to the true extent of her daughter's subversiveness. But Sylvia recognised Eliza as one of her own and wished, selfishly, that Megan could have chosen another friend.

'Thanks,' said Sylvia. She knew she didn't look good.

'You look like an old man!' said Eliza Jenkins, clapping her hand to her mouth to contain the giggle that threatened to bubble out.

'Thanks, Eliza,' said Sylvia as her mum said simultaneously, 'Eliza! Be nice!'

Megan had been silent, but Sylvia could read the discomfort on her face. The cancer itself was so hidden, even her mastectomy had been concealed from the world. This was such a flamboyant statement of what was wrong with her, she could understand why her daughter hated it.

'I had to do it, Megs,' she said. 'It was going to fall out anyway and this way it's more even.'

'But your hair was so pretty,' said Megan. 'You don't look like a mummy without it. You don't look like you.'

'It'll grow back,' said Sylvia. 'One day.'

Paul was the one she dreaded the most. She chickened out as she heard the front gate clink, rushing upstairs for a headscarf and looping it around her head.

'What happened here, then?' said Paul. He was trying to sound light-hearted, she could tell. Since Rosa, she could see the joins in Paul's good-naturedness. She was starting to understand that it was a stance he assumed, not just a genetically bestowed preponderance of serotonin.

'It started falling out,' said Sylvia. 'So Nush shaved it off. We drank Champagne.' Her attempt to make it sound like a fun event sounded flat. It hadn't been fun. Not at all. Nush had stopped after a single glass.

'Working first thing tomorrow,' she had said. 'Got to take Ryan back.' So, Sylvia had finished the bottle herself. Carly Jenkins had probably been able to smell the sour alcohol on her breath. She almost certainly hadn't been safe to drive.

'Let me see,' said Paul, quietly. Another physical revelation, so quick on the heels of the last.

'Ok.' She untied the knot in the headscarf. Her fingers felt rough against the silk.

'Oh, Sylv.' Paul held her then, not tenderly like a lover, but squeezing her tight, like a drowning man clutching a piece of driftwood.

'I think she looks cool,' said Jude. He and Megan were watching, from the kitchen table, where they were eating soggy fusilli.

'Ooof, you're hurting me, Paul,' said Sylvia. But still he held her, as if releasing the embrace and stepping back to look at her again was too much. Finally, he let go. He didn't say anything else but turned towards the children as if he couldn't bear to look.

Sylvia's eyes filled. So, this was how it was going to be now. She would be unseen. Unregarded. The invisible woman.

44

Now

'Hello? Is that Jude's dad?' said the female voice. 'It's Carrie from the school.' Paul pictured the receptionist, her hair always twisted on top of her head into an intricate bun, like a stale Danish pastry. One of the people, once entirely peripheral to his life, who had now assumed a more central role since Sylvia's death.

'Is everything ok?' said Paul, glancing at the surgery clock. It was only midday and he was about to start a complicated operation on a whippet's distended bowel.

'Actually, there's been a bit of an incident,' she said. Paul pictured Jude nipping another child, refusing to sit down on the carpet, throwing a piece of Meccano.

'What's he done now?' he said, wearily.

'Nothing. Actually, your son had a little dizzy spell earlier. He fainted in the playground. He seems absolutely fine now but we think you should come and get him. He might need to see a doctor.'

'I'll send someone to get him right away,' said Paul. For a second he wondered if he should drop everything and rush to the school. But he only needed a couple of hours. He flicked through the recent numbers on his phone. Nush. Natalia. Barbara. These women who he had grown so reliant upon in the absence of his wife. He opted for Natalia. She was always so accommodating, made things so easy.

'Natalia, I am so sorry to ask but can you collect Jude? The school rung and he's been a bit poorly. Fainted.'

'Oh, my goodness, poor Jude. Is he ok?'

'Yes, I'm sure he is,' said Paul. 'Probably just ran around too much without drinking enough water. It's just I'm about to start an op ...'

'I'll be there,' she said.

*   *   *

Jude was sitting on the sofa with Alvin when Paul finally got back, watching ninjas battling with sticks on the screen. A bit pale, perhaps, but otherwise reassuringly his usual self. Scuffed knees and a biro tattoo on the back of his hand.

'Dad!' he said to Paul. 'I fainted at school.' He sounded proud.

'I heard. Poor you. How are you feeling now?' He put his hand on Jude's forehead, which was moist, amphibian.

'Oh fine,' said Jude, airily, his eyes already straying back to the screen.

Paul went to the kitchen where Natalia was softening onions in a pan. She was playing music on her phone and there was a bunch of red tulips lolling in the centre of the kitchen table, which she must have bought. Paul certainly hadn't.

'Thanks for saving the day.'

'No problem,' she said. 'He seems ok, I think – nothing to worry about.' She smiled at him, reassuringly, and reached for the pepper grinder, so at home in the kitchen. Paul thought of all the times he had come home to Sylvia, standing in exactly the same place. Instead of Natalia's measured welcome, she would usually rush into his arms, shouting, 'Thank God you're home. The children are driving me mad! I've decided we're going to have to sell them.' The thought of his wife made him pause. She would have almost certainly overreacted to Jude fainting, would never have been able to display Natalia's calm response to it. But, nonetheless, he didn't think he needed to take Jude to the doctor unless it happened again. Children fainted all the time.

* * *

'Paul. Darling. Is everything all right? The children?' Barbara on the phone. She sounded as if she were out, there was the sound of genteel conversation in the background, silver scraping porcelain.

'Yes. We're ok. Well, Jude passed out at school today, actually. But he seems totally back to normal now. They're both asleep.' Paul was sitting on his bed, stroking the fur around Ted's ears. Softer than the rest of him, finest velveteen. He had resisted having Ted in the bedroom for a long time – he had always insisted Sylvia couldn't, after all – but in the last few weeks he had relented. Something about the little dog soothed him, even more effectively than the pills.

'He fainted?' Barbara's voice was concerned. 'Jude?'

'Yes,' said Paul. 'But he's fine. I really don't think it was such a big deal. He was on the trampoline again before dinner.'

'But you'll take him to the doctor to get checked out anyway? No, no ice, please.' He could hear her instructing someone in the background.

'I'm not sure that is necessary,' said Paul. 'It was just a touch of low blood pressure, I'm certain. I need to make sure he keeps hydrated at school. He'd forgotten his water bottle.'

'I could come and see him in the morning,' said Barbara.

'Really, there's no need ...' Paul thought of Barbara turning up as he tried to get the children out of the house. Exhorting Jude to brush his teeth, wash his face, put on his shoes. Simple tasks that, with five minutes to get out of the door, always bloated into impossibility. The idea of doing it with an audience even worse.

'It's no trouble,' said Barbara. 'I'll see you at eight.'

45

For my sister

Dearest Tess (Tessy, Tesselate, Tassle, Test, plus all the other dubious nicknames I gave you),
I don't really remember life before you were in it. My memories appear to start the day you were brought home from hospital, wrapped in that felt baby blanket you still sleep with, although I know you'll try to deny it. I was so over-excited about having a little sister, I remember trying to kiss you too enthusiastically and our parents telling me to stop.

I couldn't believe my luck. I'd longed for a companion and there you were. Scrunched but perfect. The sweetest sidekick. And with every day that passed, you only became more engaging. Smiling, reaching, laughing, learning to bum shuffle. Even as a baby, you had that ease in yourself.

As soon as you could walk properly, you followed me around, always entranced at whatever make-believe game I had started, happy to be Robin to my Batman. I took your devotion entirely for granted.

There were so many things that belonged only to us. Such as the hairdressing salon we set up for our beleaguered, shorn Sindy dolls, the favoured spots on the cliff where we would play, the injured grasshopper we kept hidden in our room for a week, dying a slow death while we remained convinced we could nurse it back to health. The times you would climb into my top bunk and we would stare at the glow stars on our bedroom ceiling holding hands, breath in sync, before falling asleep.

After Barbara left, it was you that comforted me. A pattern that continued as we grew up. You always told me things would be ok, that we'd be ok, because we had each other. Whenever anything notable in my life happened – good or bad – you were the first person I would think about telling. You still are.

When I was being melodramatic – which, let's face it, was often – you had a particular knack for making me see sense. You could always take the sting out of things, make me laugh at my own absurdity.

Now I'm so terrified that our secret stories, the ones we shared for so many years, will just melt away, because they are too weird and specific to try and explain to anyone else. Like the message we wrote every year in each other's birthday card. 'Happy Birthday Sizzle!' The word you used for sister when you were three, before you knew better. Every time we'd howl with laughter when we opened the envelope, but writing it down now, I see it wasn't really that funny at all. It was just shorthand for our history, what we'd shared.

I don't think I'm going anywhere after this. How I wish I did. But if I did believe in heaven, I think it would most closely resemble a July evening on the cliff when we were kids. Playing a game of tag with whichever random children were staying in the nearest holiday house, running across heather under the yawning sky. A sense of absolute freedom and bliss, my little sister just behind me somewhere, trying to keep up.

I assumed you'd always look at me in that way you did, as if I had all the answers, as if I was something special. I never imagined that I'd be the one to ruin things.

I'm just so sorry for what I did. So desperately sorry. The thought of the betrayal still won't go away. It's like the itch of a phantom limb. I don't know what I was thinking. It was so reckless, so stupid, so self-involved. I'd do anything to take it back, to have been better.

I want you to know that I've told Paul. I've written him a manual, for how to look after our family, for when I'm gone, and – in the end – it was so obvious to me that I needed to be honest. I want my children to know you properly, you see. That's really my final wish. I couldn't have had a better sister. I can't think of a better auntie for Jude and Megan. You're the key to a certain version of me, the original and perhaps the truest. But they can't be close to you if there are still secrets lingering around, making things weird.

I wish I could tell you how it feels. Lying here, right

now, knowing that I haven't got long. I couldn't explain it to anyone else. Not even Paul or my beautiful children. Certainly not our mother. But if I hadn't changed things between us, I'd be able to tell you, I know I would. You could always grasp what I meant, even if I didn't articulate it well. Sibling telepathy. So, let me explain it now because I know you can take it. There are intervals of relief, when I'm truly in the present, making the most of whatever I have left. But at night, the loneliness rolls in. The fear. I try to be brave but I'm just so scared, Tessy. I'm leaving when I still had so much to do.

I'm thinking now of that final afternoon, when you came to my house unannounced. It had been so long since we had made proper eye contact. It was too difficult. But that, at least, was how it used to be and I hold the memory close now, a comfort, as I come to the end. No barriers, just light, warmth, tenderness. We talked about Mum and Dad, those summers outside, the history nobody but us could ever know. Your hands in mine, your face opposite, so like my own, a mirror to my better self. If I shut my eyes, I can see it now.

I love you so much. I always did.

Sylvia xxx

46

Then

After a while, Sylvia understood that a part of her enjoyed the horrified glances she drew in the street. She had been looked at for so long by other people admiringly, she wasn't ready to slide into the background.

It was painful not to be found attractive, but her bald head carried with it drama. Sideways looks, the mothers who clamped a hand over their curious child's mouth, were preferable to being completely ignored.

This was particularly true on the gauntlet of the school run. The first time that Abigail Greenwood saw Sylvia's denuded head, she saw the other woman's eyes pop with a kind of fury. She knew what Abigail was thinking, behind the sympathy that she would doubtless exhibit: Who would do that? Who would draw attention to themselves like that?

Sylvia had feigned nonchalance for so long, but now she really didn't care. Cancer had focused her mind on what really mattered. Paul, Megan, Jude and Rosa.

But it was Megan who broke her resolve in the end. The look on Megan's face at school pick-up time. The fractional raise of Eliza Jenkins's eyebrows, barely perceptible.

The wig was nicknamed Donald. A sandy-peach-coloured bob, which had cost close to a £1,000, it let Sylvia pass unremarked on the street.

'You look lovely today,' said Abigail approvingly, the first time she wore it on the school run. 'You must feel so much better.'

Sylvia bit her tongue and tried not to scratch her head. Despite his vast cost, Donald was itchy and uncomfortable. She just nodded. Since she had been cruel to Natalia, she'd tried to stay her tongue more often. Cancer was no excuse.

Natalia had been avoiding her ever since and Sylvia's guilt had mushroomed. She sometimes dreamed of the other woman and of their two lost babies, swaddled and asleep.

That morning, she sought her out and gestured to Donald.

'Strong look for me, wouldn't you say?' she said to Natalia, who frowned and looked unsure how to respond. 'Don't worry,' said Sylvia, gloomily, 'I know it looks terrible, I'm only joking.'

'Ah,' said Natalia, the corners of her eyes crinkling. 'A joke.'

'I wanted to say sorry,' said Sylvia, scratching the nape of her neck. 'I am sorry that I didn't want to hear about your daughter. That I wasn't sympathetic. I'm sorry that happened to you. I've just been having a hard time ... processing everything.'

'Ok,' said Natalia.

'Ok what?' said Sylvia.

'I accept your apology.' Natalia smiled. 'Life is hard, but unless we can share it with other people, it's pointless. That's what my mother always used to say.' She reached out and gripped both of Sylvia's hands. 'You are a special person, Sylvia, and I forgive you.'

'You forgive me?' said Sylvia, echoing the words. Until Natalia has said them aloud, she hadn't realised that was, in fact, what she longed for.

'I do,' said Natalia. 'We all make mistakes.'

*   *   *

It was after that that Natalia's meals started. Her hearty dinners, delivered without fanfare to their doorstep.

'She's making me feel even worse,' Sylvia groaned, after a particularly labour-intensive batch of pierogi were delivered with a shy smile. 'I was a cow to her and she's being so generous.'

'Don't worry about it,' said Paul. 'She obviously likes you. Don't look a gift horse in the mouth and all that. And these things are delicious.' He popped a neatly moulded dumpling into his mouth.

'But what does she want from me, Paul? I feel like she needs something I can't give. I can't repay all this. I can hardly get out of bed at the moment, I'm so exhausted. Her husband and family, apart from Alvin, are all in Poland. It's like she wants to be part of our family somehow. She wants us to adopt her.'

'Don't overthink it,' said Paul. 'She's just being thoughtful. She's been a lot more helpful than most of the other parents at the school.'

'It's true,' said Sylvia. 'But I don't even want this food. I know I'm supposed to keep my strength up but I feel so sick ...'

'I'll eat it,' said Paul.

'She's not the one, Paul,' said Sylvia, quietly, watching him chew. 'Not her.'

'What are you talking about?' said Paul. 'She's just being kind.'

47

Now

'What made you suspect?' said the consultant. He was a large, florid, cheery man, in quite a different mode from Dr Z's millennial smoothness. He looked as though he drank heavily, skied, holidayed in the Dordogne.

'I just … it was actually his grandmother,' said Paul. 'Her own mother died in slightly mysterious circumstances and she put two and two together, worked out that maybe there was some kind of family history. He always got sweaty when he was running around and then, well, he fainted at school.'

Paul thought of the morning after he had told Barbara about Jude fainting, how she turned up before the school run, already in heels and make-up, as if she had been awake for hours. She had clopped straight towards the kitchen dresser, where the photograph of Dora had been propped up since Jude had unearthed it.

'I couldn't sleep last night,' she said, musingly, picking up the picture. 'You know they never knew what my mother died of.' Barbara had looked at Paul. 'But I remember my father was convinced it had something to do with her *heart*. I think you need to take Jude to the doctor after all.'

Paul had slowly nodded, his eyes snagged on the back of his son's head. Barbara's words made his previous dismissal of the fainting incident seem foolhardy. So he had braved his aversion to the doctor's surgery and argued persuasively for a referral.

'Well, it was very clever of you both,' said the consultant, agreeably. 'He has got a weak valve and it could have caused significant problems for him. But, luckily, it's easy enough to repair these things nowadays. A fairly major operation, but he'll be all right.'

They both glanced at Jude, who sat uncharacteristically still in the chair. He was staring out of the room's window, at a patch of grey London sky in which, improbably, a seagull whirled.

'Do you hear that, Jude?' said Paul. 'You're just going to need an op, but it's going to make sure that you're good and healthy. So you can run around.'

'He should notice he has more energy,' said the consultant, smiling as he wrote.

'That's not really been an issue,' said Paul. 'He's always had plenty of that.'

'Ah, a boisterous boy?' said the cardiologist. 'I've got three of those at home. Older now. Teenagers. You and your wife must have your work cut out.'

'My mummy is dead,' said Jude then, expressionlessly. 'She died of cancer. Breast cancer.'

'Oh goodness, I'm so sorry ...' said the doctor. His smile dropped and Paul felt a burning need to resurrect it, to restore the man's refreshing optimism. You sensed that, despite his profession, the things he must have seen, this was someone who expected good things of the world. Well-fed holidays, trips to the opera, chilled glasses of Sancerre. A gloss of everyday civilisation, like thick paint covering mortality's cracks.

'It's ok,' said Paul. 'It's all right. Really.'

'That's a really hard thing to go through when you're so young,' said the consultant.

'She sometimes comes to watch me when I'm going to sleep,' said Jude.

Paul was uneasy, concerned the doctor would think he had encouraged Jude's imaginings.

'Ah, a ghost?' said the doctor, hands on his knees and leaning slightly forwards.

'You believe me?' said Jude, looking the doctor in the face. 'Nobody else does.'

'It's ok,' said the florid doctor. 'Life is a funny old thing. I'm a doctor and I still believe in the unexpected. What's important is that you are going to be ok, Jude. You are going to be well and you are going to have a fabulous life.' He turned to Paul before asking gently, 'Are *you* ok, Dad?'

Paul shrugged. No one had asked him how he felt, even when his wife was dying. Nobody ever really had. It wouldn't have occurred to Miriam. Discussing feelings wasn't her thing. And through Sylvia's illness – and death – he had been the sounding board for other people's responses to it.

'It will probably always be hard,' said the older man. 'But it does get easier. Not so all-consuming. And your boy is going to be fine. Better than fine.'

*   *   *

Jude had thrown the covers back. The figurine he had fallen asleep clutching – a plastic ninja like the ones he loved to watch on screen, probably made by a child his age in a distant factory – had fallen from his hand. He looked so sweet, so vulnerable in sleep. Impossible to imagine the rage he could manifest and inspire.

Paul watched his chest rise and fall, as well as he could in the half light of the room. The idea of Jude being in any way at risk seemed ridiculous. He was a life force, as irrepressible and infuriating as his mother had been. But she had gone and Jude was just mortal, after all, too.

'I'm sorry, Jude,' he said quietly. He wasn't sure what for exactly. But he knew that he repented, for not trying hard enough to understand his child, for wishing for so long that he was someone different. 'Things are going to change.'

Jude murmured something in his sleep, as if in response. Paul couldn't understand what it was, but the words sounded happy. He noticed how damp he was, the hair around his temples darkened with moisture. He thought of Sylvia's pulse, towards the end. How he would loosely hold her wrist, as if in pure affection, pretending not to check it. That thread of life that kept an individual tethered.

Eventually he lay down, uncomfortably squeezed in the

single bed, littered as it was with toys. As he drifted off, he imagined he glimpsed Sylvia for a minute, standing by the door, watching them both, her expression peaceful.

48

For my mother

Dear Mum,

It's so hard to write this to you. Words are your thing, after all. And how to find the right ones to say goodbye? I know I'll lack the requisite eloquence, insight, tenderness. But I have to try, because some things just can't be said aloud.

Having my own children should have helped me understand you better. But instead it did the reverse, dilating the gap between us. With the weight of a baby against my chest, I found it harder to comprehend your leaving. When Megan called for me in the night, I remembered doing the same for you after you had gone, the ache when I realised that you weren't ever coming.

William did his best. But no man can ever be a mother, as I'm terrified Paul is going to find out. The muscle memory of carrying someone inside you for nine months persists. When a mother bears a child, their cells mingle.

It's an actual scientific fact. Both turn into chimeras, harbouring fragments of the other.

Cells from Jude and Megan are knitted into my body, bones and brain. Likewise, my cells still float in you. A comforting thought. That you'll be carrying a part of me, still, when I'm gone.

Perhaps you can use that essence to help Paul with the children. Pride always stopped me telling you the ways in which I saw you in both of them, but they were there. Flickers of continuity. The lines around Megan's mouth when she smiled, Jude's implacable self-belief.

In all honesty, the thought of you in the cliff house, hanging laundry and weeding the vegetable patch, seems farcical. You belonged somewhere else, you followed your own destiny. It's just taken me until now to see that clearly. I'll never completely understand it (why couldn't we come, too?) but in many ways, you were a better role model than I realised.

After all, you've never put the weight of your own happiness on me, as so many parents do. I never worried that I owed you something – quite the reverse. Even now, you have never burdened me with the weight of your own grief. I witness it sometimes, when I catch you looking at me, but you don't parade it. You showed me that we are responsible for ourselves. The importance of work and fun. Of just getting on with it.

Indirectly, you offered up a masterclass in the ambiguities of motherhood. When you first go home from hospital with a bundle to keep alive through the night, it's terrifying, yet also straightforward. Looking after them well becomes so much more complicated as the years go by. Before having children, I assumed it was possible – desirable – to make things perfect for them. I now appreciate that 'good enough' is just that.

There are so many memories of happy times before you left, that suddenly, miraculously, I find no longer hurt. Milk teeth treated with the reverence of diamonds. The walk we used to do, up to the coastguard station on the top of the headland, with the 180-degree view of the sea. The stories you'd made up along the way, about fairies living in the granite, mermaids darting over rip tides. Afternoons on the beach, wrapped in a towel after a swim, tucked in the crook of your arm, squinting at the horizon.

Even the later ones have lost their sting. The times Tess and I came to see you in the city. Our introduction to oysters, pavlova, bitter marmalade, the finer nuances of the class system. How to pop prosecco corks and discuss politics. All the stuff outside William's frame of reference. An education.

It's just so hard, isn't it? Life. All of it. Confusing, messy, wonderful. It always feels like you're working towards something, but now I understand that's not really true. I see clearly that you did your best.

I always loved you so much. Even my anger was only because I always wanted more from you. More love, more attention, more time. As if you were a cake that could be constantly sliced.

I know that when Tess and I fell out, it broke your heart.

But it wasn't her fault, I want you to know. It was mine. So I've done my best to mend it now. The best legacy I could think of to leave.

I've been trying to describe the feeling I had when you hugged me the other day. A sort of sad, sweet ache in my chest that lingered for hours after you had left. Then I realised that it most closely resembled homesickness. But rather than being homesick for a location, I was homesick for a person. You. My mother. The place from where I came and now, I feel convinced, the place to which I shall in part return, carried in your shirt pocket. Safe at last.

Your loving daughter,

Sylvia x

49

Now

His key in the lock. The house quiet, but signs of Natalia's presence. The alpine smell of her preferred fabric conditioner, an undertow of fried garlic. Her phone on the side, next to a pile of ironing. She insisted on pressing his boxer shorts into crisp corners. An indulgence he was starting to take for granted, although he couldn't quite shake off the lingering sense of Sylvia's scorn.

His afternoon appointments had been cancelled at the last minute. He was looking forward to collecting the children from school himself, the look on their faces as they came to the door. Ted climbed out of his basket, moving slowly to greet Paul.

'Where is she, boy?' said Paul. Probably redistributing laundry, squeezing bleach, harvesting Lego from Jude's carpet. How hard it would be to cope without her. She was running the house, no longer merely cleaning it.

He moved out of the kitchen, slipped off his shoes to go

upstairs. There was the sound of movement from his bed-room, the squeak of the floorboards. He paused outside the door. It was easy to imagine for a second that it was Sylvia inside, getting ready for something, ready to throw her arms around his neck. He pushed it open.

'Paul!' Natalia's face was aghast. 'I didn't expect you back yet …' Behind her Sylvia's wardrobe was open, his wife's garments – which he had hung up again neatly – exposed. Natalia's own sober clothes were folded on the armchair and she was wearing the green satin dress that Sylvia had wanted Paul to keep for Megan. It was alarmingly low-cut and Paul averted his eyes from her sharp collar bones, the cleavage normally kept under wraps. In an instant, Natalia's face had reddened with embarrassment, the colour seeping down her neck.

'What … what's going on?' said Paul. 'That's Sylvia's,' he said, gesturing towards the dress. Stating the obvious.

'I know. I'm so sorry,' said Natalia. Her face so flushed it looked painful. 'I just … I suppose I just wanted to know what it would feel like … to be her. Sylvia. To imagine just for a minute.' She stared at the floor. 'It was stupid. I know. I'm so sorry. I don't know what I was thinking.' She crossed her arms, holding onto her elbows, refusing to look at him.

Paul didn't reply for a moment. He stared beyond her, at dust motes dancing in a sunbeam. Beneath his own mortifi-cation lay a thin seam of anger. How dare she?

'I'll let you get changed,' he said, moving away. 'Then I think we should talk.'

* * *

306

'Why doesn't Natalia make supper any more?' Jude squirted ketchup over his flaccid fish fingers, mournfully.

Paul's eyes met those of Nush. She had dropped Ryan off for a sleepover and was drinking a beer, perched on a stool at the kitchen island.

'She got too busy with other stuff,' he said. After the dress incident, he had told Natalia he didn't need her help any more. As he said the words he had felt relieved. The question that had been lingering between them finally resolved. By that point, Natalia had stopped blushing, had resumed her accommodating diffidence. But she, too, seemed accepting, agreeing without complaint. Then Paul had finally rung Svetlana, who was cleaning, but nothing else. No mopping up of the indefinable domestic load, no proxy mothering. He was going to have to find his own way.

'So, what happened there?' asked Nush, after the boys had gone into the garden and Megan had left the room. Paul told her the story of finding Natalia wearing Sylvia's dress.

'Well, don't say I didn't warn you,' said Nush, laughing, slapping her thighs.

'It's not funny,' said Paul. He still felt embarrassed by what had happened, complicit. But as Nush continued to chuckle, hysteria rose in his own throat, bursting out into something halfway between a sob and a laugh. Shame dissolving.

'Jesus,' said Nush. 'She *was* keen. That tickled me. It's so weird.' She ran her fingers through her hair in a gesture that suddenly occurred to Paul he liked. He had never been able to fathom her romantic misadventures, but she was someone who grew more compelling as you got to know her. The dimple that appeared in her right cheek as she talked. The ragged rim of golden brown around her pupils, which segued into a darker hue. Even the whorls of grey hair that sprung from her temples no longer seemed like an admission of defeat.

She was so different from Sylvia. So much plainer and calmer. He was shocked to find that he liked this divergence. For so long, his life had been set by Sylvia's tempo. Frenetic, exciting, anxiety-inducing. He had almost forgotten that it could be another way. There was something of Alice's calmness in Nush, but she was less conventional.

Jude slipped in from the garden.

'Can we get an ice cream, Dad? Please? From the cornershop?' said Jude.

'It's freezing, Jude,' protested Paul. 'It's not ice-cream weather.'

'It is for me,' said Jude. 'I don't feel cold.' And it was true, Jude had always run hot, warmed by his own kinetic energy. He hated coats, the restrictive bulk of them. It had been something he and Sylvia had fought with him about constantly, as the weather started to chill. Jude had generally won, tearing up to school in his polo shirt, playing football in the park in shorts in sleet. But since their trip to the consultant, Paul had become more insistent, not allowing Jude to play outside without his jacket.

'How about I make a hot chocolate?' said Nush, deftly redirecting Jude's focus.

'Yay, hot chocolate,' said Jude, jumping up and down on the spot. 'Ryan, Megs, come in. We're going to have hot chocolate!'

Megan emerged back into the room, shucked off her own coat, her limbs colt-like as she moved. Paul could see Sylvia. He was starting to realise that she would always be with him, in the form of Jude and Megan. Her gestures and mannerisms surfacing like flowers under melting snow.

'Can we have cream on top?' said Jude.

'Jude,' said Paul, wearily. 'You are completely incorrigible.'

'He's all right,' said Nush, in that way she had that made him believe her. Everything was all right for Nush. She saw accidents, disease and death on almost a daily basis, but the core of her was steady.

'What's incorr—' said Jude, stopping and frowning.

Megan stood beside him and smiled. 'It means that you never stop,' she said. 'Nothing puts you off.'

Jude looked up, smiled fractionally, as if graciously acknowledging a compliment.

'He is completely incorrigible,' she said. 'But we like him that way, don't we, Daddy?'

Paul smiled, only later turning her words over in his head. Perhaps he did like his son this way, just as he was. It was an idea he was only just getting used to.

50

*For Megan Clarke, to be opened on
the occasion of her 18th birthday.*

Dear Megan,
Lying here, writing this to you, I'm overwhelmed with
memories. They keep flying up, moving together, like a
murmuration of starlings into a twilit sky.

The baby you were. So serious and sweet. Your gummy,
open smile. And the hours we spent together. All the good
stuff, before things got hard. Jumping in muddy puddles,
stories on the sofa, babycinos dusted with chocolate,
choosing clementines in the fruit shop. Eternities spent
walking slowly between the library, the park and our
living room. That funny thing about motherhood, as I'm
sure you'll discover yourself one day – time stretches and
contracts, simultaneously.

Nobody could have asked for a better baby. You made it
easy on me, from the start. I was a selfish, overgrown girl
before I discovered I was pregnant, but the minute I heard
your heartbeat, everything changed. Mistakes happen, but

sometimes, my love, they can turn out to be the making of us.

You were always so gentle, calm and bright. I remember taking you to be weighed, at the mother and baby clinic, when you were about six weeks old. It was freezing outside, sleet pulsing down from dark afternoon skies. You were toggled up in a snowsuit, just like all the other babies. But while they all screamed as they were stripped down, you were totally unfazed. As I transferred your body to the weighing scales, so like a butcher's, I saw another mother, frazzled and jiggling a bawling baby, glance over at you enviously. Such a perfect little girl.

I kept waiting for the catch. Jaundice, or colic, or sleep issues. I anticipated a problem, syringing orange-flavour Infacol into your rosebud mouth, corking it with a dummy, swaddling you tightly in muslin. But it didn't come. You fed well, slept well and were happy to lie in your cot, looking at your mobile while I had a shower. You rolled, sat up and clapped precisely on schedule. Your father and I were novices, but you showed us the way. When you laughed at four months as Ted sniffed your little feet, I thought I'd never heard a nicer sound.

You taught me so much about how to approach life. How to get the best out of it. And although I didn't seek it out, becoming your mother was the single best thing I ever did.

Can you remember being Mary in your reception nativity play? You were a shoo-in for the part, speaking your lines clearly for the audience, subtly rescuing the angel Gabriel's tinsel, when it fell off his head. You were the star, but you wanted it to go well for everyone else too. So innately generous. I remember sobbing loudly in the audience. A happy sadness. The anticipatory nostalgia of knowing you were going to grow up, that I couldn't inhabit that moment forever.

If I shut my eyes, I can picture you now. Eighteen. You're beautiful, I'm sure. Headturningly so. But better than that, you believe in yourself. You aren't looking for outside validation, as I constantly did at your age. Rather, you're aware of your own value and what you have to offer. I'm heartbroken that I didn't get the opportunity to see all the things you'll accomplish.

But I also wish that I was able to be there when you needed me. Life isn't easy for any of us. Even those with your natural gifts. I wanted to pick up the pieces of your first heartbreak, counsel you through tough job interviews, show up uninvited with soup and grapes when you got sick. I wanted to help you with your own baby one day. To give you a rest when you thought you might lose your mind from lack of sleep and push a pram through the park like all those other proud grannies.

I wanted to be there.

My reassurance, as I write this, is that I'm leaving you in the best possible hands. You're lucky to have the father you do. He gave me a life that I never thought I could have and showed me the value of everyday joy. Of trusting yourself and not looking for drama.

So, what advice can I offer, that he hasn't, in the years I've been gone?

I'd start with this: don't ever let other people define you. Their opinion doesn't matter. Don't mix your drinks. Steer clear of synthetic fabrics. When men say they prefer women who don't wear any make-up, smile and then decide for yourself. Red lipstick and black eyeliner can be great fun. And you should never sniff at fun.

Don't stop reading books as your responsibilities inevitably mount up. Remember the particular magic of disappearing into another world, the shift of perspective it affords.

Trust your gut. It took me years to listen to mine, but it's almost always right. Keep a lightness of touch in all that you do. Exercise. If in doubt, go for the navy blue. Eat full-fat. Never turn down a kitchen disco. Look for the friends who are nice to you – sounds straightforward, but it doesn't always work that way.

Enjoy your brother as much as you can. The relationships we have with our siblings are perhaps the most important of our lives. They continue to shape us as we get older, much as we might try to convince ourselves they don't.

And, above all, remember to trust in love. To live and manifest it, as you once taught me how to do. Life can be dreadfully confusing and painful. Trying to figure it out, to understand it all, can feel futile. But loving is easy. You can do that every day. And it will always show you the way.

Mummy xxxx

51

Now

'Wow, it's got big,' said Megan, looking at the holly tree, which, while still dwarfed by others at the crematorium, was afforded a plucky air by its shiny leaves and red berries.

'She would have been four today,' said Paul. He couldn't stop himself from picturing a little girl hoisted onto his shoulders, resting her chin on the top of his skull, where the hair was growing sparse like an ailing lawn. So easy to transpose fancies onto someone who never got the chance to exist.

'Why did it happen?' said Jude, squinting at the tree. 'I know that she never opened her eyes, but why?'

In the last months, Paul had grown closer to his son than before and Jude had also grown calmer, despite his mother's absence. Although there were still notable exceptions, like that morning, when he had jumped headfirst from the double bed, splitting his forehead in the centre. Paul had steri-stripped the wound, sighing but swallowing the shouts.

'Sometimes in nature things go wrong,' Paul said. 'We

don't always fully understand what happens. We can't explain everything.'

'Like Mummy?' replied Jude.

'Yes, like Mummy.'

'Shall we put the flowers here?' said Megan, placing the bunch of tulips, bought in haste from a supermarket, at the base of the slender, greyish trunk. Paul nodded.

'I can't believe the leaves have prickles,' said Jude. 'It's epic!'

'Right. Mummy wanted to make sure that we remember Rosa properly, so perhaps we should all say something about her.'

'But we didn't know her,' said Jude. 'That's stupid.'

'Well, maybe we could say something about what it was like to wait for her?' said Paul. 'I remember feeling happy and excited that we were going to have another baby. I was worried about the sleepless nights but looking forward to carrying the new baby in the sling and seeing her smile for the first time.'

'Ok,' said Megan. 'Well, I think I was a bit worried about how Mummy was going to cope. You know she could get a bit cross sometimes and stressed. But I couldn't wait to have a sister.' Her eyes lit up at the remembered prospect.

'I wanted someone to watch *Ninjago* with,' said Jude, sorrowfully, and both Megan and Paul laughed.

'Silly! She was a girl, she wouldn't have liked *Ninjago*,' said Megan.

'She would have done,' said Jude. 'Some girls do.'

'Can I say something?' Tess and Flora had been standing at a slight distance, respectfully. Paul nodded. Since the visit to Cornwall, Tess had started to become a part of their lives. She had rung Paul after reading Sylvia's letter, crying, promising she would be there for Jude and Megan in a way that she hadn't been able to be for her sister. When Paul had subsequently told her that it was going to be Rosa's birthday, Tess had insisted on bringing Flora to the informal memorial.

'I never really acknowledged what happened properly,' she'd said to Paul. 'I mean, I rang her when I found out, of course, but I should have dropped everything to be there. I don't know how she got through it.'

'She never really did,' Paul said.

Stepping forwards, hand in hand, Tess motioned for Flora to put the bunch of flowers she was holding at the base of the holly tree. Scrappy asters, like little purple stars, which Tess had brought all the way from Cornwall on the train. The little girl did it tentatively, looking around at her mother for approval.

'Good girl. I just wanted to say ...' Tess cleared her throat. Looked at Jude and Megan. 'Your mother was the most remarkable person I've ever known. I'm sure that Rosa would have been an incredibly special little girl. I mean, just look at both of you. I'm so sorry for what happened. For everything your – our – family has lost. We need to hold each other close.'

Megan hugged her aunt in response and Flora joined in on the other side. Then even Jude stepped forwards, putting his arms around them all.

'Group hug!' he shouted.

* * *

Paul stayed up late that evening, to have some time alone. Tess and Flora were in the spare room, co-sleeping.

'We'll stop when she's ready,' Tess had said, implacably, reminding Paul of the nights he and Sylvia had moved Jude and Megan to their own rooms when they were barely eight months old. The tip-toed victory dance that his wife had done outside their closed doors.

He checked on the children, Jude no longer sweating since his operation. Megan's room, he noticed with pleasure, was slightly untidy. She had taken down her books and toys to show Flora but forgotten to replace them in the usual serried ranks.

Paul loped towards the kitchen. Perhaps a drink. But first a tablet in the dishwasher, a wipe of the surfaces, food in Ted's bowl. Sylvia's tasks that he had finally assumed, with Natalia no longer insulating him from them.

He stood up, away from the carrion smell of dog food, and waited for the clatter of paws.

'Ted?' Paul said, but there was nothing. And that's when he saw him. Ted. In his basket, perched on the tartan blanket that Sylvia used to lovingly wash, but at an awkward angle, his head lolling back uncharacteristically.

'Ted! Boy?' Paul was by the animal's side, crouching. Touching the small flank confirmed his suspicion. It was cold. At some point in the previous hours, the old dog had died, at last. After all those years of diabetes, which had rendered him wizened and near-blind, it had started to feel like he might go on forever. Paul stroked the top of his silly, inbred head, where the black hair was threaded with silver, like his own.

They had aged together. Never the dog he would have chosen for himself and for so long his rival for Sylvia's affections. Yet the love had grown nonetheless, undeniable and sweet.

52

For Jude Clarke, to be opened on
the occasion of his 18th birthday.

Dear Jude,

I debated for weeks whether to write this to you. Your instinctive dislike of sentimentality is so like my own. And how to write a letter like this, that isn't cloying?

Then, I woke up this morning and decided to do it anyway. In my own truncated life I learned too late that cynicism gets you nowhere. If I can teach you that simple fact by writing this, it will be a job well done.

But I promise this – no false sentiment, no dissembling. Everything I say is the gospel truth. So, you know I really mean it.

You were not an easy baby or small child. The most active, self-determined person I'd ever met, you simply weren't suited to being an infant, to being trussed up and ferried around the place. Some babies sit in their bouncy chairs for hours, whereas you leaned forwards, trying to escape. You ran as soon as you walked, often in the opposite direction from me. There were days – so many days – when you would test my patience and I'd end up shouting at you, stamping my feet, as if I were the toddler, not you.

You always had a nose for the absurd. Do you remember that phase when you insisted on eating all your meals in sunglasses and a cycle helmet? At first I tried to make you stop, but the tantrums weren't worth it and eventually I gave up, getting used to the sight of you chomping chicken nuggets in your weird get-up. Or that stall you had outside the front door? I suggested lemonade, but instead you sold bloodshot eyeballs made of Play-Doh, in surprising numbers.

You always kept me on my toes, but you also made everything exciting. An adventure. Your joy for the things you liked easily matched your antipathy towards those you didn't. Cake, dinosaurs, skeletons, footballs, a just-right stick – you revelled in a catalogue of disparate, simple pleasures.

I wonder what you love, now that you're turning eighteen? I scarcely dare to think about it, frankly, but I know your enjoyment will be similarly strong. I can relate to that. I always saw myself in you. Your enthusiasm, your motormouth, your need to move. Your sheer intensity.

Before your father, some people made me feel like I was too much. But he always accepted me for who I was – no, more than that, he made me feel like I was special. I'm certain he will have made you feel the same. But if there's any room for doubt, know it. From the very first evening I had you in my arms, I did. You had kept me awake all night feeding. Every time I tried to put you down, you would squawk for more.

I was so tired that I grew nervous I might drift off, so I propped myself bolt upright in the bed with a bank of cushions, staring at your features in the low lamplight. Exhausted, I hadn't bothered lowering the blind in our bedroom. As the new day began, a smudge of palest yellow behind the rooftops, you turned your face towards the dawn. I will never forget it. Your tiny face searching for the rising sun. You were always so perceptive, so keenly aware of your surroundings. Nothing ever escaped you. That's a gift. I hope you use it well.

I love you so much. I am so sorry I can't see you right now, as you hold this letter in your hands. I wish I could be there, embarrassing you by trying to smush your cheeks and reminding everyone of what a terror you were. When you were a toddler, I used to smother you in kisses, crazed by your cuteness. I felt pangs when I thought of you growing up, but I always took for granted the fact I'd see it happen.

Know this. The worst thing about this wretched illness, of which there have been so many terrible things, is saying goodbye to you and Megan before it was time. I had plans. I was going to show you so many things, teach you so much stuff, set you out to navigate the world. I am furious I didn't get the chance.

Make good choices. Don't be reckless. Floss. Be as moderate as your irrepressible, sparkling nature allows. Look after your dad and sister. You and Megan have different personalities, but that's a blessing. You have so much to show each other. And you always, instinctively, loved each other deeply. When you were born, Megan was so proud. She used to sit outside the bedroom door while you had a nap in your carrycot, insisting that she was keeping you safe. Later, she would worry as much as I did when you decided to climb that high tree in the park, chewing her lip until you got down. Sometimes love looks like cuddles and soft words, but equally often it's shown through anxiety and admonishments.

You never liked colouring, much preferring to draw your own bizarre, bloodthirsty pictures. But if Megan was doing it, you'd join in, valiantly trying to stay within the lines. She was the only person you ever really cared about impressing.

Make sure, when you do settle down with someone, I imagine (nay, hope) years from now, that you do your fair share of the chores. I adore your father, but I didn't love pairing his socks. Remember that women aren't delicate creatures with an innate propensity towards housework. By and large most people in the world want the same things. To know their children are safe. To earn enough, doing a job they don't hate. To love and be loved.

I see now that I had all of that, even though my life is ending sooner than I thought it would. And who can say fairer that that? All I can ever wish for you, my darling, is the same. I feel in my tired bones that you're going to have a wonderful, exhilarating time. Choose well.

Mummy xx

53

When

From where Paul sat, his back pressed against sun-soaked granite, their bodies looked like dolls. Jude. Megan. Tess. Flora. Barbara in the wide sunhat of a 1950s starlet. A line of dinky humans in the shallow surf. He saw Jude plunge headfirst into a wave and emerge spluttering, shaking his hair like a wet dog. Holding hands, evidently shrieking, Megan and Flora jumped away.

Paul picked up a handful of sand and let it trickle from his fingers. Tiny shell fragments. Purple, pale pink, curious monochrome pinstripe. From a distance, the sand looked uniformly yellow, but up close it was anything but.

Hard to think, a year ago, he had taken the call from Khadija at St Luke's. Only a year since Sylvia had gone. Another trip around the sun, as his wife said each year, bemoaning her birthday. Yet so much had changed.

Tess had decided that they should spend the anniversary on that beach, Sylvia's childhood favourite. Only accessible by an alarmingly steep footpath, the sea a livid turquoise. It was actually a nudist beach, which had predictably fascinated Jude, although the only visitors taking advantage of its status seemed, disappointingly, to be a particular breed of ageing hippy, the men and women's sagging skin sexless and inter-changeable.

They had been seeing more and more of Tess and Flora. Weekends, half term in the bell tent at Brean, even a tentative nut roast at Christmas. He would never warm to Danny, but he could see how much Jude and Megan enjoyed spending time with their aunt. The glimpses of their mother that she afforded. That was the trade-off, why he had taken the cliff house for the summer, found a locum for the practice, hot-footed it out of the city.

'Did you do my whole back?' said Nush, lying next to him on a towel on her stomach, reading a paperback. 'I feel like you missed a bit.'

Paul looked at her soft shoulders, the thick straps of her swimsuit, so different from the scant triangles of fabric Sylvia had always favoured. Yet she was so much happier in her body than his wife had ever been, genuinely didn't seem to care what other people thought.

'What, here?' He leaned forwards and dropped a kiss at the apex of her spine. 'You mean this bit?' Her skin tasted of ocean, an acrid lick of sun cream. Despite the freezing water, she had been the most enthusiastic swimmer of them all, entranced by the Cornish sea. Her and Ryan joining them for a fortnight in the cliff house was the first formal acknowledgement of her and Paul's relationship. Ryan had been climbing the rocks with a bucket for hours, looking for crabs.

Paul couldn't pinpoint exactly how it had first started. When they had stepped from being one thing to another. It had happened fractionally, like a sunrise. One evening, after she had dropped Ryan off, he had realised how badly he didn't want her to leave, touching her hand and asking her to stay too. Not long afterwards, she had helped him take Jude to the hospital for his operation. Her reassuring presence allaying Paul's fears. It had gone well, just as Nush had said it would. He knew he would never stop missing Sylvia, would remain subject to grief's tidal pattern. The surprise was that he could feel such fledgling happiness too.

'Yup, that bit. I feel like it's burning.'

'I definitely didn't miss it,' said Paul, stroking the patch of skin, firmly, definitively.

'Come for a swim with me?' said Nush, getting up.

'Another one?' said Paul, but stood up and followed her down towards the shoreline. He paused for a moment, before they reached the others, watching Jude and Megan splashing, already so different from how Sylvia had known them. Relentlessly growing, changing, unfurling upwards. Then he tilted his head backwards, smiling, and looked up at the unbounded blue.

ACKNOWLEDGEMENTS

My amazing agent Sophie Lambert and everyone at C&W, including Katie Greenstreet, Alexander Cochran and the foreign rights team.

The accomplished Orion team. Clare Hey and Charlotte Mursell, dream editors both, also Victoria Oundjian, Virginia Woolstencroft, Lucy Cameron and Olivia Barber.

My Dutch publisher and the team at Nieuw Amsterdam.

Charlotte Philby, for the multi-platform chat, the red wine and always being one step ahead. My other book club ladies - Alex Joyce, Charlotte Haworth, Louise McMahon, Julie Johnstone and Hannah Worthington, I hope this doesn't split opinion. Sarah Swash, Eleanor Ireland and Malin Vester, I miss you. Catrina Davies, you can still feed Nelson. Tom Duggan, seventeen forever. My UCL bookworms Lisa Pickering and Emily Crump. And my City compadres, Kate Maxwell, Vanessa Jolly and Esther Walker. Chris Lines, too, for the kickstart of a commission.

Rick and Henrietta Newman, Jon and Hannah Simons, Arif and Farah Morbiwalla, Kate and Theepan Jothilingham, Abi and Matt Simmonds, Helen Lightbowne and Jenita Rahman, Mim and Pierre Humblot.

My erstwhile section editors - Tony Turnbull for giving me a shot at *The Times*, Sally Brook at *The Sun*, Maggie O'Riordan at the *Daily Mail* and Harriet Green at *The Guardian*.

My Faber crew: the outstanding teacher and writer

Richard Skinner and all my talented classmates, especially Sif Sigmarsdóttir and Douglas Wight for invaluable feedback.

Louise Dean, too, for thoughtful, eclectic advice. Emily Pedder and Penny Rudge, for the extra eyes.

Rachel Porter and Karen Sonego at Scriberia for all the enjoyable scriptwriting. And Alex Depledge for a great year.

Stavroula Kalaitzi - for tender care, the gift of time and tahini bread.

As I wrote this book, I was moved by the bravery of the women, everywhere, whose lives are changed by breast cancer. The broadcaster Rachael Bland's account of her illness will always stay with me, as will that of the writer, Nina Riggs. And my older sisters, Abigail and Naomi, the courage you both showed is just one of the many ways you've inspired me.

The rest of my family. Will: for all the yoga and everything else, I'm so proud of you. Ellie and Ruth (PBs): I love you. Baby Sara, here's to another summer holiday in the cove.

The next generation: Jessica, Isaac, Rose, Sheba, Nina, Ruan, Kit, Caitlin, Matthew, Bruno and Clara.

Derek and Christine, Juliet and Christian, Simon and Kirsty, the best in-laws I could ever ask for. Neil and James, too.

Mum, for a childhood full of all the right things. And Dad, no longer here, but always on my mind.

Finally, the family I've made. My astonishing children - Isobel, Felix and Sebastian. I love you more than words can ever express, more than all the stars in the sky. I hope you know it.

And Andrew, my love and first reader. Your good humour and kindness are an ongoing example. You've taught me so much.

CREDITS

Rebecca Ley and Orion Fiction would like to thank everyone at Orion who worked on the publication of *For When I'm Gone* in the UK.

Editorial
Charlotte Mursell
Clare Hey
Victoria Oundjian
Olivia Barber

Copy editor
Francine Brody

Proof reader
Natalie Braine

Audio
Paul Stark
Amber Bates

Contracts
Anne Goddard
Paul Bulos
Jake Alderson

Design
Rabab Adams
Joanna Ridley
Nick May
Helen Ewing

**Editorial
Management**
Charlie Panayiotou
Jane Hughes
Alice Davis

Finance
Jasdip Nandra
Afeera Ahmed
Elizabeth
Beaumont
Sue Baker

Marketing
Lucy Cameron

Production
Ruth Sharvell

Publicity
Virginia
Woolstencroft

Sales
Laura Fletcher
Esther Waters
Victoria Laws
Rachael Hum
Ellie Kyrke-Smith
Frances Doyle
Georgina Cutler

Operations
Jo Jacobs
Sharon Willis
Lisa Pryde
Lucy Brem